COMMON MODE FAILURE

Ian McKinley

COMMON MODE FAILURE

DOUBLE DRAGON

Pulse Arrival, Hanoi, Vietnam

The aging KLM A380 was on final approach for landing, third in line in the usual mid-morning stack of heavy tin being squeezed into the busy airport. Captain Richard Mackenzie was sipping coffee, keeping only a bored eye on the autopilot that was doing all of the work – not that there was much to do as, despite some threatening clouds on the horizon, the conditions were almost perfect with a five-knot headwind and only slight turbulence from the Emirates behemoth ahead of them. He glared at it. *A bloody electric wide-bodied jet, I wouldn't even have thought that was possible when I started flying three decades ago and now I'm going to be on the scrapheap along with this old bus when the next increase in carbon credit rates finally kills off fossil-fuelled planes for good.*

All of a sudden, the multi-coloured display panel went black and the cockpit became strangely silent – absolutely nothing apart from the faint sound of air rushing past outside. *Must be what it's like in one of those electric bastards,* then the shear impossibility of this occurrence hit the captain. *Complete power failure in all systems, including all redundant back-up. Just not possible!*

Now he could hear the first sounds of panic from the passengers, which increased in volume when someone started hammering on the cockpit door. *Electric lock and armoured door to keep out terrorist nutters. Well, there's nobody coming in until we get power again.*

His co-pilot, Richard Koenig, had stirred from his dose and was looking around in an almost comical state of confusion. At that point the plane stalled and started to plummet towards the ground. Although both pilot and co-pilot automatically fought with the controls, a strangely calm area in the back of Mackenzie's head had already recognised that this would have zero effect on a fly-by-wire jet that was completely blacked out. *It should be impossible, or at least one in a million, but somehow statistics don't seem to mean anything anymore.* He had several seconds to ponder this thought after watching the Emirates flight explode into a city suburb, just short of the runway.

Mackenzie was an expert sky-diver and well familiar with ground-rush, but experiencing it in a cockpit was a novelty that held him transfixed, a contrast to his screaming co-pilot who seemed to think that the brace position was going to help him in some way. *Hey, that's the Hilton...* was his last thought before the 380 turned it into an inferno.

Pulse Arrival, Gotthard Rail Tunnel, Switzerland

Vreni Fricker was driving the high-speed goods train through the Gotthard Alp-transit when the controls suddenly went dead and the tunnel went dark. This was anomalous enough, but the emergency brakes failed to engage and only the slight uphill gradient acted to slow the train down. As her eyes adjusted to the faint green phosphorescence that identified the escape hatch from the cab, she also began to make out the blur of a similar green from the tunnel itself, also showing escape routes. Over the next five minutes, she marked her decreasing velocity by their rate of progress past her window while trying to work out whether she would be able to stop before the train crested the invisible rise ahead and started to run downhill towards Italy. As a precaution, she turned the handle that opened the side escape hatch and wondered how slow it would have to be for her risk of injury to be low enough to justify jumping.

By the time that the train had slowed to a fast walk, Vreni's sense of responsibility had taken over and her focus had shifted to stopping the train completely, ensuring that runaway either forward or backward was prevented. Although never having had cause to use it, she remembered that the locomotive possessed a hydraulically-operated parking brake which, if timed just right, might be fit for the job. *The tricky thing's to apply this at just the right moment – too early and the brake will simply burn out, too late and I risk cresting the summit and starting irreversible acceleration.*

She wiped sweat from her eyes, straining to determine if the train was still slowing. It was now crawling along and she could easily jump out, but forced herself to wait. Suddenly she spotted a phosphorescent number on the tunnel wall, indicating the maximum elevation of the route, and immediately started pumping the hydraulics with all her might. A terrible screeching resulted and the train slowed further while the smell of burning brake-pads filled the air. The hydraulic pump then jammed and Vreni bailed out, realising she could do no more.

The movement was almost imperceptible, but the train was still creeping forward while smoke issued from the locked parking brake. Fighting an irrational urge to jump in front of the locomotive and attempt to stop in by brute force, she cast about in the deep shadows to try to find a solution to this challenge.

"Chocks, where're the bloody chocks?" Vreni cursed aloud when finally remembering the steel wedges that were required to be placed on the lines when locos or wagons were parked in stockyards. She painfully barked a knuckle while searching along the side of the train, relying more on memory than on vision. "Yes!" she pulled the heavy wedge free and dropped it in front of the second bogey, jumping back as it exploded with a deafening screech and a hail of sparks. Within seconds, she reached the first of the goods wagons and pulled another chock free. This one was simply pushed forwards, again accompanied by sparks and the scream of tortured metal. A third chock and the train finally stopped, but Vreni worked her way further along, applying the wedges to both sides of the wheels, as the train was long enough to straddle the summit and there might also be potential to slide backwards.

A quarter of an hour later, the exhausted driver clambered back into her cab and, as specified in the operational manual, settled down to wait for the recovery team. *Normally this'll be fairly quick, but I've never heard of a complete power loss ever happening before. Maybe there's been a big accident, so the wait might be longer. Anyway, nothing further that I can do, so I may as well try to take a nap.*

Pulse Arrival, Amman, Jordan

After almost a decade on the CIA most wanted list, Achmed had almost forgotten his real name. He changed identities every month, whether there was any indication that they had been compromised or not. He also changed cities, countries, even continents. Anywhere that Islam was fighting the infidel and bombs were needed.

The common or garden terrorist has no need of my skills – they could concoct an acceptably powerful explosive device from material that you could pick up in any department store, following a recipe downloadable on the internet. The open internet, that is, not any kind of dark net. But I'm anything but a hoi polloi raghead.

Achmed was fluent not only in Arabic, French, German and Italian: his native tongue was English, but the class of English possible only from his Eton and Oxford classics background. The scion of a Saudi family that built a fortune out of brokering contacts to the country's royalty – rather than being part of it – he knew that he would always be an underling of the host of Princes born to privilege. Rebellion thus came naturally, under the cover of a religion that he had once earnestly believed in, but was now nothing but a route to his ultimate goal.

A fucking bomb-maker, that's what I am on the CIA list. True, I do put bombs together, but that's just for the fun of getting my hands dirty – and the cred that accrues from the cannon-fodder that I use to deliver these devices. 9-11, that's when the power of the attack manager was revealed. It wasn't only a cost-effective way to hit the enemy at home, the economic fallout vastly amplified the impacts of the initial attack. It's not just knowing how to make bombs, but planning their use so that it has the maximum possible impact.

"Jesus, fuck, but I'm good!" he congratulated himself, just before the device he was working on exploded, setting off the entire inventory of bomb-making materials that he had stored in the basement. If they had ever been able to reconstruct what had happened, the authorities would have been pleased to find that the charred mass in the sub-basement comprised thirty-seven martyrs who had already decided that their early deaths would be rewarded by hosts of virgins in the afterlife.

Of course, there is no afterlife, but, if there was, enough fresh virgins would have been supplied by those vaporised in the kindergarten directly above the bomb factory; not only the infants but also their young teachers, who had turned a blind eye to the activities in their basement.

Pulse Arrival, Nagoya, Japan

The day started so well. It was a beautiful spring day in Nagoya and the cherry trees scattered around the University were in full bloom. As a visiting professor, I lived on campus in a very neat – if rather small – apartment that was just five minutes' walk from the Department of Environmental Engineering and Disaster Management. A rather strange discipline juxtaposition to most Westerners, but typically Japanese. *In any case, a three-month boondoggle as far as I'm concerned: time to catch up on the literature, write some papers and give the odd lecture. A holiday away from the cut and thrust of international technical consultant work.*

It being a Sunday before the start of term, the building seemed deserted when I entered mid-afternoon, intending only to sort out accumulated email. After a couple of hours, I switched off the desktop peripherals linked to my pad and settled back to savour a coffee from my thermos, admiring the sakura through the window. Suddenly, a post-doc crashed through the half-open door of my office. I started in surprise, spilling hot coffee on the cuff of my shirt while turning in my chair to face this most anomalous intrusion.

"Shoko, what's up? You look like you've seen a ghost." Indeed, the normally quiet and demure young woman was wide-eyed and visibly shaking. "Has something happened, is someone hurt?"

Shoko responded in a babble of Japanese, then seemed to pull herself together while she clenched her hands into tight fists. "Sensei, it's the control room. There's something very shit... I mean shitty... Shit, you must come to the control..."

I could feel a cold shiver going up my spine. *We've been monitoring increasing seismic activity in the region of Mount Fuji and it's really only a matter of time until something bad happens.* I jumped to my feet and grabbed the shocked girl by her elbow. "Okay, let's go. Fuji, is it?"

We were cramming though the door when she resisted my push for a moment. "No, it's not Fuji, I think. Worse..."

I was going to respond to this when I noted that I was being diverted towards the stairs. "Come on Shoko, we're going to the sub-basement, it's faster to use the lift."

"Lift doesn't work, all is out."

As I let myself be led to the stairs, I noted that the ubiquitous air conditioning was silent, light was limited to that from windows and the emergency fluorescent lamps. The twinkles of flashing LEDs were strangely missing from the offices and labs that we passed. "Power cut," I muttered, aware that I hadn't experienced such an event in a developed country for decades and guessed that this could be a novelty for young Shoko, causing her to freak out.

"Yes, there's electric only in the control centre," Shoko confirmed in a trembling voice. "It's all a shit!"

13

I could never remember this polite young student's English being less than perfect or her using even such mild curses, so this further confirmed how upset she was. I almost tripped as I tried to keep up with her headlong clatter down the stairways. "Shoko, slow down, you'll break your neck – or I'll break mine. I'm not as fit as I used to be."

I caught a slight trace of a smile and noted her shoulders relax a little as my joke registered. I am a great believer in pre-emptive excuses and this is my usual mantra whenever some of the young post-grads talked me into doing some sport with them. Just before I thrash them running up hills, swimming, mountain biking or in the dojo. Not that I am especially fit – just that Japanese science and engineering students are notoriously sedentary, work incredibly long hours and live on junk food.

I puffed and panted in an exaggerated manner while we hurtled down seven flights of stairs and then along the corridor leading to the DMRC – our disaster monitoring and response coordination centre. After the darkness since we hit basement levels, this was an oasis of light and the normal background buzz from the banks of electronic kit filling the main control room.

The glass door with its embedded mesh of thin copper wires slid aside as we approached and silently closed behind us after we entered the large circular room. I automatically glanced at the Fuji monitoring system and breathed a sigh of relief when I confirmed that there was nothing beyond traces of the usual continuous background microseismics and acoustic emissions. There was, however, one warning showing: *loss of all signals*. I quickly scanned around the circumferential work stations, it looked like similar warnings were showing on them all. *Okay, this must be a must be a truly huge scale power outage*.

Shoko dragged me over to a chair facing a bank of monitors that I did not immediately recognise. Clearly this was what had worried her – a baffling series of red warnings was scrolling down the screen. "What's this…?" I ground to a halt as I caught sight of the bilingual banner over this niche. "Self Defence Force link: this should only be active if Japan is being attacked. There must be an error somewhere."

The young researcher dropped into the chair and issued commands in rapid Japanese while her fingers flashed over a touchpad and the wall of screens switched to status overview mode – luckily for me defaulting to English. "It was this that set off all the warnings, this EMP."

"An electromagnetic pulse that's big enough to knock out our entire national monitoring network? That doesn't seem possible. Okay, it would explain why everything is running fine inside our Faraday Cage and that we're picking up stuff only over a nuclear-hardnet, but an EMP would have to be local, regional at worst. It looks from this as if it's national."

"That's what I thought, Sensei, but look at this…" Strangely, working on the problem appeared to have calmed Shoko, although I felt as if her initial terror was being gradually transferred to me.

15

The screen displaying an electromagnetically dead Japan zoomed out, to show all of South-East Asia.

"Jesus fuck! Even an all-out nuclear exchange couldn't totally black out such a huge area."

"So, it's some kind of equipment fault. I hoped it would be something like that. At first, though, it really looked like the start of a nuclear war."

I grabbed a chair from the neighbouring work station and pulled it over so that I could sit beside the student and take a closer look at the monitors. I took my palmtop from its pouch on my belt and it immediately linked to the control centre. This made me feel a bit better for a moment, until I remembered that it, like everything in the DMRC, was military specification and hence its survival did not prove a lot. My bespoke expert system took charge and the results of a preliminary synthesis flashed onto the main screen.

Earlier I had thought that I was on the verge of pissing myself, now I felt as if I was about to lose control of my bowels. "No, Shoko," I whispered, "this isn't a nuclear war – it's a hell of a lot worse than that!"

PA+3 hours, *Golden Harvest*, English Channel

Captain Lee had almost begun to relax. He had been on the bridge ever since the massive bulk ore carrier had lost all power just before entering one of the busiest sea lanes in the world. He had been preparing to decelerate from normal oceanic speed to the crawl required for the Channel transit into Rotterdam when everything went dead. That shouldn't be possible but at least, looking on the bright side, the pebble-bed reactor that powered this juggernaut was inherently safe and, even without power and left completely to its own devices, would shut itself down safely. This process was driven only by the immutable laws of physics.

Unfortunately, it was also physics, specifically Newtonian mechanics, which caused his real concern. With a mass of over one million tons and a hull constructed to reduce drag to a minimum, this ship was going to take a long time to stop. Due to loss of all communications, he was powerless to issue a warning to other ships in the vicinity; but the coastguards must have noted this by now and he could entrust that task to them. What he couldn't understand was why a helicopter had not yet been out to investigate. Indeed, the sky seemed strangely clear of all aircraft.

Captain Lee again lifted the binoculars to peer through the squalls of rain, aware that this was the first occasion he had used such ancient technology since taking command of this ship. A grey mass seemed to be emerging from the gloom dead ahead. "What the hell are these guys doing?" he muttered under his breath, catching the attention of the two other men who shared the bridge with him – Flynn, the Exec Officer, and Flaherty, the systems analyst.

"Despite this shitty vis, they can't possibly have missed us on radar. This monster has a profile like the bloody Empire States Building," Flaherty commented, peering through the sheeting rain.

The ghostly shape ahead was rapidly gaining substance as it neared, a very large white vessel that wallowed in a bizarre manner.

"Christ, it's one of those mega-cruisers," Flynn gasped. "It's not supposed to be possible, but it looks to have also lost all power. Those babies are designed to be dynamically unstable, to increase manoeuvrability. But look at the way it's bouncing about now – makes me feel sick just to look at it. There's going to be a lot of spew to mop up on that boat."

Lee automatically punched down on a large red button, one of the few controls that was not a touchscreen or voice operated, and was shocked for a moment by the absence of the blare of the ship's horn. "We're going to ram her and there's not a bloody thing we can do about it. Anybody have a clue what powers her, is it also a nuke?"

"Hydrogen fuel cell, I'm pretty sure. I think there's a cryogenic tank that runs the length of her keel," Flynn supplied with a frown. "It's well shielded though and supposed to fail safe, pressure release valves below the waterline, if I remember correctly."

"So, it's a potential fucking Hindenburg if they also lost power the same time as us."

"But, Captain, that can't be right. Why'd we both lose power at the same time," Flaherty objected.

"Occam's Razor," the captain glared ahead as if hoping to remove their victim by mind power alone. "It's either a coincidence that two ships that are designed never to lose power have not only done so but are about to collide with each other, or it's some kind of external cause."

"You mean like some kind of terrorist hack?" Flaherty asked.

"Not a fucking clue, lads. But, whatever the cause, I'd get strapped in for collision if I was you. We're almost four hundred metres from the bow and, although our closing speed seems to be only about fifteen knots, we're going to ram her amidships and will probably cut right through. Even something as bloody big as that cruiser. It's going to be a big bump though and that's without whatever happens to the hydrogen."

To Lee, everything thereafter seemed to take place in slow motion. A first shudder as the elongated prow made first contact, immediately followed by a shockwave that visibly ran along the deck towards them, ahead of a wall of flying debris from the stricken vessel. The jolt reminded Lee of a large earthquake he had experienced on the 50th floor of a Tokyo skyscraper, but with much more noise, despite the thick armoured glass of the bridge.

The first hundred metres of the ship was hidden by mist for a moment, before the cloud of hydrogen exploded in a fireball that closed inexorably as the ore carrier ploughed through it. Lee was frozen to the spot, eyes wide like a rabbit in headlights. *The hull of this ship may be unstoppable, but that probably doesn't hold for the superstructure.*

He was right.

PA+6 hours, Cupecoy, Sint Maarten

Not the best start to the day, I groaned as I was wakened by the sound of a truly stentorian fart – shortly followed by a stench that would have stripped paint off the walls if, of course, there were walls and if they had been painted. The fuzzy miasma, confirming my woolly memories of far too much alcohol consumed the previous evening, slowly dispersed while I became aware of my surroundings – the balcony of a villa in the Caribbean island of Sint Maarten that had been my home for the last month. *Shit, never even made it back to the bedroom, wonder if it was wild sex or booze that caused that?*

Another explosive fart brought my attention to my bed-mate or, more correctly, sunlounger-mate, who was sprawled on her stomach beside me. From my current viewpoint, the small brunette looked very presentable: trim, with a tight little arse that was spoiled – or enhanced, I wasn't sure which – by tattooed gothic text. *Lasciate ogne speranza, voi ch'intrate. Abandon all hope, ye who enter here, from the Divine Comedy.* I grinned although, truly, I had not a clue whether I had abandoned such hope during our alcoholic encounter or not. *Probably not, given my present shape,* I concluded, not sure whether to be glad or disappointed about this.

The sun had yet to rise, but the pre-dawn cacophony of tropic bird and reptile calls was beginning to drown out the susurrus of the surf and the rustle of palm fronds in the morning breeze. I rolled to my feet without disturbing the gentle snoring of my partner-of-the-night and headed indoors to ease the growing pressure on my bladder and find a prophylactic to an imminent hangover, not necessarily in that order.

As I walked into the living room, I noticed the absence of the air-curtain that usually maintained the boundary between in- and out-doors. Also, the house did not offer its usually air-conditioned chill. *A power cut? How quaint! Anyway, I've lived here long enough to find my way into a dark toilet and relieve myself without mishap.* After a quick piss in the guest toilet, I headed to the kitchen and ordered, "analgesic, medium strength," to an unresponsive dispenser, realising then that loss of electric power could be more than a tropical paradise novelty.

"No coffee, fuck, how'll I survive this?" I muttered under my breath as the reality of my position began to dawn. I opened the door of the huge refrigerator, still surprised that this was not accompanied by an internal light, and grabbed a gallon container of grapefruit juice by reflex alone. I drank directly from the plastic flagon, immediately refreshed by its cool tartness. *At least the fridge hasn't had time to warm up.*

The coffee craving was building in line with the throbbing behind my brow. *Fruit juice isn't going to sort this out. In the absence of stronger pharmaceuticals, I've got to get some caffeine into my system.*

I walked back out onto the terrace and leant on the fence rail; no sign of life at this early hour, but also no flashing lights at the resort entry barrier and dark traffic lights beyond that. *Not just a fuse gone in the villa: looks like power is out in the entire complex. So how am I going to get coffee? I'm a scientist, I must be able to do that.*

The first step was straightforward, searching out a mobile barbeque that I remembered was part of the villa facilities, although I hadn't considered using it until now. Then I had to find charcoal, lighter fluid and matches. It took a while, but eventually I had the barbie fired up with a kettle sitting on it, all such activity not disturbing the sleeping woman in the slightest.

I found a cafetière and a large jar of coffee beans, feeling quite pleased with myself until I poured a load of beans into the electric grinder and realised that this was something else I had forgotten. *Bollocks! How do you grind beans without a grinder?* The kitchen seemed to be equipped with every gadget known to man – all of them defunct in the absence of electricity.

I was stymied for almost five minutes until I simply went for the minimum option and poured the beans onto a thick wooden butcher's block and started chopping them with a large, razor-sharp, Sabatier knife. I kept chopping until I saw that the kettle had started to boil and then poured the product into the cafetière. While the coffee was infusing, I wandered over to inspect the woman more closely, smiling again as I re-read the inscription on her bottom. *What the hell's her name? Cecilia, could it be? That seems to ring a bell.* I admired her golden tan, noting that it was only slightly paler in the shape of a small bikini bottom. *Didn't she have a friend, they were dive instructresses or something? No, it was two friends, wasn't it?*

With a feeling of foreboding, I strolled back through the kitchen and quietly opened the door to the master bedroom. Sure enough, two pairs of bronzed legs protruded from a crumpled mess of sheets. I eased the door shut and headed for my coffee.

Although it was a bit thin, the coffee helped drive away my immanent headache and I felt a lot less fuzzy around the edges. The line of clouds offshore turned from grey to white cotton wool, indicating that the sun had now risen. *Looks like it's going to be another fine day in paradise. All I need to do now is work out how I'm going to give these girls breakfast if the power doesn't come back on.*

***

The smell of frying bacon evidently had more impact on my sleeping beauty than the noise that I had made setting up the barbie. "Jesus, fuck!" she muttered, scrabbling around for a towel that she put over her head. "It's goddam bright here, close the curtains or something."

"You're on the terrace, which doesn't come with curtains, I'm afraid," I explained gently, realising that her evident misery seemed to reduce the remnants of my throbbing hangover. "You could go through to the bedroom, if you want, and squeeze in with your two pals, I suppose."

"Fuck, no," the muffled voice was just discernible, "licked to within an inch of my life is

24

just what I don't need at present. Pain killers, can you manage that?"

I was just about to reply in the negative based on my previous experience with the defunct auto-dispenser, when I remembered that I had a travel first aid kit somewhere. *Why didn't I think of that earlier?* I checked that the bacon would be okay for a few moments and then hurried off to the cupboard that stored luggage and other travel kit.

I found what I was looking for immediately, in the side pocket of the large backpack that I used for adventure travel. I dry swallowed a heavy-duty analgesic and then took its mate to the terrace, stopping only at the fridge to fill a tumbler with a mixture of grapefruit juice and a rather flat prosecco that was left over from the previous evening.

"How about this, pain relief to be washed down with some hair of the dog?"

An elfin face emerged from the towel and opened blood-shot eyes. "Fuck, it's even brighter now. Give me that shit." She grabbed the pill and gulped the Morning Glory in a most inelegant manner, followed by an even less elegant burp. "Wake me tomorrow, preferably after sunset," she groaned before covering her face again with the towel.

"Well, all the more bacon for me," I noted to my unresponsive guest, before jumping with surprise when a finger poked me on the shoulder.

"Well Cecilia is as wasted as usual, but we're both happy to take you up on the bacon sarnies."

It was the pair of dive instructresses that I vaguely remembered from the party, who I had magnanimously offered a bed at my place despite the fact that they were clearly much more sexually interested in each other rather than me. I did, of course, have an ulterior motive, fancying my chances with their pretty buddy. Les Girls had the sense to retire early, but I had ended up in a heavy drinking session with this Cecilia. Once again, I admired her trim body, completely exposed while she lay snoring, covered only by the towel across her face.

The taller, rather chubby girl seemed to read my mind. "Yes, she does have a very nice bod, I've got to admit…"

"…though a total alkie," her partner added. "Okay for the first couple of drinks, then goes into overdrive. Unstoppable. Better admired from a distance I'd say…"

"Not that it stopped you giving her a good shagging…"

"…then she was sick all over my bed…"

"…well, you were trying to get her to have a go at wet sex…"

"I'll tell you what, ladies, you keep an eye on the frying pan and I'll hunt up some rolls. Coffee?"

"Straight black for me."

"White with three sugars."

While making their coffee, I took the opportunity to closely inspect the lesbian couple. I had some recollection of them being called Lee and Marge, but had no idea which was which. Inspection was eased by the fact that the tall, well-built one was wearing nothing at all while her partner was clad in only a minute transparent tanga.

26

They were both muscular and evenly tanned all over but, while the former possessed a fine pair of shapely breasts, the latter was completely flat chested, although with prominent brown nipples that sported large golden rings. *Very pretty, even if a bit on the young side for me.*

I returned to the terrace to be met by a couple of wide grins. "You don't remember who we are, do you?" the more robust girl started, getting straight to the point.

"If he spent an evening drinking with Cecilia, he probably doesn't even remember who he is himself..."

"Actually, I do remember you," I broke in. "Lee and Marge, isn't it?"

They burst into laughter and I wondered if I had got them completely mixed up with some other couple."

"Well, that was close at least. I'm Margie and was actually responsible for introducing you to your nemesis when you tried to chat me up in that bar last night."

"And I'm Lynn, who you ignored completely – evidently being more impressed by the size of mammaries rather than their exquisite form."

Margie lifted the objects of discussion to show them off better. "What do you think, Chris? Chris is your name, isn't it? We didn't get further than first names."

"Yes, correct, Chris Herzog. And they are indeed a very fine example of nubile breasts at their best. But I can't be accused of focusing only on

27

size, don't you remember those Yankee women from the bar."

The girls burst into delighted laughter. "Christ on a bike, they were fucking huge – all over. There're farmers who'd dream that their milk Jerseys had udders like those."

"By comparison, you must have seemed as flat chested as me…"

"Well, before I think too much more about breasts and end up having to go searching for bromide, why don't we have some breakfast and have a chat about what's happening in the world?"

"Why not, assuming that anything has happened in the world that's of any interest to those like us, living in paradise."

"Well, let's focus on Saint Martin then." I surreptitiously flicked a switch to confirm that power was still out. *Actually, I haven't seen a single ship go by or any of the early morning arrivals or departures from SXM.* The approach path for Princess Juliana International airport directly faced my terrace and, now that I thought about this, it was more worrying than the power cut.

We settled down around the table on the balcony with coffees and bacon rolls, one each for Margie and me and two for the diminutive Lynn, while I updated the girls on the power cut situation.

Margie was dismissive. "Well, a power cut in Northern Canada, where I come from, would seriously fuck you up. But here, the worst thing that could happen is that your beers warm up."

"Or the fat Yanks don't visit. That's how we earn our daily bread, remember," Lynn pointed out, more pragmatically.

"Well, the fat Yanks already on the Island can't escape until the power's back on, so it really doesn't matter."

"But how do they pay? Remember, no power, no cash cards. It would have been okay a couple of decades ago when folk still used paper, but now? How's that going to work?"

"Lynn, you know you're not just a pretty face, that's the key problem in a nutshell." I closed my eyes to think through this concept before slowly continuing. "Lots of stuff that depends on electricity we can work around – with candles for light, fires for cooking, bicycles for transport. But the cashless society needs electricity to function. How could it work without it?"

Margie still wasn't convinced. "Okay, even say the entire island is blacked out for a week. We can work with IOUs. It's doable because it has to be."

"You know, I've got an old electric watch that stopped just over six hours ago, which seems to be the time that the island lost power. How do you figure that – coincidence? Ever since I noticed it, I've been thinking about what could kill a watch and also black out an entire island."

"Calm down now, Chris, we don't even know that the entire island has lost power…"

"We've had nobody come round to tell us that power will be restored, or even explain why it's out. There are no flights in or out or any boats sailing past."

29

"There you're wrong, I can see a boat out there heading towards Simpson Bay," Margie pointed.

"That's a sailing dingy or a sailboard, with no electrical power at all. Where are all the big yachts and floating Gin Palaces that parade past here, the cruise ships or even fucking jet skis? Not a sausage, nothing that requires any kind of electrical power."

"He has a point," Lynn piped in to my defence, "it's all a bit spooky. But, Chris, you seem to have an idea about what is going on. I thought you were an accountant or something similar."

I groaned, realising that my capacity for pulling avaricious women was going to take a hammering if I explained. *But there's no fucking option.* "Well, I probably said that I work for Zurich Re, so that's an easy mistake to make. Over the last couple of decades, re-insurance has become huge and many of the companies were historically based in and around the Caribbean."

"And just what has reinsurance got to do with blackouts?" Margie sounded a bit miffed, as if she realised that she was missing something important, but had no idea what it was.

"Quite a lot, actually, as I'm one of the guys who works on regional disturbance scenarios – so a poorly-paid boffin rather than an over-paid, under-qualified accountant wanker."

Lynn smiled. "Well, that really seemed to come from the heart! So, mister boffin guy, what's going down here?"

I really was beginning to like this girl and felt disappointed that she was one of the lesbians. On the other hand, I conceded, Cecilia had a much better bum.

"What's the inane grin about?" Lynn smiled to take the bite out of her question. "If you say it's the end of the world and we've got to live in the basement with you and shag like rabbits to repopulate the planet, you're in for a good kicking."

My grin widened. "Yes, well it's actually Doctor boffin guy to you – or Mister Doctor Doctor boffin guy, back in Germany where I picked up my degrees. But it's true, repopulation of the planet has got to be our top priority..." I managed to duck a thrown sandal, one of mine I think, but was well hit by a cushion and a suspiciously soggy pair of shorts, the latter adorned with a painful array of studs and buckles.

"Okay, okay," I conceded defeat, "what this is all about. My day job is all about calculating the risks of big disasters, so these're what I know. Now, what we have here is nothing like anything I've ever looked at..."

"...so, you're no use to us at all..."

"...but, my dear Lynn, it's got all the trademarks of an incident causing common mode failure. I actually only spotted it when you mentioned the cash problem – probably something to do with the time of the morning..."

"...or the amount of booze consumed last night! So, if it was a common mode thingy, what does that mean for us, for the island?"

"I wish I knew; I really wish I did. That's the problem with catastrophes like this – at the beginning they're hard to spot and, by the time you have spotted them, they're pretty well out of control and the best that you can do is try to survive until the worst is over."

"And how do we do that?"

"Back to my original answer, more clearly expressed: I do not have a fucking clue!"

PA+9 hours, Nagoya, Japan

I stood and stretched, realising that Shoko and I had been working constantly for over eight hours, with breaks restricted to toilet visits and trips to the coffee machine in the small kitchen that was attached to the emergency sleeping area. "Okay, Shoko, we should take a break now. There's some beer in the fridge, isn't there?"

"Yes, Sensei, I'll get it." She scuttled off and returned moments later with a large can and two small glasses. She also had a large packet of dried squid. Although not my favourite snack, this made me realise how hungry I was.

"Okay, we've been covering different monitoring networks and we now need to bring this all together. You should think about it as if it's a research project and you're outlining a paper for some scientific journal." Although the young woman had been working steadily, she clearly had spells when the magnitude of what we were looking at overwhelmed her and I hoped that this artifice might help her look at things in a more objective manner.

"Well, Sensei, it seems clear now that what I thought were nuclear EMPs, maybe a preliminary to a full-scale nuclear conflict, were actually solar. Something like a coronal mass ejection, but much bigger. This is what you originally suggested," she sounded impressed.

"Yes, a lot bigger. But what about the solar weather satellites? They should have picked this up ages ago."

"Yes, they should have. I checked back and there was a gigantic CME event five days ago. This was directed almost 180° from Earth's present position, so not an immediate concern. It did, however, have an associated EMP that knocked out the entire monitoring network: it's noted as some form of common mode failure, as all units of the entire satellite swarm were of identical design."

"But this isn't the EMP from this morning," I frowned, "that one would have hit us 8 minutes or so after we lost the satellites."

"Certainly not, but the sun monitoring people recorded it and effects at this distance were negligible. Their conclusion seemed to be that we had been lucky to be far from the path of the CME and, as the big ones are relatively rare, there was not a special rush to put replacement monitors in place."

"But this wasn't a normal solar storm, nothing that we've ever seen before?"

"No, it looks like the original event was only a precursor, like the fore-shocks before a huge earthquake."

"So, how's it being interpreted?"

"Before everything went down, it seems like a lot of exotic options were being considered, like impact of a mini black hole or something similar. Anyway, there were no solar activity warnings issued."

"Seems to be a typical Black Swan..."

"A black swan, Sensei, what's that to do with this?"

"It's a technical term, Shoko, used to describe things which are assumed not to exist because nobody has ever seen them."

The girl looked puzzled. "But there are lots of black swans, you can see them in the pond at the zoo."

"Yes, well, in Europe all native swans are white and this term was introduced because this local observation was assumed to be a universal truth and hence it was a complete surprise when black swans were discovered – in Australia, I think. In this context, the impact of the initial large CME event was interpreted in terms of past experience with these occurrences, not considering that we could be experiencing something new."

"So, this is something completely novel, that's never been seen before."

"Well certainly something that wasn't noticed in the past."

"A global-scale blackout that wasn't noticed?"

"Yes, it would've been obvious enough any time over the last century or so, but before electrical power was developed, what direct effects would be observable?"

"You think this is something that might have occurred many times?"

I thought a bit before answering, wanting to avoid simple arm-waving. "Could be, there's no real way of telling. Now we know that such events occur, we could look at old records, maybe searching for spectacular aurora recorded further from the poles or some kind of paleomagnetic signals in geological material. The thing is, I doubt that there'd be anything that'd help us assess the impacts of this particular event."

"And what are those impacts? That's what you've been looking at."

I had been wondering exactly how much to reveal, but suddenly decided that it would be unfair not to give the young woman everything that I had. *After all, she's doing post-doc research in disaster management so she, if anyone, should be able to handle it.* "Well, we're lucky that we have the military network, as a reasonable part of it is still functioning." A series of maps appeared on the main display screen, showing sparse active satellite coverage and hardened cable links. "However, it looks like almost everything civil is down."

"Is everything knocked out or just electrical power?"

"Difficult to tell, but all communications that aren't military spec are down. I'd suspect that any sub-systems that are shielded like ours may still be operational, but we won't see them as they'll have lost external links."

"So, like this, built in a Faraday Cage, you mean?"

"Or deep underground or underwater. Unfortunately, these are some of the worrying cases: underground missile silos or nuclear subs."

"So, there could be a real risk of a nuclear conflict, especially if launch systems have a default to respond to what looks like a pre-emptive attack."

"I worried about that, especially when I looked at the military radiation monitoring network…" the map on the main screen morphed to show a time step animation of an increasing number of hotspots.

"Shit! This shows someone used nuclear weapons…"

"No, worse, those're nuclear power plants."

Shoko looked horrified. "So many of them… But, there don't seem to be any in Japan. Aren't we covered by these monitors?"

"Just shows that even clouds like Fukushima Daiichi and the nuclear threats from North Korea can have silver linings. The passive, fail-safe defences for the Japanese reactors and their hardened control bunkers seem to have really paid off here. You also see that most of the European reactors also seem to have survived, at least so far."

"But the US, there're dozens!"

"Lots of old plants and a complacent industry. Anyway, the nukes are the failures that're easy to spot. The thermal images are more horrifying…" now the map looked like one of the old *world at night* satellite images, picking out population centres.

"Those can't all be fires, surely."

"Maybe not all, but probably most of them. There must be a huge number of potential ignition sources if all power is lost in a refinery or other major industrial complex, or even a densely populated city. With no power backup or communications, automatic suppression systems and external fire-fighting are lost also – so fires will grow until they burn out."

"Again, it looks like Japan has not been hit so hard…"

"Strict building regulations and high-quality construction. Most of the big fires shown are industrial." A graphic compared data from Japan, Europe, Africa and South America. "The squalid slums of the new megalopolises must be holocausts. It really doesn't bear thinking about."

Shoko seemed stunned as she began to grasp the full scale of the catastrophe. "So, this is what you meant when you said this was worse than a nuclear war. How could you have known so quickly?"

"We've known for decades that over-population was driving us towards dangerous instability on a global scale. All we needed was the right initiator and we hit a tipping point, when the house of cards falls down. Global loss of power, even if only for a few hours, is certainly enough to start an autocatalytic collapse."

"You think that power will come back after a few hours?"

"No, that's the problem with this kind of collapse, it has an inherent hysteresis: you lose functions rapidly, but it takes a very long time to get them back – if you actually ever get them back at all."

"So that's the house of cards, you're talking about? A small touch will make it fall down but a long careful effort is needed to build it again."

This young woman is impressive; I would expect most people to be gibbering wrecks when faced by a disaster of this scale, but she just works

38

her way through it. "Exactly, so this is what we need to know now: what do we have that is critical and can be fixed? And then, how do we live without anything that isn't fixable?"

"You say *we*, but who do you mean? Who do we help and how do we define triage?"

I scowled as I looked directly into Shoko's eyes. "That is an extremely good question. I just wish I had a good answer to it!"

PA+12 hours, Mooloolaba, Australia

Jimmy Ramage had only been about one hour into a two-week jetski safari when the machines just died. He had reached the wreck of the HMAS Brisbane and the team were preparing to raft together to form a base for snorkelling when everything went tits-up, not only loss of power, but all comms and navigation. In technical terminology, the group was truly fucked.

As tour leader, he worked his way through all the accident responses that had been drafted before they left base. Despite the fact that the fuel-cell powered, magnetohydrodynamic jetskis were effectively indestructible, having completely sealed electronics and no moving parts, failure of one was a scenario that had been considered. However, failure of all five, simultaneously, due to some kind of common-mode defect, had never been considered. Such failure, combined with loss of all communications, was simply too unlikely to be worth considering. So, he knew from the start that, unless power was restored in as mysterious a manner as it had been lost, he was on a hiding to nothing.

For the next hour or so, the safari participants seemed more amused than concerned, dreaming up conspiracy theories to explain the situation. It was true that these safaris were unpopular with environmentalists and the local communities that they bypassed, but they were not against the letter of any law and hence could not be stopped until Government got around to re-drafting relevant regulations. Given current priorities in Oz, now suffering from multiple impacts of anthropogenic global warming and loss of its coal exports, this could be decades in the future.

Jimmy went over the inventory of supplies, realising now that the distribution of load between the five machines had been less than optimal. The aim had been to spend nights at established camps along their route, but they had emergency supplies. Apart from anything else, it made the trip seem more exciting for the punters.

Unfortunately, all drinking water was in the specially constructed tank of number three, driven by Yoko, the timid Japanese school teacher who had been bringing up the rear and was thus further adrift than the other 'skis. Food was split between numbers two and four but, as most of this was dehydrated survival rations, it was of limited use without Yoko's water. It might actually be edible with added fresh water, but palatable only after cooking – and the microwave was built into number five. His machine carried the tents, miracles of miniaturisation and creative use of smart fabrics, but worthless out of sight of land.

For a while the tour group could talk to each other, even if the volume of shouting had to increase as they slowly drifted apart. Drifting not only further from each other, but clearly also in a current that was taking them further away from land.

The team all wore wetsuits and were warm enough for the first few hours. Then the rain started and things began to get really miserable.

Jimmy looked at his watch, an ancient Tag Heuer automatic that he had inherited from his grandfather, just before last traces of light vanished from the autumn sky, noting that it was now a full twelve hours since the original loss of power. It was also five hours since he had seen any of his party. *Why the fuck hasn't a search found us by now? I've lit flares every hour, which must be picked up on the satellite network that monitors coastal shipping. So why am I still drifting alone?*

He was cold, stiff and dehydrated, so almost missed the ringing of a bell from somewhere to his left. He was about to dismiss this as an auditory illusion before he remembered the small Japanese bell that Yoko had ceremoniously hung from the handlebars of her jetski. *It's got to be the 'ski with the water.*

Jimmy shouted, calling on Yoko for a quarter of an hour without response while the diminishing sound of the bell indicated that they were drifting further apart. His natural tendency was to stay with his 'ski, but he knew that his chances of survival dropped rapidly without water. "Fuck it," he cursed, his voice more of a croak, as he finally made up his mind, strapped on fins and slipped into the chilly water.

The swell was gentle but, at water level, the sound of the bell came and went as he breast-stroked in what he prayed was the right direction. After a few minutes swimming he glanced back and realised that he could no longer see his own jetski. *So that's it, I'm fully committed, trusting my life to the distant tinkling of a bell.*

Swimming in the dark with only an auditory clue for guidance was very much more difficult than he had imagined. For a few minutes it seemed like he had lost it completely and felt the rush of warmth as his terror caused him to piss himself. He fought down the urge to break into a racing crawl, but stroked steadily in what he thought was the right direction. On the crest of a particularly large wave, he was rewarded by a faint ringing sound and he increased his speed in the direction indicated.

After a further fifteen minutes the bell was more distinct and he realised, belatedly, why this swim was taking so long. A faint breeze was pushing the higher profile of his target, while simply blowing over his head. This clue allowed him to better orient on his goal and, after another ten minutes he could make out the dim shape of the 'ski in a faint greenish light which seemed to be due to some kind of auroral display.

Jimmy was exhausted when he carefully clambered on board, wondering what could possibly have happened to the Japanese girl. Some company would have been nice but, most importantly, he now had the water. In the ghostly half-light, he moved to the rear of the seat and searched for the clasps that allowed the front part to open, exposing the storage compartment. Yoko's kit bag would be on top and the water container would be at the bottom, acting as ballast.

43

After several moments of scrabbling about he finally located the clasps, noting that they were lying open. A sudden premonition made him feel sick to his stomach while he wrenched the lid open, making him hesitant about searching therein. When he finally forced his hands inside his worst fears were confirmed – the compartment was completely empty. Tears ran down his face as his final hopes were dashed. *The question's no longer if I'm going to die, but when and how drawn out the process is going to be.*

PA+1 day, Nagoya, Japan

I was momentarily disoriented when I woke up in the narrow camp bed, very aware of the nubile body in my arms. At first, I thought that we were both naked, but some careful exploration indicated that, although I certainly was, the girl was wearing panties and a bra.

I tried to relax and ignore a throbbing erection while I went over the events of the previous day. Initially it seemed surreal enough to be some kind of dream, but the fact of the woman in my bed was clear evidence that it was much more than that. We had been in the DMRC all day and, in the evening, decided to spend the night in the attached sleeping quarters. Here, at least, we had light and access to hot food and cold drinks, things previously taken for granted that those outside our bunker would now be beginning to miss.

Our DMRC was a fully functional, although passive, part of the Japanese national disaster management system. Basically, it was a centre for research and training of the operators who ran the active centres, which were scattered throughout Japan and coordinated responses on a regional basis. Although emphasis was very much on natural hazards – earthquakes, typhoons, volcanoes – it also incorporated the military network that would activate in times of war or large-scale terrorist attacks: nuclear, chemical, biological or cyber. As such, the DMRC had a lock-down mode, in which it could be sealed off to provide a self-sustained refuge for a full team of 20 operators. For these 20 staff, there were provisions for a month, so we had large reserves as long as there were only the two of us here.

Last night, Shoko and I had discussed this in depth over beer and snacks. Would any of our colleagues show up in the following days and, if not, should we try to fetch them? The problem was that, without the information that we could access in the centre, would anyone recognise how serious the situation was? For the first few hours, the blackout would seem like an anomaly, a serious nuisance, but not a cause for panic. At least not in Japan, where every household kept emergency supplies of water and food.

From what we could see from the monitoring system, even in Tokyo, still one of the world's largest cities, things weren't so bad. Unlike many capitals, its two major airports, Narita and Haneda, had approaches over the sea and agricultural land. There had been a few helicopter crashes in the city, but nothing like the carnage that plummeting jets caused to other major urban areas. The city's famously efficient public transport system died instantly but, apart from those trapped underground, this was mainly an annoyance, as the centre of the city is relatively compact and the policemen in the numerous Kobans are always on hand to help guide those whose idea of a Tokyo map was restricted to the metro network. In addition, the majority of Tokyoites owned a bicycle and, in times of trouble, were generous in lending these to neighbours or even complete strangers.

In other countries it would be very different. Accidental fires would be compounded by arson, with shortages of supplies leading to widespread looting and rioting. With police, fire and ambulance services neutered by lack of transportation and communication, entire districts of major cities would become war zones. Within twelve hours, untold millions of refugees will be aimlessly fleeing urban centres, reversing the flow from the countryside that had been the global trend over the last few decades.

I was relieved to learn that Shoko's parents, living in Shinjuku near the centre of Tokyo, were both doctors and would probably be well integrated into the disaster response centre in the hospital where they worked. For myself, I was twice divorced, the first time acrimoniously, so I had no idea where my ex-wife and son had ended up, and the second time parting on good terms after my wife decided that she preferred women to men. She and her new wife had *gone back to nature*, farming somewhere in rustic Eire. *They probably haven't even noticed that global civilisation had just fallen apart – and probably won't for some time.*

My story had greatly amused the young Japanese researcher. "How long were you married, Sensei, the second time?"

"Just under 10 years."

"And she didn't know that she was a lesbian for all that time?"

"Well, after my first catastrophic marriage, I was a bit more careful and we had a sort of open relationship. This actually lasted for several years –

about five – before we finally decided to get married during a trip to Gretna Green." I spotted the confused look on Shoko's face. "It's a kind of crazy place is Scotland where people used to run away to in order to get married," I explained.

"Oh, like Las Vegas?"

"Well not exactly. But, anyway, we both had our own close friends and occasionally that got physical – either separately or together."

"So you were, what do you call it, *swingers*?" The girl laughed, plainly amused by the concept.

"Again, not exactly, but something like that. I know that things are a bit more relaxed nowadays, but we considered ourselves quite progressive. Probably hard to believe when you see the old fart that I've become, but I was pretty dynamic in my younger days."

"So, the groups included your wife and other women, you liked that?"

"I think it's maybe time to change the subject," I could feel myself blushing and hoped my tan would disguise this. "So, do you have a boyfriend?"

"Not at present – or a girlfriend either," she grinned mischievously. "I want to work hard and finish my research here: then I can think about boys, or maybe girls."

"Yes, well, whatever rocks your boat. At least we both seem to be in the position where we have no close family members to worry about…"

"…actually, I have my grandparents, my father's parents. But they live in Hokkaido, on a dairy farm in the very north. On a clear day they can see Russia from their house window."

48

Grandparents! Christ but I feel old compared to this young girl. "I expect that's probably a good place to be. As safe as anywhere else. But there's nobody in or around Nagoya that you feel obliged to look after?"

"Only the other senseis and students. But they should be able to look after themselves, I guess."

"No special friends amongst them, there're some cute boys – and girls," I teased.

"They're all friends, but nobody special. They spend all their time studying, working on projects and stuff like that."

"Right, so now we get back to a question you asked a while ago. Triage. I guess we focus at present on looking after each other and seeing if there's anything we can provide to help recovery actions. If any of the other DMRC members turn up, we'll bring them into our team, but we won't go chasing them."

"Would that even be possible? You need your e-ID to get into the department at weekends or holidays, and the power is off now. Could anyone at all get into this building?"

"Good point. I suppose we're locked in by ourselves at present. Anyway, it'd be an intelligence test for them. But if they can get to the sub-basement, their hardened comm units will let us know that they've arrived and we can let them in."

"I didn't notice, but I guess that means that you've closed the bulkhead door now, Sensei."

"It seemed a sensible precaution, as we still don't know what direct or indirect effects this solar activity will have and how long they will persist."

"So, you think that maybe it's not all over. There could be more."

"Not a clue, that's something to check in the morning. I don't know about you, but I could do with an early night."

***

There were two sleeping rooms, each with eight cots and a communal bathroom. I nominated one as mine and wished Shoko good night, giving her a brief reassuring squeeze before I wandered off in search of toiletries.

I fell asleep as soon as my head hit the pillow. I had not been asleep long when I was wakened by the slim body slipping into bed beside me. "Shoko, what're you doing?" I whispered in surprise.

"Sorry, Sensei, but can I sleep with you? I'm so frightened." Indeed, the slim girl seemed to be shivering.

"No problem at all, you probably just need a well-padded father-figure to reassure you. Anyway, just lie here for a bit and you can go back to your own bed when you feel a bit better." I stroked her silky hair and felt the tension gradually drain from her body. I had just noticed that her breathing had become shallow, indicating that she had fallen asleep, before I also drifted off.

So, now, here I am, with a hard-on that would normally be a source of pride at my age, trying to avoid rubbing it against her thigh. I'd never have thought this would have been possible twenty-four hours ago. But, pleasant though it is, I've got to find a way to extricate myself pretty soon before I wet

50

myself – which would really betray me as the ancient crumbly that I've become.

***

I managed to extricate myself from the sleeping girl and slide out of the cot with minimum disturbance of my bedmate, just about to congratulate myself, when I was pinned by a pair of beautiful dark eyes. I immediately felt ashamed of my old man's body: sagging muscles and belly covered with white hair, white straggly pubes and, especially, my sizeable erection.

"Oops, I'm choking for a pee. It does this," I waved vaguely towards my dick before I scurried off towards the bathroom.

After relieving myself and taking a quick shower, I peered cautiously into the dormitory, relieved to see that my bed was now empty. I quickly dressed and then headed for the kitchen, where I switched on the coffee machine and laid the dining table for two. About fifteen minutes later Shoko joined me, now wearing form-fitting overalls and towelling her hair.

"If you need clean clothes, there are these in lockers in the sleeping area. I can also put your clothes through the laundry, if you prefer."

At least she doesn't seem traumatised by the sight of my naked bod and happy to forget all about last night. I sighed with relief. "Okay, lass, what would you like for breakfast? I've put out some fruit juice and the coffee is ready. Would you rather have tea? What do you eat in the morning?"

"Please sit down, Sensei," she directed me towards a chair and poured me a mug of coffee. "I

51

will get this sorted out. What do you want for breakfast?"

"I've already put a couple of the deep-frozen croissants in the microwave, so you just need to push the button. That's enough for me."

"Are you sure. I was going to use this dehydrated egg to make omelette and zap some toast. Don't you want some."

"Not for me," I poked my paunch, "already too fat."

"Not really fat, cuddly," I recognised the mischievous grin from last night. "Most of the post-grad boys have fatter bellies."

Oops, this is going in a tricky direction. I wracked my brains to try to find a way of diverting the girl onto a different track. "Yes, well, let's have breakfast and then we can plan the rest of the day."

"What were you thinking of, Sensei, maybe having sex with me?"

I choked on my coffee, spluttering as some of the hot fluid went down the wrong way. I stared at the girl, wondering if I had misheard, but her salacious smile was unmistakable.

"Shoko, I'm sorry about what happened this morning. It's just an old man thing, the result of pressure on my bladder."

"So, you don't want sex with me?" The minx pouted provocatively. "Do you prefer boys? We could do anal if you wanted."

Again, I choked, even worse this time. *What the fuck happened to demure, shy little Shoko. Has her brain been fried by some kind of exotic solar radiation or has she simply had a breakdown*

52

overnight? I suppose the sight of my erect penis might do that to a girl of a delicate nature.

"Shoko, of course I'd love to have sex with you, but not when you're clearly in a state of shock. I'm not only old enough to be your dad – actually maybe your granddad – but I'm also your teacher. Relationships, sexual contacts, between teachers and students are never a good idea."

"Yes, but we have to talk about this. We're stranded here like castaways, maybe for months. You're still my teacher, sort of, but you've been saying that we work as a team. Team members have sex sometimes, don't they?"

"Mmm, maybe, but let's talk about this later," I could sense that I was babbling in my haste to change the subject. "So, we finish breakfast and then into the control room – find out what's happened overnight and think about whether we can focus on recovery or if the sun has still threats in line for us."

"Okay," she agreed, "but we need to check how long we're likely to be trapped together. It'll be like Robinson Crusoe. I loved that book when I was a kid. I was always sure that Robinson had sex with Man Friday: what do you think?"

"That's something that I don't even want to contemplate," I muttered under my breath, focusing on my croissant, while avoiding coffee in case the young woman came out with another of her outrageous comments.

***

When we entered the control centre after breakfast, I still had half a cup of lukewarm coffee.

53

"So, what do you think about testing to see if solar activity is still causing problems."

"I've been thinking about it, Mike-sensei, and I think the best place to start would be the military net notice boards."

I noticed this new familiarity, but decided not to rise to the bait. "That's an excellent idea – so what do we have?"

Her fingers blurred over the touchpad. "This is a US defence link to NASA, the one that I got the original solar weather stuff from. They seem to have a think tank working full time on this, trying to see what they can get from surviving satellites."

"The military ones, I guess. There's probably not too much to be obtained from them except profiles of failure rates."

A graphic flashed onto the main screen. "That's exactly what they're doing," she sounded very impressed by my wild guess. "There was steady attrition over the first six hours, but things are now holding steady, with the main problems being degraded performance of the survivors."

"That's a good sign, it could be that the ones lost were only semi-hard and the ones remaining are the truly nuclear-hard beasts, but more likely that the worst is over."

"That seems to be the consensus also from the NASA gurus. Would you care to speculate what else they've been up to?" Clearly a challenge to my seeming omnipotence.

"Interrogation of the deep space missions?"

"How did you know that? Have you already looked at this board?"

"Not at all, but it would be the obvious way of checking if the EMP-type pulse was 4 pi or more localised, say in our orbital plane. Also allows a check if it propagates at light speed and allow some guesses about energy density, as this drops off with the inverse square of distance."

"So, there really wasn't much point of following this lead, was there?"

"I've no idea – was it light speed propagation or not?"

"It says here that the leading edge certainly is, within measurement limits…"

"That's boffin-speak for yes," I explained. "And was it 4 pi?"

Text scrolled down the screen until I called out. "Stop! There it is." I highlighted the relevant text.

"Distribution consistent with an oblate spheroid," she read. "That's supposed to mean something to me?"

"It is indeed, my dear," I could see the opportunity for revenge for the way I had been teased over breakfast. "Your task for today is to interpret these findings in terms of making response recommendations to the Japanese team."

"But you already know the answer; this is a waste of my time!"

"I have an inkling of an answer, but I could be wrong. If we independently come to the same answer, then that is an indication that, maybe, we're onto something. It's the scientific method and good training for you!"

"Training, how can you be thinking about training now when everything is so…, so…, shit? I don't need training now!"

"On the contrary, my dear, I can't think of a time when your training is more important. To get through this, Japan, the world, will need as many disaster response experts as can be found. You'll be like gold dust."

She seemed mollified by this hyperbole. "Alright, Sensei, I guess that you're correct. I'll do it. But please don't call me *my dear,* you make me seem like a little schoolgirl."

"Fine, Shoko, but if we're working so closely together you can drop the sensei bit, just call me Mike."

"Okay, Mike, that's good with me. Does that mean that we're going to have sex?" The girl's eyes gleamed as she turned the tables on me.

Fuck! Hoist by my own petard! How do I get out of this? "Well, we can talk about that later, but for now concentrate on your job. This is very important. Remember that we are in an incredibly privileged position – there are lots of people who have died, or are going to die, out there. We are amongst the few who can, possibly, save lives."

Shoko was evidently moved by this thought. "That's the thing that I really wanted to ask you Sensei, Mike, how many are going to die?"

I thought of prevaricating, but decided that here honesty was the best policy. "There's no rigorous way of calculating this…"

"Without the boffin-speak!" she glared at me, daring me to give a straight answer.

"Okay, dead before we get over this, at least two to three…"

"Millions?" Her voice was a squeak as she interpreted my answer in terms of some mental calculations that she must already have carried out.

Got to take her down gently here! "Yes, well, under best possible conditions the death toll in Japan might be as low as that. Realistically, we should reckon it being a fair bit higher, factor of two or three, say."

"In Japan?" her voice was so low as to be almost inaudible and all colour had drained from her face.

"Yes, as we discussed previously, due to high risk of natural hazards, both the defence and response systems here are second to none. With a bit of luck, it could be kept to a few million."

"And globally?" she whispered.

"Ah, yes, well, that's the two to three – billion. This is a *four horseman* event. The initial deaths will only be in the millions, tens of millions, but then things will fall apart. Conflict, starvation and disease will give the really big numbers. If we could keep it to three, we'd be doing well."

"Three billion, thirty percent of the world's population is going to die?"

I swithered, my mental commitment to honesty vying with my desire to avoid freaking the girl out more than she already was. "Look at it this way, if we were left with seven billion, we'd still have a factor of about three more people than we had in the middle of last century, when our fundamental, low tech, infrastructure was more or less intact, rebuilt after the Second World War. Is that really sustainable while we recover from a global destruction of the high-tech infrastructure that allowed such over-population to occur?"

"So that's what you really believe, three billion people are going to die."

"No, three billion are certainly going to die – but I believe that the total will eventually be higher, much higher. In the absence of a miracle, I'd guess about seven. If we can't get our act together, maybe more than nine. That's why what we're doing is so important."

I explained this to Shoko but, in truth, I was also talking for my own benefit, reminding myself what the stakes were.

***

We had previously discussed the concept of *triage*, but I had already applied it in my own mind. Something that I definitely do not want to get into with Shoko before she has sorted out some of the big stuff that I have already laid on her. In some ways, it is already defined by the hardened military communication network that has good coverage in North America, Northern Europe and the more advanced countries of East Asia and Australasia. These are our primary targets. Africa and the Middle East are, despite their development potential and huge populations, basket cases that cannot be helped. They will sink or swim on their own and the mortality rate will be horrendous. Similarly for India and a lot of South America although, on a regional basis, the prognosis might be slightly better. Oceania, together with remoter island countries in all oceans and seas, might be inherently better off, especially in areas with low population densities and good agriculture and fisheries. They would be better left to their own devices, with only a bit of protection to ensure they are not ravaged by larger, predatory neighbours.

These global goals were, however, all well and good, but had to be seen in a local context. Presently I was locked in a basement of a Japanese University with a rather loopy, even if distinctly cute, young student. Our immediate priorities thus had to be to help the Uni, Nagoya and then Japan. *The rest of the world will just have to wait.*

***

We had a break for lunch, comparing notes on our progress while eating truly anodyne microwaved burgers, washed down with coffee. *It is certainly a standard of life beyond anything accessible to 99.99% of the planet at the present moment, but I need to stock up on booze. There's got to be both a quality as well as a duration to life.* There had been a couple of beers in the fridge used by the trainees, but the rations packed for the lockdown phase betrayed the pedestrian tastes of those involved.

So, while Shoko was working on developing a solution to the catastrophe, I was planning a raid on the refectory wine cellar. It was not a coincidence that I had access to the database of all comestibles stored on the university premises; this was just one of the normal functions of the centre so that, in case of a disaster, distribution of any food and drink available could be optimised. In terms of food, almost everything on the inventory was too short-lived to be of interest. But stores of alcoholic beverages were also included – the focus of my search.

Amongst the diverse Departments at the university was the delightfully named *Catering and Restaurant Management Engineering*, which had a demonstration restaurant integrated into the more industrial student refectory. The good news was that all university buildings were connected at basement level by a network of tunnels, to allow movement between them in case of the tropical downpours associated with typhoons. The bad news was that the bulkhead doors that limited such access were electrically controlled.

I memorised the route and then called over to Shoko, who was staring glumly at some cryptic data. "I'm just off for a wee walk to stretch my legs. I've shut off lockdown mode but, given that we haven't seen a trace of anyone else so far, I doubt that this place will have filled up by the time I get back."

"Are you going outside the building?" She sounded perturbed by this thought.

"No, not yet anyway. It's not smart until we know a bit more about the local situation. I'll just have a perambulation through the corridors. It'll also be a bit of an experiment – I'm taking head lamp to test if it continues to function outside our Faraday Cage."

"Do you want me to come with you?"

"No, you get on with your work here. There'll be a test for you at lunchtime."

The girl groaned and rolled her eyes theatrically, but returned to her screen without any further complaint.

There was enough remnant phosphorescent emergency lighting for me to make my way up to the B1 level. There I easily found the large metal door that provided entry to the underground connecting tunnels. As normal, it was securely closed, being opened each morning during term time by the security guys. The door looked immovable, but I spotted what I was looking for: a glass-covered panel, with a lever plainly visible behind it. This was associated with a paragraph of red Japanese text, but I ignored that and broke the thin glass with my elbow – just before I noticed a little metal hammer on a chain that was evidently supplied for this purpose.

Although the door was heavy, the rails that carried it were well greased and, with a bit of effort and much grunting, I was able to slide it open. Now I needed the torch – it was pitch black inside. To my relief, the torch functioned perfectly and I strapped it to my head so that everywhere I looked was lit by its powerful beam. A set of wide steps took me into the labyrinthine tunnel network, but bilingual signs made finding my way to the refectory easy.

Although, on the surface, the walk to the student's canteen took only about 5 minutes, the underground route was more circuitous, clearly cutting through the basements of other university buildings. I had to repeat opening of bulkhead doors four times before I eventually came to that leading into the refectory. My goal was at the back of the special restaurant kitchen on the 4th floor, so I braced myself to trudge up five flights of stairs, switching off my torch when I left the basement and my way was lit by sunlight streaming in from numerous windows.

On the third floor, I was stopped by a strange smell and cast about, finding what looked like spatters of blood on the walls and a long trace of red on the otherwise, spotless white-tiled floor. Fearing that someone had been hurt, I rushed along the corridor, following the spoor of gore around a corner, where I almost tripped over the body sprawled on the floor. I bent to check the boy's neck for a pulse, but his temperature alone was enough to confirm that he was dead – probably for at least several hours. Cause of death was also obvious, he had been stabbed and slashed many times, probably with the large kitchen knife that still protruded from his back.

I cautiously made my way back along the corridor, only now noticing a vandalised cigarette machine in a side niche just before I reached the stairs. More worryingly, I could also hear faint noises from the floor above.

Jesus, how much do I really want this booze? Despite this sensible reconsideration of my actions, I felt myself slowly slide up the stairs, making as little sound as possible. On the 4th floor, the door to the restaurant had been smashed open and the noises were clearly coming from therein. I peered through the doorway and could then see that, on the other side of the restaurant, the door to the kitchen had also been kicked open. The noises were also more distinct, the crunching of broken glass and some truly awful singing. I even recognised the song from my student days, some rugby ditty about sticking your finger in a woodpecker's hole.

Curiosity overcame discretion and I tiptoed towards the kitchen. Looking in, it seemed to be deserted, with immaculate steel worktops and neatly hung racks of utensils. To the left was another door, somewhat more robust than the others. It looked like the lock had been hacked off with an axe but, as I approached, I saw the tool responsible discarded on the floor – a large kitchen cleaver of the type beloved by Chinese chefs.

I carefully picked up the cleaver and its weight in my hand gave me fresh courage. I had to push the door open, resulting in a loud creak and the singing breaking off mid verse. "Who's there? Is somebody there? Fuck off! I got here first, so you find your own fucking booze."

I recognised a distinctive antipodean accent, Australia or New Zealand, but the voice was also slurred, sounding very drunk. I pushed the door further open and looked in, my weapon at the ready.

The young man was tall and well-built, but dishevelled and swaying on his feet, surrounded by broken wine bottles and cigarette buts, clutching a very expensive bottle of cognac in one hand and his smoke in the other. Although I was pretty sure that this was the homicidal maniac responsible for the murder I'd seen, he was clearly little threat in his present state. "Fuck off, I told you, go to fuck! I work here and this is mine! Who the fuck're you? Don't you understand fucking English?"

I could feel rage building in me. *Fucking gaijin. I'd forgotten how many of us there now are in this country. The Japanese are civilised and respond well to crises – but fuckers like this screw it up for everyone.* I lifted the cleaver high and saw the man's jaw drop when he spotted it.

"What the fuck, mate, screw the nut! You're not going to hit me with that fucking thing, are you?"

I actually considered it for a moment while I looked him over: long blond hair and scrappy beard over a deep tan, denim shirt and jeans, fancy trainers. *Could be either one of the older students or a younger member of staff. In any case, I can hardly slaughter him if I'm unsure of his guilt.* The guy seemed to have decided that I was having second thoughts and started to relax before I kicked him in the groin as hard as I could.

His scream of pain as I made contact was followed by another when he dropped to his knees, lacerating his jeans on the shards of glass that covered the floor. Just to be on the safe side I kicked him again on the side of the head, rendering him semiconscious on his bed of broken bottles. I then grabbed his hair and dragged him along behind me as I retraced my route.

He seemed to be coming to while I bounced him down the stairs and I thought about giving his head another kick. *He's not a threat at the moment, so just hold back. He can't answer questions if he isn't conscious.*

We had now reached the body of the boy. I banged the drunk's head against a wall and stared

64

into his bloodshot eyes. "Why did you do this? Why did you kill this boy?"

"Him, was it him," the man was struggling to focus on his victim. "He was stealing my fucking fags! I told him they were mine, to get his own, but he wouldn't listen. It was his own fucking fault!"

"Good, so we agree the penalty is now death for not listening to you. I really don't think that you'd listen to me, so you can't disagree with this." I raised the cleaver.

"No, fuck it, you can't! I was drunk at the time!"

"That's an explanation, not a fucking excuse!" I swung as hard as I could and buried the chopper in the back of his neck, almost decapitating him. *Suffer not a mad dog to live, it'll just end up biting you in the arse some day.*

I forced the entire incident out of my mind and got to work. First of all, finding one of the collapsible trolleys that the Japanese use for shifting stuff and then loading it with crates of beer and boxes of fine wines. I heaved the heavily laden cart to the lift, pressed the button, waiting for about 10 seconds before I rapped myself on the side on my brow. *No bloody electricity of course! Bollocks!*

I thought about abandoning some of my swag but, given the effort involved in getting it, I simply groaned and started schlepping it down the stairs, box by box, then finally returning for the trolley. *Well, at least I'm getting my workout for today. And I always claimed that booze made me fit, not that I was necessarily thinking about it this way.*

After working my way through the underground maze, I was relieved to find a ramp that bypassed the final stairs into my department's basement. However, I then had to lug everything down into the sub-basement.

I was completely knackered when I finally reached the centre, but tried to hide it with a cheerful, "Honey, I'm home!"

Shoko did not even look up from her work. "What's honey got to do with anything?"

"Forget it, just a line from a very old movie. Anyway, I'm back with the shopping."

Now she glanced at me in surprise. "Mike-san, what's all that stuff. Where did you get it?"

"Just some extra liquid supplies from the refectory. Something for a rainy day."

"Rain, is it raining? Anyway, you went there and all you got was alcohol? The food here is all dehydrated or deep frozen. Couldn't you have picked up a few steaks, maybe some fish?"

I felt ashamed that this had not even crossed my mind. "I'm just starting with the heavy stuff," I lied. "I'll take a big backpack later, after lunch, and bring back food."

"Okay, I'll come with you and give you a hand."

I thought of the bodies and their resting place, signpost by a trail of blood. *No way that Shoko needs to see, or even know about that!* "No, we've got traditional division of labour here: I'm the man, so I search out the food and bring it back to you. You're the woman so you do the cooking and cleaning." As the words left my mouth, I realised

66

that such sexist lines would get me well reamed anywhere in the western world. However, I might just escape with my balls intact in Japan.

Shoko was thinking this over and I was beginning to worry that she really was more westernised than she appeared. I relaxed a bit, however, when a grin spread over her face. "So, we're playing at traditional roles, husband and wife kind of thing. That would also extend to sex, so it'd be only missionary position for you, would it?"

I groaned aloud, which seemed only to encourage my tormentress. "Of course, if it's back to hunting and gathering, you should bop me over the head with a club and drag me back to your cave to have your evil way with me. Would that turn you on?"

"Jesus, Shoko, where do you get all this stuff?"

"English comic books, of course," she laughed, turning back to her work station.

***

Before we had lunch, I changed into overalls and dropped my clothes in the washer, having noticed several bloody stains on my trousers and shirt. "Dragging beer and wine up and down stairs is sweaty work," I announced by way of explanation to an evidently uninterested Shoko.

"Are you really going to give me a test on this solar stuff?" she enquired, indicating what was foremost on her mind.

"Most certainly," I grinned, "do you want to make a formal presentation or just talk through it while we have lunch?"

"Informal would be much better," she was clearly happy to have this option. "I'll set up lunch now. What do you want?"

"Maybe one of those disgusting microwaved cheese toast things?"

"Croque Monsieur. I thought those tasted quite nice."

"Whatever, as long as there's beer with it. Now we have reserves, we don't need to ration it."

While Shoko sorted out lunch, I tried to anticipate what she might have found out. The initially good news, confirmed by my functional headlamp, was that the solar wave of destruction had passed beyond Earth's orbit and hence we could plan to start recovery. *If we can be sure that the event has ended: that's the crunch! There was a precursor that took out the solar monitoring network, so can we be sure that there isn't something bigger yet to come? This has a critical impact on our strategy. If we're through the worst, we should start rebuilding as soon as possible to minimise the degradation of infrastructure – and loss of life – that this phenomenon has caused. If it's only a warning of something even bigger, however, we need to carefully harbour the resources that we have left to avoid losing any more, even if that does increase global hardship in the short term.*

I was extremely pleased that Shoko captured the essence of my musing in the introduction to her synthesis. "Best guesses on what we actually experienced and the chances that there's more to come," as she put it. "In terms of the first, the

68

geometry of the shockwave – oblate spheroid or just about 4 pi – indicates that the initiating event occurred over the entire surface of the sun. The leading edge is EM, probably with a very high gamma component, so propagates at light speed. This is followed by a wide band of slower particles, intense enough to cause massive secondary EMPs in the upper atmosphere."

"Even if they're slow, this still indicated that this was a long-term process on the solar surface, not just a single flash event."

"Which would imply…" now she was teasing me.

"That it wasn't a surface event, but something that occurred at a specific depth throughout the entire star.

"Mike-san, sometimes you really piss me off," she sighed in frustration, "How can you possibly know this shit?"

"Reading New Scientist cover to cover," I responded, smugly.

The girl frowned. "I know the New Scientist site, it's pretty good, but what's *cover to cover*?"

"Originally it was printed on paper, so cover to cover is reading the entire contents every week."

"That's not possible, must be gigabytes, even without graphics."

"It was less when I was young and dinosaurs roamed the earth. Anyway, maybe not read, more scanned."

She raised a sceptical eyebrow, but evidently decided not to take this further. "Anyway, the bottom line is that, although it is only a small fraction of a percent of the total, a gigantic mass of material has been lost from the sun. The consensus of the solar physicists is thus that a further event is extremely unlikely and, even if it did occur, would have a long lead time."

"What do they mean by *long*," I asked, suspiciously.

"Best guesses lie between a million and a hundred million years."

"Well, that's good news," I sighed. Responding to Shoko's glare I expanded. "This Black Swan event has no precedents, so we have to consider anything numerical as guesses, at best."

"But guesses from the best minds in the field…"

"Yes, maybe, but guesses, nevertheless. I would always assume a further couple of orders of magnitude uncertainty on anything they come up with but, even in the worst case of the minimum time being 3 or 4 orders of magnitude out, this indicates that we're in good shape."

"But something like this could happen again in another thousand, or maybe a few hundred years. We build up, only to have the house of cards knocked down again."

"Yes, maybe this isn't as novel as we think it is. But we're in much better shape now, aren't we?" I raised an eyebrow to indicate that the student was on now.

"I hadn't thought about this yet, but I can give it a try…"

"Good start, get your apologies in first," I smiled in encouragement.

"Okay, why things are better now... I suppose because we know that events like this are possible."

"Excellent!" I clapped my hands in admiration. "That's 50% of the answer – and the rest is..."

The girl closed her eyes and grimaced. After a couple of minutes of silence, she shrugged despondently. "I don't know, I really don't know. I'm just not as smart as you!"

"You're certainly as smart, you're just not as old. So, what else have we learned, together in this basement?"

"In the centre, maybe, we followed what was happening... That's it, we have the technology to provide counter-measures. Even if it is just a by-product of the development of really stupid weapons, we can already survive such an event. In the future, we'd maybe be able to see it coming but, even if not, could ensure that the complete system failure that we've experienced would not happen again."

"Exactly, well done!" My intended paternal hug ended up with me getting a number of kisses to my neck before I could pry myself free.

"Right, less of that, there's work to be done! We need to integrate everything that we've learned and use that to develop guidelines for future defences."

"And what about aiding recovery here and now?"

"Yes, well that comes automatically as part of the package," I blustered. *Now's not the time to mention the other way that things would be better, removal of a large proportion of the population, the excess of which was a root cause of global vulnerability to perturbations. Stabilisation somewhere about 1 – 2 billion would probably be ideal, but I doubt that Shoko would see that as a benefit at the present moment.*

***

After lunch, I had a quick trip back to the refectory with a large backpack, originally designed to carry medical supplies, but ideal for my purposes. Before proceeding to the fourth floor, I first stopped off to move the two bodies further along the corridor and onto a balcony that was normally used by smokers. *We could be here for a while and can do without the smell of decaying corpses.*

I couldn't work up the enthusiasm to wash the corridor clear of traces of blood, but did brush up broken glass from the floor of the restaurant larder. I then looked though the walk-in refrigerator, removing choice items that would go off as it slowly warmed up. In line with its role of showcasing the culinary skills of the students, the selection was impressive – caviar, wagyu beef, lobsters, scallops. I mentally thanked Shoko for pointing me in this direction and, when the rucksack was packed to bursting point, broke the lock of a cage protecting their choicest wines. *Not sure what we'll eat tonight, but a Chablis Premier Cru and a twenty-year-old Opus One should cover the options. I really hope the power doesn't come on tomorrow and I end up having to pay for this stuff.*

Grunting under the weight of the backpack and with an outrageously expensive bottle of wine in each hand I slowly slogged my way back to our refuge.

This time Shoko was standing at the entrance to the centre, evidently waiting for me. Seeing me at the end of the corridor, she rushed along and relieved me of the wine. "Mike, there's been a nuclear attack on Pakistan. Multiple warheads, hitting all big cities and industrial centres."

"Fuck! I knew the Indians couldn't make their ICBM silos nuclear hard, but I forgot about their one fucking submarine. Luckily, the Pakis have nothing nuclear to retaliate with but, if I know these smart buggers, they'll probably have a MAD response lined up. We just have to hope that it has gone down along with their communications, but I've a bad feeling about this."

"But, Mike-sensei, surely any weapon that isn't nuclear hard, protected against EMPs, will be useless now. The Indian ones survived only in a submarine."

"Okay, that's your test for this evening – list up some of the EMP-proof WMDs that I might be worried about. But, before that, you need to look at my sack full of swag and decide what we're going to eat tonight. The world may have gone to hell in a handbasket, but at least we're going to dine in style.

***

It was a truly exceptional meal, the exotic Beluga Caviar starter accompanied by the white wine, followed by a Japanese beef and lobster tail *surf and turf*, washed down with the Californian super-red. The simple preparation and accompaniments were perfectly suited to the food, betraying either Shoko's facility with such gourmet fare or beginner's luck. I favoured the former and she the latter. *In any case, memorable.*

Shoko had seemingly drunk more than usual and appeared to be rapidly losing inhibitions. "Okay, my dear, time for the exam," I announced in an attempt to cool her down, receiving a painful kick to my shins in response.

"No, Mike-sensei, I've had too much alcohol. We should go to bed now."

"No bed, for either of us, until you've passed your exam."

She staggered from her chair and pushed her way onto my lap. "So, if I pass my exam, we will have sex."

I stroked her hair, trying to work a way out of this. "Okay, you score 100% and we'll do anything you like, would that be okay with you?"

She started nibbling my neck. "But if it's only 99%, what then?"

"Okay, anything like 100%, more than 90% say, would be good enough. But I think you're too drunk now, maybe it'd be better if you went to bed, your own bed, now. You can sit the exam tomorrow."

"Yes!" she bounced from my lap, almost causing me to fall off my chair. "You're very cute, Mikey, but you don't listen," she ruffled my hair provocatively. "You think Japanese can't handle alcohol, but my family are from the borders of Russia. We have vodka – or the nasty local equivalent – from our mothers' nipples. Let's have the exam now, while I'm in my zone."

Fuck, Fuck, Fuckity-fuck-for-fuck's sake! I'm a man of the world, three times her age, and stuck my leg right into that fucking bear-trap! "Really, now, are you sure?" I swithered pathetically.

"Definitely, this was the question about EMS-proof WMDs, was it not?"

There was something about her enunciation that indicated that her alcohol tolerance was not all she claimed. Actually, she still seemed at least half-cut. *This may be my chance to initiate damage limitation.* "Okay, what can you tell me about those, with special consideration of application to the current India – Pakistan situation?"

"That last bit wasn't part of the original question," she pouted, "but I think I can manage anyway – at least 90%. Both countries have nuclear missiles, but Pakistan might consider itself vulnerable to a first strike. The entire point of these nuclear weapons is the MAD philosophy – mutually assured destruction – so if there was a risk of the nukes being circumvented, there'd have to be a backup. This backup has to be credible, resilient and also known, or at least suspected, by the top Indian military. An obvious answer would be portable, suitcase nukes placed in city centres."

"But these would be knocked out by the EMP," I pointed out.

"Yes, but if you had a critical mass of plutonium, you could probably rig up something completely mechanical to cause an explosion. I remember seeing this in a comic one time," she added as if this was a convincing supporting argument.

75

"Well, it's certainly theoretically possible, although I have my doubts about its practicality – especially if a purely mechanical setup didn't exist from the beginning. Building something suitable without electrical power or electronic support would be extremely tricky."

"But it is an option, isn't it? Even if it was a small explosion, a dirty bomb would have huge effects under current circumstances. So, how many points do I get for that?"

"Say 15% - possible but extremely unlikely."

She looked for a moment as if she was going to argue, but then meekly continued. "Okay, other WMDs: the traditional ones are chemical and biological. Chemical is particularly easy as all you need to do is tip a sack of something sufficiently nasty into a drinking water supply."

"Of course, but water distribution networks will be knocked out…"

"But people still need to drink. Even if they are taking water from a reservoir with buckets, the poison could have devastating effects. This, of course, would be even worse if a highly contagious bioweapon was used. Actually, you wouldn't even need to get to the water supply for that: anywhere that people are gathering would do. If it has a slow initiation time and populations are being evacuated, it could spread throughout the entire country."

"Yes, those are the two obvious biggies and you've identified how they could be applied under present conditions. You're actually very good at this – more comics?"

"A bit," she admitted, "a lot of that stuff is fairly dystopic. So how many points?"

"I guess I have to give you 50%, to be fair – so now you have a total of 65% and the easy answers are out of the way."

"Alright, then there are conventional explosives."

"Remember WMDs."

"Yes, but what makes a WMD is not what it is, but the impact it has, isn't that right."

"Correct, of course" I admitted, seeing that my ploy to put her off track had failed.

Her smile indicated she was well aware of this. "Okay, two ways to employ explosives as WMDs: have a huge amount of them or use them somewhere that the impact is magnified. Or both together, I suppose. Under normal circumstances, a huge explosion in a city centre would cause chaos, especially if it was acknowledged to be a terrorist attack. The impact might be less now, given the chaos that must already exist, but a bomb in any sensitive facility close to a city centre – a large chemical plant or a refinery – would not help things at all."

Shoko hesitated for a moment, gathering her thoughts. "Most of the obvious targets, power, communication, water, transportation, are already knocked out. But I suppose you could make things worse if the aim was retaliation. There's probably key infrastructure, bridges, tunnels and the like, that are essential for the supply to, or evacuation of, major urban areas. A few bombs on these choke-points and the situation becomes even worse."

"That's certainly good for 20%, any other key targets for another 5?"

"Disaster management centres," she answered immediately, with a satisfied grin. "That takes me to 90%, doesn't it?"

"Yes, well you just need to get over 90% to win."

"I think you just don't want me to win, for some strange reason," she scowled at me. "Don't you like to have sex?"

"I love to have sex, but just don't get the opportunity much these days."

"Well, you're in luck today," she laughed, "cyber attacks!"

"After an EMP, really?"

"Of course, especially now. Just think how helpless we would be if we hadn't got the military network. The Indians and Pakistanis have been at each other's throats for decades, so must have sleepers in place in their military command systems. You'd probably need to be on the inside to have a chance of infiltrating a high-security communication network, but they've had plenty of time to set that up, probably actually via IT support. I would guess that this would be the priority target because, without it, the impacts of any other WMDs in place would be even greater. Well, that must be worth a few percent," she concluded, smugly.

"That really was extremely well done, Shoko," I conceded. "I avoid ever awarding 100% as a matter of principal, but that could be 99…"

"Or 99.5, maybe?"

"Okay, 99.5%. In any case you certainly won the challenge."

"So, it's time for sex now?"

"Maybe, but beforehand you'll have to tell me how your English became so much better during your presentation. It has always been good, but it became more colloquial, with a really advanced vocabulary."

"I'll tell you all about that afterwards, pillow talk," she promised as she pulled me to my feet and dragged me in the direction of my sleeping quarters.

PA+1 day, Cupecoy, Sint Maarten

It must be a day since the power went out, and still not a peep from the powers that be. Must be fucked up beyond my wildest imaginings.

The three girls were still staying with me and we were now well provisioned after a visit to the local Carrefour. To our surprise the manager had forced the shutters open and distributed candles throughout the shop to provide some kind of light. He greeted everyone who arrived and told them to give their name at checkout, where the girls would make a list of the items taken. "You can just come back and pay when the power comes back on," he explained." Anyway, everything that was refrigerated is free, but take only what you need so that others can share. We've got a big deep freeze room in the back which we aren't touching at present, but if the power's still off tomorrow we'll start taking stuff from there."

To my surprise, there were very few takers of this generous offer. *Probably either not aware of how serious the situation might be or not prepared to walk to this location – or not fit to, if I think of the old, obese Americans who seemed to be the majority of off-season residents of the resorts and villas in the Cupecoy area. Might be a bit different in Simpson Bay, Marigot or, especially, Philipsburg.*

In any case, Margie, Lynn and I filled three trolleys with charcoal, water and food, while a subdued and rather ill-looking Cecilia filled one with beer, wine and spirits. The manager smiled as we left. "It looks like folk are planning on living on steak and vodka for the next few days. A week of this and all we'll have left is cornflakes." He seemed to regard the chances of power not being restored soon as being negligible, but I was already planning how to stock up for the long haul.

***

The factor convincing the girls to stay had been when the toilets failed to flush. This was just after an extended brunch, when an offer of another Morning Glory had been sufficient to entice Cecilia into our company. After searching out a pair of dark sunglasses from somewhere, she hoovered this drink as quickly as the first, then shot off in the direction of the loo. She returned shortly afterwards looking very unhappy. "You know, the bog won't flush and there are only drips from the taps. And there's no light, I had to leave the door open," she added as an afterthought.

"Yes, well, the power's out," I explained, "there's no electricity at all."

"Your toilet's electric, is it?"

"It's gravity feed from a tank, I guess, but the tank would be filled by an electric pump. Fresh water was going to go at some point anyway, as the island's supply is produced by desalination."

"Fuck, I wish you hadn't told me that," Lynn groaned, "now, of course, I'm choking for a pee."

"Luckily I do have a reserve toilet," I smiled.

"Do you indeed, where? I've really got to go soon."

"There!" I pointed at the turquoise sea that extended to the horizon. "It's certainly big enough for us all."

Lynn seemed a bit unsure, but Margie slapped her on the shoulder. "Come on, I need a pee too, we may as well get it over and done with. You coming as well, Chris? Want to have a group piss?"

"I'm okay for the moment, thanks, but I can watch from the terrace here to see how you're doing."

"Don't you think I know how to take a pee by myself, or is it just an excuse for voyeurism?" Maggie enquired.

"Oh, the latter of course. Nothing more erotic in my book than a pair of urinating lesbians." I treated them to my best leer. "However, you also need to watch out for the swell, it's quite big today."

"Fine, well, you can get started with this..." stepping behind her partner and whipping her miniscule panties down.

"Marge, fuck, what're you doing, I nearly pissed myself there," she jiggled about in a manner indicating that she had almost reached her limits of bladder control.

"Well, let's go. How do we get down there Chris?"

"Out the front door, left and then there are steps down to the beach after about thirty or forty metres."

"Right, we're offski," the girls rushed out together and appeared moments later on the beach.

I stood at the rail of the balcony and shouted down. "It's better a few metres further along the beach, as it's all sand there with no rocks."

The girls ran into the surf and turned to wave at us, chest deep in water. "Look at me, you perv, I'm peeing," Margie shouted, just before a large wave caught her from behind and propelled her sprawling up the beach.

I heard a laugh from my side and saw that Cecilia had joined me, still clad only in a pair of sunglasses. "Yes we can both see that," she shouted back while her friend was sucked back into the swash while she struggled to crawl forward on hands and knees. "I just dread to think where all that sand is ending up," she giggled.

An arm went round my waist and her hand slid lower to stroke my willy, reminding me that I was wearing even less than her, not having sunglasses on. "Want a quickie?" she whispered. "I don't suppose we got that far last night, did we?"

"Not a clue," I confessed, "but, considering the state I woke up in, it's rather unlikely. I've probably still got enough alcohol in my system to reduce a rhinoceros to impotence."

"Doesn't look that bad to me," her manipulation was indeed inducing a growing erection. "That pair will certainly start cavorting about in the water, so we've probably got about a quarter of an hour. Unless, of course, you prefer the urinating lesbians."

"Mmm," I pretended to ponder this question, "normally I'd go for the pissing rug-munchers, but I am, after all, your host and it'd be impolite of me not to accept your kind offer."

"Stop messing about then," I could just make out her rolling her eyes behind the dark shades. "Unlike you, I need a bit more effort to get me ready, so we need to get going," she led me to the sun lounger, where she lay back with her legs widely opened. "Get your laughing gear into action there and let's see where that leads."

I looked at what was on offer. *No way I need to be asked a second time.*

***

I must have dozed off for a moment, the archetypal male post-coital response. The giggles woke me, as I was sure was intended.

"What do you think, technical merit first?"

"I don't know, maybe five?"

"Out of six?"

"No, out of ten, stupid!"

"Okay, I could go for that, now artistic impression."

"Well, there was a lot of grunting, I suppose that must lose points."

"That was her, not him, we're rating him, remember.

"Well, he was certainly going at it hammer and tongs – but isn't that technical merit?"

"Depends on the orifice involved, I suppose."

"He seemed to have covered pretty well all of them from what I could see…"

Clearly my partner could take no more. "Would you two comediennes just fuck off? I haven't had a shag for ages and I don't need you

84

spoiling it." The muffled voice seemed to be emanating from beneath my right armpit.

"Good that you're awake now Cecilia," Lynn laughed. "So how was it for you? Points out of ten."

"Nine, so would you please go to fuck."

"Nine, wow that's high. But was it technical performance...?"

"...or artistic merit? You can score that separately for each orifice."

"Go! To! Fuck!" my lover groaned. "Jesus, that pair really do my head in..." she added sotto voce.

"Oh, I thought you'd had the odd fling or two with them?" I whispered in her direction as the sound of laughter faded in the direction of the living room.

"Does the thought of girl-on-girl action turn you on? Will I tell you some stories – or do you just need to think about what that pair will be up to now?"

"Why don't we start with your stories and see where it gets us? I suspect you're going to be disappointed, though, I'm pretty shagged out now, in more ways than one."

"Shagged out? You consider that shagged out? Just wait until I'm done with you and you'll really know what that means."

She was completely correct, and thereafter I slept until sundown.

***

We ate dinner on the terrace: barbecued steak and vegetables washed down with beer, or gin-and-tonic in Cecilia's case. The girls followed this with some of our free tiramisu accompanied with white

85

wine, while I had cheese and crackers with red. I had remembered to pick up some ground coffee, so we ended with espresso-strength cafetière brew to go with large cognacs.

Typically, it was Lynn who introduced the topic that we had been avoiding all evening. "Okay, Herr Doctor Doctor, you've now had all day to think about it. Can you tell us a bit more about what's going on here? Everyone else is surprised that the power isn't back on yet, but you seem to be preparing for a much longer outage. Why would that be?"

"It's the fact that everything electrical or electronic is out, not just the things that depend on mains electricity. I don't even know how that's possible. The cell-phone network fine, but the phones themselves? My bloody battery-powered watch, for fuck's sake. The hazard warnings along the road that're solar powered and the cars and buggies that run on fuel cells. There's only one thing I can think of that'll do something like that…"

There was a moment of silence. Then Cecilia could resist it no longer. "For fuck's sake, cough it out. It can't be that bad!"

How on earth do I put this? "Okay, my only explanation would be a massive dose of radiation…"

"Fuck, there's been a nuclear war and nobody told us about it…"

"…and we're all going to die of cancer…"

"…and if we didn't, our children would have green skin and three eyes."

86

"Not that we were thinking of having children in the foreseeable future, anyway," this last contribution to the babble from Cecilia.

"Well, that was the bad news; the good news is that, due to the fact that we're not coughing blood or having our hair fall out, the radiation was probably something that effects electronics more than it does humans."

"Couldn't you have given us this good news first," Lynn seemed rather pissed off.

"But isn't there a weapon that does that – a cobalt bomb or something?" Cecilia asked.

"A cobalt bomb is actually specifically designed to kill as many people as possible, like a neutron bomb, killing people but doing less damage to infrastructure. But you're probably thinking of something like high-altitude hydrogen bombs designed to produce electromagnetic pulses. Those could do the trick."

"So, cutting out the technical waffle, the answer is *yes*. So what would this *or something bomb* do to us? Are Lynn and Margie going to have green children, assuming that they can find a suitable source of sperm?" she raised an eyebrow in my direction, breaking the tension and causing all three girls to smile.

"You have to realise that I'm not an expert here, but I could imagine that, if it was in the right part of the EM, electromagnetic, spectrum, you could fry all kit using modern microelectronics without serious health impacts to animals – that includes us."

Cecilia rolled her eyes theatrically. "Okay, Chris, try that again with all the bullshit and arse-covering caveats stripped out. Have we got radiation poisoning?"

Fuck, why are scientists so crap at this? Our training destroys our ability to communicate with non-scientists. I drew a deep breath and carefully enunciated, "No, I think we'll all be fine."

She walked over, sat on my knee and patted me on the head. "There, lover, that wasn't so hard was it? So what do we do now? Presented in the same manner please."

"Apart from us all heading to the bedroom to start repopulating the planet, I assume?" I received two kicks and a slap to the back of the head as answers.

"Okay, but you have to realise there are two end-member scenarios..." another two kicks and a slap, "...there's something that I can only guess about that influences my answer. The question is – could this be a local or regional effect, or is it much bigger?"

"And that affects us how?" Cecilia emphasised her question by biting my earlobe.

"Ow, that's painful!" Another couple of kicks and a slap and I forced myself to refocus on the answer to the question. "If it's regional, help will eventually come from outside. I have no idea what would cause a super-power to want to nuke the Caribbean but, in any case, once the dust settles..."

"Don't you mean fallout settles?" Lynn asked, apparently seriously.

88

"No I don't think radioactive fallout is an issue here, but anyway we can expect help to come from the areas that aren't affected."

"And how long would that take?" Cecilia enquired.

"Depends on the initiating event but, given that we've seen nothing at all so far, I'd say more weeks or months rather than days."

"Months, really, you think it could be that long?" Margie seemed to be struggling with the concept."

"Definitely, so that is what we have to bear in mind over the next few days when we plan what to do."

"Right, so we should start planning for that now?" Margie asked.

"Wait a minute," Cecilia interrupted, "what if it's not regional but much bigger, like you said? What does that mean?"

"Well, I've not a clue what could cause that, but if that's what we have, we can forget about help completely. This is it – TEOTWAWKI – we're on our own."

"Teo what?"

"The end of the world as we know it…"

"This is possible?"

"It's not more impossible than what we're experiencing at present. I recommend that we focus on assuming months before help arrives, but keep in mind that it could be a best case.

For the first time that I could remember, all three girls were reduced to silence

PA+1 day, Chicago, USA

Liz Schwartz was an office cleaner, working the night shift on the upper floors of the Sears Tower, more than 100 stories above downtown Chicago, when the power cut occurred. As she had been near a wall of windows when both inside and outside suddenly went black, she knew exactly what had occurred and that the outage affected the entire metropolitan area, as far as the eye could see from her high vantage point. She couldn't remember any power cuts at all happening in recent years, so guessed that this must be something serious, a major problem that might not be repaired rapidly. As if to confirm this foreboding, a distant fireball exploded, which seemed to be somewhere around O'Hare airport. Her skin went cold as she unconsciously whispered the words, "Nine-eleven."

Abandoning her cleaning trolley, she followed dim phosphorescent lighting to the elevator hall, where the three other cleaners were assembled in a dim huddle. Mike, the floor superintendent, had already taken charge of the others, Mary and Heather. "That's you, Liz, isn't it, so we're all here now. I think we should just settle down now and wait for the power to come back, it can't take long."

"I'm not sure about that, Mike," Liz spoke up to fill the resulting silence. "The entire city is out and there seemed to be a big explosion up around O'Hare."

"We were all working lakeside, so we didn't see anything special," Mike responded. "Maybe we

90

should go to the office that you were in and have a look."

The others followed meekly as Mike led the way, the shape of the tall, bald Negro unmistakeable in even the faint light. He bumped into a desk and cursed under his breath. "Damn emergency lights should be brighter than this."

The group spread along the windows, staring in shocked silence at the points of fire that dotted the otherwise black landscape. "There's a lot more now," Liz observed. "Five minutes ago there was only the one, which looked like an explosion." As if to make this point, another distant fireball appeared.

"I guess that's somewhere along lakeshore, although it's difficult to tell without the streetlights," Mike observed.

"You know what's really strange," Mary piped up, "there's no lights from the planes heading for O'Hare. I used to love watching the line of flashing red lights, they just seemed to be endless."

"Well, a power cut ain't going to put out no plane lights, that's for sure," Mike pointed out.

"No, but remember 9-11. All the planes were grounded then, I remember it when I was a girl. Not a single plane in the sky, it was really weird."

"Oh, Mary, I wish you hadn't said that," Heather sounded worried. "I remember all those bodies falling from the Trade Centre – and we're on floor 101. I'm getting out of here."

"You're going to walk down 100 flights of stairs?" The very concept appeared bizarre to Mike.

"Rather walk than fall!" she replied. "We can just go slowly, take our time, then if the power comes back, we can take the elevators the rest of the way."

"Maybe that's actually not such a bad idea," Mike conceded, "better than just standing here in the dark. So, are we all going?"

"I definitely am," Mary confirmed. "My husband's always nagging at me to get more exercise, so I can start now."

"Me too," added Heather, "you've got me really worried now."

"We you can go without me," Liz decided, "I live way out in the burbs and there's no way I can get home if the trains ain't running. I was caught up in a riot one time, when there was that police strike ten years ago, so I'd rather be up here, I can tell you. Anyway, if no planes are flying then nothing can crash into the tower."

The others tried to persuade her to go with them, but Liz was adamant and so now had been alone for about twenty-four hours, dozing in a chair that she had dragged to the window in an executive's corner office. Over that time she had left the office only to visit the toilet, which she knew well enough to negotiate in the dark, and the cleaner's kitchen to pick up some snacks and cans of soda from a slowly warming fridge.

After daylight, the fires were increasingly blanketed by palls of smoke – the clear sunny day seeming strangely incongruent given the chaos that was sure to be breaking out below. From her elevation it was impossible to make out details, but roads contained only a few immobile vehicles and filled instead with groups of people. It looked a lot like aerial footage of the last riots that she had watched, with the anomalous absence of the phalanxes of police cars with their flashing lights. *Surely the police aren't on strike again, not at a time like this.*

Now it was dark again, revealing that fires were more widespread, scattered throughout the city. And also still no flashing lights to indicate the police, ambulance and fire services at work. Once again she congratulated herself for her decision to stay put and hoped that the other cleaners were okay.

Liz prided herself on her honesty, which was very important for a cleaner. She regularly found valuables that had been dropped or left behind on desks, but always either put them in a desk drawer, if the owner was evident, or handed them in to Mike, who sorted out lost property. However, she knew the desk in the office she had annexed contained cigarettes and, although she had stopped smoking over a year ago, the craving was building in her.

Finally, she decided that, after a full day with no power, the rules had to change. Even in the dark she quickly located the packet and lighter, enjoying the flare of flame as she lit up. She did not even bother to go to the smoking room, but remained in the office, casually flicking ash onto the floor. In some ways this action seemed even more of a rebellion than stealing the cigarette. *Well, that won't be the worst thing that's happening in the Windy City tonight*, she mused, aware that, after a day

without police control, downtown would be a
veritable hell on earth.

94

PA+1 day, Paris, France

Sylvie Blanc huddled in the middle of the huge crowd filling the Champ de Mars as she watched the city burn.

When she awoke early in the morning to a blacked-out world, it was mainly an annoyance. She couldn't make coffee or even boil water, so breakfasted on a rather soggy banana and the dregs of orange juice from a cool, rather than cold, fridge. This observation made it clear that the power had been out for some time. There was no TV or radio and even her mobile phone was dead, so she had no idea of what was causing the problems or how long they might last.

Sylvie groaned aloud when she realised that she had to walk down six flights of stairs, as the elevators were also out of action. The front door of her apartment block had an electric lock, but someone had already smashed this and wedged the door open. She peered out cautiously, noting that the street was surprisingly empty, with a couple of cars and a truck abandoned in front of a dead traffic light. The few pedestrians looked either confused or angry, so Sylvie swithered on what to do next. Normally she took the Metro to the bank where she worked, but it seemed that all power in the city might be out. *Is it worth even trying to struggle into the city centre, when that's likely to be more chaotic than here on the outer edge of the 7th arrondissement?*

She peeked out of the door again and this time noticed a couple of large plumes of smoke, gradually becoming aware that, despite these, it was almost silent, without the sirens and horns that formed an almost continuous backdrop to Parisian life. Now she felt really scared and, without thinking further, climbed back up the stairs and locked herself into her flat.

She spent the day by the window, high enough now to see the blazes that seemed scattered over her entire field of view. Most grew gradually, while a few burned out. But all this with no sign or sound of the emergency services that should be flooding the area. She sipped wine and chewed on stale crackers as the entire world outside became increasingly surreal.

By sunset, the streets were getting busier – but more of a rabble than a crowd. It was clear that the shops and restaurants at ground level were being looted and that absolutely nothing was being done to stop it. Even worse, first one and then a second shop started to burn. There were also arsonists in the mob.

Now Sylvie was really terrified, aware that her own building had shops at street level, which would also be under attack. She quickly dressed in hiking gear and packed a rucksack with essentials, before again heading downstairs. As she pushed her way into the unruly crowd in front of her door, she realised that her decision to leave had been made none too soon – already smoke was issuing from an Indian restaurant in the neighbouring building.

So now she had escaped from the worst of the rowdies, sheltering with others who looked as shocked as she was. *These morons, complete morons! They're looting shops and burning them after looting only a small fraction of the food and drink within. They seem to think this will stop the police being able to identify them, as if that is going to be a concern now. What if the power doesn't come back soon – what then?*

Sylvie looked up and could see that even the iconic Jules Verne restaurant on the Eiffel Tower was burning. *Completely mindless vandalism.* Paris had suffered many riots in the past, but this was something far, far worse. She shook her head and realised that her decision was made. At first light she'd find a bike and head off towards her parents' place in the distant Jura Mountains. A completely soporific village, where nothing ever happens – which is what drove her to the big city in the first place. Anyway, she was going home. *Even if it's the end of the world, it'll be six months before anyone notices in that place.*

PA+2 days, Nagoya, Japan

Once again, I awoke with a young woman in my arms and building old-man pressure in my bladder. *But, this time, with a touch of post coitum triste or, if not sadness, at least a bit of post-coital guilt. Actually, if I remember the Latin proverb correctly, all animals suffer from this sadness, except the rooster and the woman. Seems to be bang on in the case of young Shoko.* I looked at the contented smile on the face of the sleeping girl.

I could not help smiling also when I replayed the events of the previous night, starting with Shoko's surprising confession that she was a virgin, while in the process of pulling off my overalls. "What, you've got to be joking!" I grabbed her arms to stop her stripping me. "You're expecting me to deflower you?"

"Deflower, that's very quaint, though I don't know if it applies to me. It's just that I haven't had sex with a man, not with penetration."

"So, you're a lesbian."

"I don't think so," she seemed to ponder the question. "I've tried oral sex with boys and girls a few times, which was okay. Mostly it was just touching, masturbation until we had our orgasms. The girls were usually better, because they didn't come so quickly. Oh, and there was a gay boy too, he was very good with his hands."

"For a virgin, you seem to have had a lot of sexual experience," I observed as I allowed her to finish disrobing me. "But never penetrative sex?"

"No, not with a man."

"Not with a man? Don't tell me that you had sex with an animal?"

There was a loud crack when she slapped me hard on the bare buttocks. "Don't be disgusting, of course not. Just toys. Lots of Japanese girls have them – and I think lots of women in the West. They seem to have them in all the videos."

"Videos?" I lay back on the bunk, trying not to look down at my aged, sagging body, while Shoko did a slow striptease.

"Yes, pornography. There's tons of it on the internet for free. The Japanese stuff is frustrating as they still usually blur out the interesting bits. It's often quite kinky, though. There's a lot that's quite nasty, brutal, but if you stay away from that there's a range of stuff that I like. Mainly AC/DC group sex."

"So, the proper, well-spoken little Japanese girl is actually a porn fiend?" I smiled as she now posed nude in front of me, looking anything but proper.

"I don't know if I'm a fiend, but I masturbate regularly – most nights, if I'm not too tired. It's better, faster, with a video and a vibrator."

"Well, that's cleared up now. You really want to go ahead with this?" She was now on her knees at the side of the bed, caressing my rising erection.

"Yes, I'm absolutely sure. Ever since we found out how bad things are, I wanted to lose my virginity as soon as possible. Until now there didn't seem a rush and I wanted it to be a special occasion. But now," she looked in to my eyes and, behind the evident lust, I could see a trace of fear, "now I have to take the opportunity while I can."

"I suppose that makes sense also. I can't imagine why you'd want to have sex with me if any other option was available."

Teeth clamped playfully on my glans, causing me to squeak in shock. "Not at all, Mike," she pouted at me, "I'm very happy that it's you with me at this time. You're so kind and helpful to me and an older man is more comforting when things are scary."

There didn't seem to be an answer to that, so I just went with the flow.

***

I don't know whether losing her virginity was truly memorable for Shoko, but it certainly was for me. After some preliminary fumbling about, we moved to soixante-neuf, which was slow, gentle and very pleasurable. Just as I felt about to lose control completely, struggling also to restrain the sweaty nymph writhing on top of me, Shoko reversed her position and I entered her well lubricated vagina. We both came very quickly thereafter, although her orgasm endured much longer than mine and, after my now flaccid penis slipped free, I helped to keep her going with fingers deep inside her, a thumb rubbing her clitoris and a pinkie thrust into her bum.

"Well, that is certainly one of the best orgasms I've ever heard," I whispered into her ear when her screaming finally stopped and she subsided, panting, onto my chest. I remember hearing a faint purr of contentment before I drifted off into exhausted slumber.

***

I guess it was a couple of hours later when I woke, momentarily confused, but then realising it was Shoko sliding on top of me. "Sorry, Mike, did I wake you? I just had to get up to pee."

"No problem at all, Shoko," I slid my hands down her back and squeezed her tight bottom, "this is exactly the way that I want to wake up from now on."

"If you are awake, do you want to have sex again?" Her naked body rubbed against mine and I could feel the first signs of tumescence.

"I'd love to, my dear, but I'm afraid I'm too old. You need to get someone younger if you want wild sex all night."

"Are you sure?" She slipped to my side and took a hold of my dick, "I think this might work again."

"I'm really not convinced. But, anyway, you wanted penetration and now you've had it, so the pressure's off."

"I had you in my mouth," she took my hand and started sucking my fingers, "then in my cunt," I was shocked to hear this crudity from the softly spoken Shoko, but guessed she was repeating text from one of her porn videos. She opened her legs then and slowly pushed my fingers inside; she was sopping wet. She salaciously sucked my fingers again, now wet with her own vaginal juices. The smell of sex was overpowering and I could feel myself hardening. "Feel how wet I am," she

101

continued, speaking as if she was reciting lines from a movie, while she replaced my fingers in her vagina, "now you can get me ready for you to take me in the arse." She guided my sticky fingers into the indicated orifice, making her offer unmistakable.

By now I was fully erect and she slid on top of me, guiding my erection into place in her vagina and encouraging me to repeated stick fingers beside it and into her anus. She then raised herself and moved my dick to a much tighter orifice. "Oh, shit, that's bigger than my dildo," she grunted, but rather than allowing me to withdraw, forced herself deeper. *Maybe just another line from a favourite porno, as she seems amazingly into anal.*

I again came quickly, resorting to tongue and fingers to satisfy my partner. Already then I began to feel guilty, worried that I was taking advantage of her in some way. She was certainly an adult and extremely smart, but her use of online porn as sex education clearly left her vulnerable, acting out roles rather than anything that I would have considered as normal, healthy sex. *But, what the fuck do I know about the younger generation – she doesn't seem isolated or hung-up about her lifestyle. Whatever, I really need to be careful and ensure that it really is her exploiting me, which she has every right to do, rather than vice versa.* Sleep then claimed me within seconds.

***

I sneaked out of the bed before she woke and expected breakfast to be somewhat strained. *Of course, I completely misread this young woman yet again.* Shoko bounced out of the bedroom like a manic Bambi, full of the joys of spring and happy as a lark. I felt as if I aged a further ten years just looking at her.

"Well, Mike, wasn't that fun? I'm really glad I decided to lose my virginity with you. Do you want to have sex again? Although I think maybe we need breakfast first."

"I think I'd need hormone therapy and a shot of vitamins," I murmured under my breath as I rushed to set out breakfast for her.

"It's okay Mike, I can do it," she tried to push me back to my seat by the dining table.

"No, not at all," I insisted, "after such an exceptional night you should be pandered a bit for a change. I've already got something special, Buck's Fizz, for you to start on." The only bottle of Champagne that I had to hand was a Veuve Cliquot Grande Dame, which seemed a crime to pour into long-life, concentrated orange juice, but the feeling of guilt was heavy on my shoulders and this seemed at least some kind of nominal atonement.

Shoko was delighted to have me seat her and serve her the drink – unfortunately in an industrial glass that looked a bit like a tooth mug. I then offered her croissants, revitalised from the deep freeze, along with jam from a tin and a selection of cheeses and meats from vacuum packs. *God, she may be a slim little thing, but she eats like a horse!* I picked at the food in front of me, feeling more and more a total bastard while the girl rabbited on about her best night ever.

Realising that I was being a damp squib and risked ruining Shoko's current high spirits, I remembered her promise of the previous evening and saw this as a way of breaking out of my spiral of self-recrimination. "Shoko, last night you said that, after sex, you'd tell me why your English is so good. I mean it's always above the standard of the other students, but you usually speak as if it's a foreign language. At other times, sometimes when you're making presentations about work – or talking about sex, strangely enough – you speak as if English is your native tongue, understanding and using colloquial expressions that foreign students never do."

"Did I really promise that, Mike-san?" She fluttered her eyelashes at me, indicating that she had dropped back into teasing mode.

"You did indeed, my dear, so you're going to have to spill the beans or I'll be forced to put you over my knee and paddle your behind."

"Really, would you like to do that?" She turned around and unzipped her overalls, peeling them down to a level just below her perfectly formed buttocks.

"See, that's exactly what I mean! How do you do that? And, anyway, better get back into your kit as there's no more sex before I know what this's all about."

With a reluctant shrug, she zipped up her overalls and then plonked herself on my knee. "So, why is this so important to you? You've already said that my technical work is good; why is my enunciation, vocabulary and mastery of the vernacular so important to you?"

"Because you're an enigma. I noted that you were very smart beforehand, but your performance since the shit hit the fan has been exceptional. Could be that you're just pure fucking brilliant, as they say in Glasgow, or it could be that, under the strain that we've been under, your cover is starting to slip."

As I spoke the last few words, I felt a sudden tensing of her muscles, although I was sure she was trying to hide it. "My cover?" The disappearance of her bubbly joy broke my heart and I now felt even more of a total shit than I did when I thought I had taken sexual advantage of an innocent student, decades younger than me.

"I'm an old guy and my area of expertise is disaster management. Every disaster is unique, so the trick is to spot patterns that allow you to use experience gained in something similar, previously and / or elsewhere. This is probably my only real talent, but I'm good at it. We've now been living together for two days and I've become closer to you than woman that I lived with for decades. I adore you, I really do, and I know that you've had a very rough time adjusting to what has happened, but there's something important that you're hiding, I'm sure of it."

At first, I thought she was going to cry, then she broke into wild laughter, which worried me even more. "God, I heard that you were good, but this is better than I expected. The stuff about my virginity was more or less accurate, so my memorable last night seems even better."

Blindsided yet again! What the hell is this woman up to? "So, let's get clear about this, you are really a Japanese student with a passion for masturbation and a perverse interest in geriatric academics?"

"Sort of…" she bit my neck with sharp little teeth, evidently enjoying my flinch of pain, "…but with a bit of sponsorship. Although my father is a doctor, he used to do little jobs for the CIA, but wasn't happy with the way that they treated him. More recently, it's been work for the English and EU security services, which is why I ended up in Nagoya."

"Not because of my erudition and wit?" I feigned shock and swooning.

"Exactly because of it. There wasn't another gaijin who was more locked into the Japanese disaster management system than you. I know I fell apart just after the EMP, but we've all known that something like this was going to happen sometime. You wrote a bloody book about it, for God's sake! I was sponsored by the English security people to do my post-Doc here, with the promise of a cushy number back in Blighty if I ever wanted it. Then, of course, we were caught with our nickers down and all went tits-up, to mix my metaphors."

"So, you're a spook?"

"Not a spy, if that's what you mean. I'm just a student sponsored by a potential employer. I may have the chance to do some intelligence gathering on the side if I can get a suitable day job in Japan or the Far East, But, for now, I'm just a trainee."

I don't know whether to be disappointed that Shoko hadn't confessed earlier or relieved that the explanation is so mundane. As part of risk assessment studies over the last three decades, I had built up a lot of contacts in the Japanese, EU and NATO military and intelligence communities and was well aware that, although intelligence gathering was now overwhelmingly electronic, agents on the ground still played an important role. "So what's the story with your English?"

"My mother is half-English and completely bilingual, although she has lived all her life in Japan, apart from time spent studying in Stanford. That's where she met my father. They speak English together as much as they speak Japanese, so I was also brought up bilingual. My granny moved back to Britain after my grandpa died and, as a kid, I spent every summer with her. She lives in Scotland: Helensburgh, near Glasgow. I had lots of friends there and this helped to keep my English up to date."

"Okay, but why did you hide your fluency before things went tits-up, as you expressed it?"

"That was recommended by my MI5 contact, who said that native English speakers often feel that they're talking in private if they communicate using slang and obtuse colloquial expressions. My apparently normal level of student English encouraged that. It also helped me to bond better with the staff and other Japanese students, who'd be self-conscious if they realised my English was much better than theirs. This pidgin had really become my natural working language, until we were locked in here together."

"You seem surprisingly good at carrying that off."

"It shouldn't surprise you, after all I'm Japanese and, as you should know by now, conformity is the name of the game in education. *The nail that stands up will be hammered down* and all that shit. I had to be seen to be learning from my English teachers, even though they were usually crap. Otherwise unemployable gaijin whose only pedagogic skill was being brought up in an English-speaking land."

"Even then, your vocabulary would be impressive, even for a native Brit."

"Cryptic crosswords," she smiled. "My mum and gran were both fanatics and I picked this up from them. When we're talking together, we try to use crossword vocabulary, sesquipedalian terms and abstruse slang rather than the more pedestrian circumlocutions encountered in normal, run of the mill dialogue, if you catch my gist."

"Righty ho, good that we got that out of the way. So, where do we go from here?"

"Well, we could have sex again…"

"I think we should reserve that pleasure for night time. We don't want it to lose its edge, do we? No, I meant any other little surprises that you have for me or actions that you intend to spy on?"

"Well, if you put it like that, you could show me the coded dispatches that you've been logging on that unlisted hardnet bulletin board." She smiled

108

at my look of surprise. "See, you had me pegged as a simple Japanese student and didn't even try to cover up what you were doing – you simply assumed that it'd mean nothing to me."

Good God, this girl is shit hot. Just as well I wasn't up to anything dodgy. "Initially pegged as a simple Japanese student, but latterly as a wild, tireless nymphet," this clarification made her smile prettily. "Anyway, I'd be happy to go through everything I've posted with you; there's really not much more than we originally discussed."

"So why didn't you mention it?"

"Why do you think I didn't mention it?"

"If I knew, I wouldn't be asking you. All I know is that it's heavily encrypted stuff that's going to an address that's untraceable."

"So you've already tried to hack my communications?"

"Not really hack, just have a look at."

"A bit of splitting hairs there. Anyway, why might I have wanted to conceal this stuff from you – even before I suspected that you were anything other than the student you seemed to be?"

"Mike, you can be really annoying at times," she punched my arm. "Why does everything turn into an exam with you?"

"Because I'm your teacher and I'm trying to get you trained up. Think of it as specially focused on your future career as a Jane Bond. It's not just what a spy overhears that makes a good intelligence agent, it's what he or she deduces from what wasn't said."

"Why can't I just see what you posted?" she wheedled, "I'll let you do even more pervy things to me tonight."

"You're not doing your case any good at all," I grinned. "Just give me your thoughts on what I might have posted and why I haven't opened this site to you?"

"Well, as far as the latter is concerned, it's probably because the contents are classified; top secret or whatever the Japanese military intel use."

"Indeed they are, but I'm now happy to give you access, which will be okay under the circumstances. This'll happen, however, only after you've worked out what the content may be, which will explain why I didn't tell you all about it from the beginning."

"I guess there's probably a clue in there somewhere," her brow wrinkled in concentration. "You are the disaster management guru, so it has to be something to do with that. There's nothing that we can access here that can't be done easier in the national coordination centre, so it's not that. It must be something that you've got, or can do, I suppose, that the others can't. I know that you're really good, but I can't believe that, when it comes to impacts on Japan, you can do better than the guys in Tokyo. In fact, I guess you've probably taught classes to half of them."

"Completely correct. Although we've been hit by something that goes beyond any scenario I've ever seen considered, the Japanese team is second to none. Also, due to the high risk – and recent

110

experience – of major natural disasters, they have a superb response and recovery infrastructure."

"Bugger, somehow I knew you were going to say something like that! So, what have we talked about that's not specific to Japan? The source of the perturbation and the risk of further EMPs?"

"We got most of our stuff from NASA bulletin boards, remember. I did actually log a short note covering our discussions about the 4-pi shockwave, but that was just backup for material that will have been produced by those with real solar astrophysics expertise."

"So it's not Japan and not the sun," her face lit up and she laughed, "it's everything in between! The global impact of, and response to, this catastrophe. That'll be something that the Japanese teams have much less understanding of."

"Exactly, I knew you'd work it out. So why is this on a secure network that I deliberately kept you away from."

Her grin vanished and she waited before answering, as if afraid that her conclusion could actually be correct. "Because it's so bad," she whispered. "You've been trying to break this to me gently ever since I first dragged you down here. The tools on your palmtop let you see a different picture to that apparent to others."

"Yes, I'm afraid that you've hit the nail on the head there. I have a number of global macroeconomic models that provide a rather unique perspective on the present situation, even though they weren't specifically developed for a case like this."

"Using the patterns, analogues and stuff that you mentioned earlier?" she interrupted, technical curiosity seeming to displace her initial shock.

"Exactly, a hybrid containing both heuristic and rule-based expert systems. I've transferred the tools to the top-level international liaison guys in Tokyo and they'll make the decisions on where and how to transfer them further. I provide support, helping to formulate and interpret the different scenarios that are produced. Everything so far is focused on impacts; it'll get much more complex when we try to implement recovery and remediation."

"Well, I'd like to have a close look at these tools. But why not just distribute them openly on the international hardnet. It seems unfair to pass this only to the Japanese. At the very least they should be available to major allies like the US and the EU."

"A good question, maybe you'd like to answer it?"

"Mike! Will you please give me a break! This interrogation is doing my head in!"

"Nope," I grinned in my most annoying manner, "this was a very important decision that I made. As you noted, one that appears very unfair. I'd like you to confirm that I've done the right thing by working through it independently."

"You smug bugger, I could really get to hate you!" Her harsh words were spoiled by the traces of a smile, suggesting that she had now worked out the answer to my question.

"Stop waffling, lass, and get on with it. What am I, and the top brass in Tokyo, worried about?"

"You implied that, even in Japan, things are going to get bad. But you've also emphasised that, in cases like we have now, it's not only Japanese infrastructure, it's also culture that contributes to minimise impacts and aid recovery. It's not going to be like that elsewhere – we've already seen what happens for a tinderbox like India and Pakistan. It's going to be the same elsewhere and you're worried that this knowledge may, in itself, make things even worse."

"That's it, bang on again. We have to determine, on a case-by-case basis, if and how we can pass on this knowledge so that it doesn't do more harm than good."

"Seems like a very tricky job, especially given the internal situation in Japan, which must make it pretty low priority."

"It's not top of the list," I conceded, "but recognised to be of critical importance for planning recovery. Japan hasn't been self-reliant for a very long time and hence we need to balance attempts to substitute imports with those to reinitiate them. The latter will be a key to re-establishment of an effective global economy."

"But who is going to do all the background work to support such decisions?"

"You and I, of course," I grinned at her look of shock. "After I've shown you what I've done so far, you can start helping. I would have brought you in at some point anyway, so you've just accelerated the process. You'll just need to be toughened up a bit to get involved in the first steps of triage at an international level."

113

"I know about the application of triage in management of disaster medical responses, but what do you mean in this context? And don't turn this back into a question for me!"

"I should, really, but maybe I can make it part of the toughening up process. The concept is straightforward, break a list of all countries in the world into three groups. The first consists of those that'll be relatively little damaged and hence don't need this tool in the first place. These are mainly isolated, rural, low population density lands that can easily live from low-tech agriculture or fisheries. Life without power or electronic communications will be physically tougher, but they should survive fine until global recovery eventually impacts them, with the return of luxury goods and, probably, tourists."

"The second are countries like Japan, who will have a tough time recovering, but have the ability to use this knowledge to facilitate the process in a positive manner. Our job is thus to find other examples and make recommendation on how to proceed."

"The third class are the basket cases, who are inevitably going to crash and burn and for whom it is pointless to consider any form of assistance. It'd just be shifting deck chairs on the Titanic. Unfortunately, at least in terms of total population, I fear this will be the biggest group of all."

Shoko looked grim. "So, you think it'll be black and white, this triage, with no grey cases?"

"Of course not, black and white cases will be the exceptions, that's what makes our work so

114

tricky. Take the US, for example. Its population is going to be decimated and its cities will burn. But it possesses so much valuable infrastructure available to us via its military hardnet. So, even if we can't prevent its eventual collapse, we need to try to slow it to the extent possible."

"Even the one global super-power is unsaveable?"

"Well, that's what we need to look at. So, finish your breakfast and let's get started."

Poor Shoko looks totally shell-shocked. It's finally dawning on her how great the responsibility of her job is going to be. Nevertheless, I don't think there's anyone I'd rather have helping out.

***

We did, indeed, work very well together now that everything was out in the open, on both sides. I started by walking her through the tools that I used, emphasising functionality rather than the operational details that could be covered later. The key things were the basic assumptions that went into the specification of boundary conditions. From these, the expert system and associated knowledge base would flesh out the bare bones to develop credible evolution scenarios, which could then be refined by iterative tweaking of initial boundary conditions and evolution constraints.

Given her background and training, Shoko quickly grasped the concepts behind these codes, although was clearly in awe of their capabilities. "Can these really make useable predictions though?" she asked. "It all seems a bit theoretical, academic somehow."

115

"A very perceptive question, why don't you set up a test case and run it, see what you come up with. Use the US as an example, the databases tend to be better for it." I watched carefully as she described the conditions of complete global blackout without forewarning, using natural language input. She then refined this to add the functioning hardnet military communications, the likely irreversibility of most electronic system damage and the initiation of nuclear conflict, although currently confined to the Indian subcontinent.

"Okay, now have a look at damage to population centres as a time evolution. Throw the graphics up into the main screen." Almost immediately a map of the US appeared, with all cities having populations greater than one million identified. "This is the time zero starting point. Slowly scroll forward over the first hour with five-minute resolution."

Immediately the map filled with spots of different colours that gradually increased or expanded with time. A digital counter to the side of the map showed a number that blurred due to its rapid rate of increase.

Shoko stopped the animation and scrolled back to time t + 10 minutes. "That can't be right, Mike, it's only 10 minutes after loss of power and this digital readout of death toll is already well over a million. That can't possibly be right."

"The number that you're looking at is actually the median of the death count." My fingers flew over my laptop, which was still slaved into the control system. "Here's the range," a histogram was displayed, "as you see it goes up to over 2 million."

"How is that even possible?"

"Here's the breakdown..." again I used my palmtop to set this up. "The numbers here are colour-coded to indicate degree of confidence. The big, well-defined number is the total of passengers and crew aboard aircraft. As this occurred during the night in the States, the numbers are relatively low, but there were still about 3000 commercial flights in the air at the time, giving over 700,000 deaths when private and military planes and helicopters are included. That's associated with a highly uncertain estimate of deaths on the ground. Although many of these crashed into unpopulated areas or bodies of water, the larger aircraft going down in the cities are automatically mapped using the military IR satellites. These have enough resolution to identify fireballs encompassing hotels, hospitals and high-density residential areas, giving the estimated 50 to 200 thousand deaths."

"Other large numbers are associated with transport," Shoko observed, taking over control of the display. "Being the US, a very large number of crashes of private cars killing drivers, passengers and pedestrians, with a significant number of collateral deaths associated with commercial vehicles and transportation of hazardous materials."

"You can also see a breakdown of deaths from primary events – which are effectively fixed and would only be refined if additional data is input – and secondaries, such as fires, where impacts may grow with time."

117

"It's mentally exhausting just looking at this output, but surely it does more than calculate mortalities."

"Of course," I zoomed in on Las Vegas, "here we have a relatively simple case with little heavy industry or vulnerable infrastructure. Initial population is only a rough estimate due to the large number of tourists. The airport is, however, very busy and is surrounded by hotels, so a large initial peak in the death rate, which then drops. But we can also estimate the numbers and types of injuries – as shown here – and compare these to the number of available hospital beds, distances for injured persons to be transported and capacity of ambulance and other transportation services. The problem here is clear..."

"With communication and transportation knocked out, support is available only to those who can walk or be carried to a hospital or clinic," Shoko interjected. "Even then, with no power, only very limited treatment would be available."

"Yes, so the death rate here will gradually climb again. We can also compare the population to available services..." the graphic changed, "...and resources. Here we have food and water."

"That's clever, it distinguishes between residents, who are relatively better off, and those in hotels who will run out of water within days."

"Exactly, and you see also that these mega-hotels are identified as flashpoints for civil disruption. With loss of lighting, air conditioning, running water, etcetera, there'll be a lot of highly disgruntled punters. With no communication or transportation, police control will be effectively non-existent. To make things even worse, there will be a lot of firearms about. It's a recipe for disaster."

Shoko made the assumption of no external assistance being provided and ran the simulation forward in time, gasping as the mortality rate rapidly climbed after the first week. "If it keeps on going like this, the entire population will die," she gasped.

"Well, it's a huge city in the middle of a desert that's completely dependent on food and water provided from outside. It goes completely down the toilet unless these crucial lifelines are replaced."

"This is so depressing," Shoko sighed, "is there no good news anywhere?"

"Well, the places with low vulnerability, low-tech farming communities off the beaten track, tend not to be well covered in the background knowledge base. Maybe try somewhere in the Caribbean, one of the smaller islands."

Shoko was quickly mastering the communication interface, the map on the main screen zooming out to cover all of North America and then in to show the Caribbean in more detail. "How about this one, it seems to have two names?"

"Yes, Sint Maarten on the Dutch side and Saint Martin on the French. I visited that place once." *About ten years ago now, I guess. Good food and scuba diving, but too many American tourists.*

"Okay, here's a bit of good news straight away, their little airport doesn't have night flights, so zero deaths from air travel." The young researcher was instantly cheered up. After the past litany of death and destruction, quite understandably so.

"Now road accident estimates, range is small and again zero seems quite likely, although a number of injuries. Mainly seems to be due to the absence of heavy vehicles on the roads at night."

The display morphed to present predicted developments over the first week. "Mainly seems to be deaths due to failure of medical services, loss of intensive care facilities and a few fires. The reserves of food and water seem to be fine."

"You can also get interpretations here," I drew a cursor over the appropriate command line. "As you see, an important factor is the timing of the event, the formal population of the island fluctuates markedly when these huge cruise ships dock. But they come in mornings and leave evenings, so they don't get factored in for this analysis. I imagine the situation on board any of those boats would be fairly dire after a week."

"I don't want to even think about that. Let's have a break from this now that I've seen some reasonably good news."

"Okay, let's scan the main bulletin boards on the hardnet. You have a look at how things are developing in Tokyo and I'll scan through the international ones. We can compare notes over lunch."

"Okay, fine with me, but then we should think about going outside. I've been stuck in here for two days now and I need a breath of fresh air."

"Yes, we can do that," I agreed, hoping that my confidence in the resilience of Japanese culture was well placed.

***

The most interesting news from my viewpoint was a detailed assessment of the radiation dose resulting from the solar event. Although the exact mechanism of its generation was still a mystery, it was clear that the initial shock wave of electromagnetic radiation did the main damage to electronic equipment. Although there was an anomalous dip covering the visible part of the spectrum, a huge peak extending over the microwave to radio region was sufficient to fry anything containing an aerial, or anything that would act as such, unless it was military-grade hardened.

Bloody internet of things! A couple of decades ago the damage would have been limited, but today everything's wireless-linked or wireless charged, from my car to my bloody toothbrush. Probably an old diesel tractor would be immune to this, but a modern, autonomic, fuel-cell powered, combine harvester would have failed in so many ways that it'll now be an irreparable pile of junk.

There was, however, good news. Shielding by the atmosphere had reduced doses due to accompanying high-energy radiation – X-ray, gamma and extreme UV – at least at ground level. This was also important for later secondary radiation resulting from the slower moving particles that bombarded the earth over the following hours. At high altitude, above a few thousand metres or so,

121

things didn't look so good, however. The total radiation doses accumulated over the incident could be enough to cause illness for anyone who was outdoors for the entire period.

With a better understanding of the cause of our troubles, I joined several groups looking at recovery approaches. One of these focused on utilising old, immune technology to re-establish critical services. This included using animal power, mainly horses, and old fossil-fuelled or wind- and water-powered vehicles and equipment, mainly recovered from museums, junk yards or half-forgotten military depots. In coastal areas, lakes and large rivers, sailing ships were available, although crews would need to be retrained to do without the auxiliary motors that the larger ones normally used for entering and leaving harbours.

Another group was developing ways to repair damaged equipment. It appeared that, in most cases, the fundamental electric motors and fuel cells in vehicles were robust enough, it was just all of the smart control and communication systems that were fried. If these could be stripped out, it may be possible to replace them with something very low tech in order to restore some kind of function. Replace the entire self-driving system with a simple manually-controlled rheostat and wireless charging with a pair of jump leads and an e-car could be driveable, even if vastly below its previous performance. *The kind of things that third world garages have been doing for decades, but would require major retraining of the first world mechanics, who do all diagnosis with a computer, with most repairs involving replacing circuit boards.*

I was amazed to note that three hours has passed and Shoko had started to lay out lunch. *Excellent, I can use more good news for her as justification for a midday beer.*

***

Shoko's report complemented my own, focusing of specific ways that the Japanese were working around the constraints on recovery. The military hardnet was a clear bottleneck and an ambitious goal of establishing communication channels to all municipalities in Japan had been set. This would be facilitated by a hoard of several thousand ancient military radios found in a basement of the Ministry of Defence in Ichigayahonmurachō, which were now being distributed by sailing ship, horseback and bicycle.

Serendipitously, a major national road-racing championship had been scheduled in Tokyo for this weekend and competition cyclists were being recruited as couriers. *I love this about Japan, they're just so good at using what they have to hand to solve problems. In times of trouble, they all pull together, the exact opposite of what seems to be happening in the large American cities.*

Overall priority was still on firefighting, in some cases literally as large fires still burned in many places, but mainly in terms of finding those needing assistance and collecting those beyond it for burial.

They were also using my software in predictive mode, to try to anticipate the evolution of future

123

problems and develop solutions in a pre-emptive manner. The greatest concern was their reliance on food imports. Shoko had now been tasked with assessing the likely situation in Australia and New Zealand, with the aim of checking if any kind of external support could speed up a return of trade with these key suppliers.

Shoko was extremely pleased at having an active role in the recovery effort, but a little overawed by the responsibility. "I've done a quick check but, apart from damage to the major cities, especially Sydney, both these countries are in quite good shape. Certainly, when compared to the US. They have low population densities, lots of agriculture and fisheries, little high-tech industry, so should be able to recover quickly. They could supply us with a lot of what we need, but why should they? In the past we complemented them with our high-tech industries, but these have now been destroyed. We don't have a basis for trade."

"We should look at this together this afternoon," I stood and gave her a reassuring hug. "I think that, even if the industrial base will take time to recover, we have a hugely valuable knowledge base that can serve as a bargaining counter in the interim. Anyway, I promised you a walk – we should have a look at what the area around the University looks like and see if there is any way in which we can help."

***

We left the department by an emergency fire door, wedging it open so that we were sure we could return without breaking our way through the main door, which would otherwise stay locked until power was restored. It was beautifully sunny, but the campus was completely deserted. Apart from the absence of a throng of students and the faintest trace of wood smoke in the air, everything seemed normal. It was a very strange feeling, being alone in a Japanese city, and Shoko was clearly spooked, clinging to my arm. "I don't like this, Mike," she whispered. "Where is everyone?"

"I suspect we'll find out soon," I answered as we headed for the main gate to this part of the University campus. Sure enough, as we approached it, I began to make out the sound of voices. The gate itself appeared to be closed but, on closer inspection, it was clear that its power drive had been decoupled so that it could be slid open. The small security office beside the gate was deserted, but I could see that the door was damaged and was now slightly ajar. *Probably kicked open from inside.*

A group of what were plainly students were gathered around a notice board that stood to the side of the gate, rushing in our direction as soon as we were spotted. They helped me drag the gate open while Shoko fended off a barrage of questions in Japanese. After I emerged, I wandered over to have a look at the board, leaving my young colleague to handle the students. The display screen was dead, of course, but a sheet of paper covered in a scrawl of Japanese was pinned to it. Underneath this text, a different hand had added in English a simple summary: *University closed until further notice. For help go to student union.*

Amazing, even the students seem to have gotten themselves organised.

I was pondering this when Shoko joined me. "They're mainly worried about how to ensure that they don't fall behind with their studies now that they no longer have notebooks or internet. I assured them that special allowances would be made, so they seem a bit happier now. They'll go now and sign up for work at the Koban."

The Kobans, these're an aspect of Japanese culture that I often forget about. They'll help a lot in maintaining order and coordinating recovery. As we wandered in the direction of the student union, Shoko and I discussed these ubiquitous police boxes, which are found scattered around all Japanese town and cities. *Such neighbourhood policing previously seemed like make-work to me, but it's now evident that the local knowledge possessed by these police officers is an invaluable resource at a time like this.*

We turned onto a main thoroughfare and then the idyllic picture that we had been building was rudely shattered. Cars were scattered about the road and there had been a number of collisions. A couple of wrecks were burnt out in a station which supplied bio-ethanol for their fuel cells and part of the station itself was still smoking, although the main storage tanks seemed to be intact. *A stroke of luck there: if those had exploded it would've been very nasty.* As we passed, we also noticed pools of blood in and around some of the crashed cars, but, reassuringly, no sign of bodies.

The closer we got to the student union, the more people we encountered, whom I mentally classified as students, staff and ancillary workers. At the union itself, there was a steady flow in and out of the main entrance, which had been wedged wide open. Above this a banner had been hung with instructions in both Japanese and English. The latter were clear enough – *foreign students who need aid go to first floor left side, volunteers to provide help first floor right side.* Before being asked, Shoko explained the Japanese text. "It's like the English, but Japanese help is on the second floor. The volunteers should go to the University Koban."

"Well, let's see if we can be of any use here. You've your main job set out in the DMRC, but we should check if any of our facilities can be of value to the Uni."

Volunteers on the first floor were being greeted by none other than an exhausted looking vice-Chancellor, who I knew by sight, but had never talked to. I quickly outlined our situation and it was pleasing to see how this cheered him up immediately. "Mitchell-sensei, I am so thankful that you are assisting us at this terrible time. We have been very lucky at the University, compared to other areas of Nagoya and some of the big cities, but we have many foreign undergrads and post-grads who are mainly concerned about contacting their families. Could you help?"

"There are already Disaster Centre electronic notice boards with lists of both those who have survived and those who have died," I answered while I pondered the problem, "I could certainly add names and details to those if that would help. Do you have a list?"

He pointed to a desk, containing sheets of paper and pencils. "We're just compiling one at present; even though I had no idea what to do with it, writing this down seemed to help those involved." I somehow sensed that this deception had been preying on his mind and this probably explained why my presence was so welcome.

"No problem," I took a small slave unit for my laptop from my pocket and passed it to him. "If you can get one of the students to put all your material on this, it'll be easier for me to upload it."

"Oh, are you sure that you can spare this. Such a functional device must be very valuable."

"I had intended to pass it to the University Koban, so that they can piggy-back communications through our DMRC network. If you use it for your own needs first, you can then pass it on when you're finished. I guess many of your Japanese students have similar needs and if you sort this out here it will reduce the load on the Koban."

I was just about to leave when I suddenly realised that I had an opportunity to clear up one of my personal concerns. "By the way, I guess you already know that the university refectory contains a lot of food, but the refrigerated stuff will go off soon if it isn't used. I have already taken some food from there, but found that there had been a fight and there were two dead students." I heard a gasp from my companion and felt her hand painfully grasp my elbow, but I simply continued. "I moved the bodies into a smoker room to avoid possible food contamination, but you should organise their recovery when possible."

The weight seemed to return to the vice-Chancellor's shoulders and I regretted ruining his moment of relief. "It is extremely regrettable, Mitchell-sensei, but some students – even some staff – have reacted very badly to this situation. Especially during the first night there was a lot of drunkenness, violence, rapes. Yes, there were several murders, I'm shocked to say. In many cases, we have not yet identified the culprits."

"I'm afraid that many of these will be gaijin and I apologise on their behalf."

"No need to apologise, it is not your fault and we realise that the pressure on those from different cultures who are far from home will be different to us Japanese."

"In any case, if there's anything I can do to help prevent any possible recurrence of such acts, let me know – either via the communicator or sending a note to the centre."

As I started to leave, I took note of Shoko's irate mumbling. "Why didn't you tell me? How could you hide such a thing? There could be a murderer on the loose. You should have let me come with you."

I walked – and Shoko stomped – to a quiet bench a distance from the union in the shade of a spectacular cherry tree in full bloom, where I forced her to sit. "I'm sorry, I should have told you earlier and would have probably gotten around to it in the next day or two, but my main aim was to avoid upsetting you further. You've been subject to so

129

many shocks over the last two days, that I felt adding this to your burden was unnecessary."

This is the tricky bit, if she wants more details, do I tell her the truth of what I did or do I lie? Which option would do less harm?

Luckily the young woman seemed mollified by my abject apology and I changed the topic of conversation, reminding her of the work that she would need to start in the near future. This diverted her during our walk back to the department, clearly due to both the extent of the challenge and her desire to establish herself by doing a good job.

PA+2 days, Cupecoy, Sint Maarten

I awoke to the sound of rain battering against the window, almost drowning out the background roar of the surf. I glanced at the electric clock beside the bed, noting that its second hand was still immobile, and then turned to scan the naked brown body at my side. *Hard to believe it's just 2 days since the power went off; it seems like I've known Cecilia and her palls for ages. Maybe some kind of variant of Stockholm Syndrome? In any case, time to head for the big alfresco toilet, rain or no rain.*

I stood on the sand at the water's edge while the rain poured on me, enjoying a coolness that I now realised that I had missed since the loss of air-conditioning. While I emptied my bladder, I thought through the things that we would have to start sorting out, based on the assumption that power was not coming back anytime in the near future. *Capturing rain water, that'll be a start.*

Suddenly I was aware of giggles behind me and I spun to find Margie and Lynn sheltering in the tunnel that provided beach access, just a few metres distant. "Why are men such exhibitionists when they pee?" asked Lynn, rhetorically.

"Yes, ladies squat discretely while guys stand tall and wave their willies about," Margie added. "Probably a macho way of establishing pecking order. I mean, only guys could talk about *having a pissing competition.*"

"Anyway, Chris, if you're finished in the loo, would you mind buggering off, we're bursting,"

131

Lynn added. "Unless you want to watch, of course," she added mischievously.

"I'd love to watch, but it's ladies who make such a communal thing of visiting the toilet, going in pairs or groups," I retaliated. "And that's not just the lesbians, in case you bring up guys hanging around public toilets," I added with a smile.

I shook off and turned to depart, but already Lynn had squatted down in the surf beside me, this varying between breast and bum height as a result of the swell. "Oh, well, I suppose I get to watch whether I want to or not."

"You could close your eyes," Margie suggested as she took her place beside her partner and they grabbed each other's arms to avoid being bowled over.

"And miss this, you've got to be joking! There's no way that you're going to manage to keep a position like that in these waves." Only moments later I was proven correct when a particularly large wave rolled them up the beach, squealing and cursing in equal measure.

I watched the comedy for a few seconds more before, with great reluctance, I forced myself to head back to the villa and start preparation of breakfast.

***

After a slow breakfast that transmogrified into brunch while we waited for Cecilia to emerge, the girls and I discussed our priorities in the absence of any indication if and when power might be recovered. The rain had gone off and it had started to brighten, but the mood was sombre.

We agreed that remaining together in the villa was a good idea, but a question was whether we should try to talk some of their friends into joining us to expand our community or whether we would be better off on our own. As I was a visitor to the island, there was nobody that I knew who was worth considering, but the girls produced a list with a dozen names, who were then discussed in detail. I was a silent observer, but couldn't help noticing that anyone initially proposed by Lynn was opposed by Margie and vice versa.

Finally the list was reduced to two, a gay couple who crewed on the catamarans that were used for tourist trips around the island. "Steve and Alan are good fun, party animals who get on well with everyone. And they can sail, if we need a boat," Lynn argued.

"Yes, maybe, assuming that they're on island at present," Margie agreed with seeming reluctance. *Apparently not particularly happy, but without a good argument against them.*

"Oh, no, not that pair of poofs!" I now noticed that Cecilia had finally emerged from my bedroom and wondered how long she had been silently following the discussion.

"What have you got against gays?" Lynn angrily responded. "Half your friends are either homosexual or bi."

"What they do with their willies bothers me not a jot," Cecilia was unruffled, "it's just that that pair are so fucking camp. Good for a laugh on an evening, but living together – that'd do my fucking head in!"

"Cecilia has a point," Maggie quickly added, smiling at Lynn, "they are awfully precious. They spend more time in the loo doing their makeup than you do. Just think of the hissy fit there'd be if they ran out of eye-liner!"

The girls settled together to trade anecdotes over the outrageous behaviour of *Les Boys* at parties, while I sorted out coffee and fruit juice for my bed-mate, relieved that Steve and Alan were clearly out of contention. *But linking up with a couple of good sailors, that's not a bad idea at all. Most of the Villas here are locked up for off-season, but requisitioning a couple and encouraging some useful folk to live in the vicinity is something to consider.*

***

We had a swim together after brunch, in the bay in front of the house which had now been christened *The Loo*. Although it was still overcast, the rain had passed and, of course, the fresh water showers on the beach no longer functioned. Luckily, I had a pool on my terrace which could be used to rinse salt off our skins. *I wonder how long that'll remain usable in the absence of the automated cleaning system.*

The rinse turned into a splashing competition, myself strangely paired with Margie and Lynn with Cecilia. As we towelled each other down afterwards, life did not seem too bad at all. *Just a shame we've no music in the background: that's something I'm really going to miss.*

We then dressed and wheeled the trolleys back to Carrefour, filling only one for the return trip.

There was no charcoal now available, but we helped ourselves to a selection of mainly canned food, instant coffee, bottled water and packets of breakfast cereal, in terms of fresh food careful not to take anything that would go off before we could use it. Cecelia selected a huge package of toilet rolls before Margie replaced them with a couple of packets of small face towels. "That's what you're going to be using in the loo from now on," she noted.

"What if I need to go in the middle of the night?" Cecilia scowled. "I'm hardly going to fight my way down to the beach in the dark."

"That's a very good point!" Margie admitted with a grin, scurrying off to return with two plastic buckets. "Problem solved!"

"But we still need paper!"

"Make sure that, in the worst case, you're only going to need a pee, then a wash towel will do the job." Nevertheless, Margie didn't fight her case further when Cecilia compromised with a smaller pack of toilet tolls.

"Actually, buckets are a good idea, we can use them to catch rainwater," I went off to collect another two. "What we really need, though, is some heavy-duty plastic sheets so that we can collect rain over a larger area."

"No idea about plastic, but there are sails a plenty in the Marina," Cecilia offered.

"Good idea," Lynn added, "sails will be much easier to rig up and a hell of a lot more robust than plastic sheets. We could also get all the ropes that we need at a chandler, or even any of the abandoned

135

yachts in the harbour, I suppose. Of course, if we had Alan and Steve, they'd be able to rig them up for us."

Cecilia rolled her eyes theatrically. "Don't you think we'd be able to tie some sails to the balcony without the help of a couple of shirt-lifters? Or even straight lads for that matter," she added quickly to pre-empt a response from Lynn.

"What about me, I could help," I contributed.

"You can fetch and carry, but we'll handle the ropes," Margie replied with a grin.

"Why's that? I can tie knots. I was even a Boy Scout for a little bit."

"Spent much time on boats, have you?"

"No, but I'm not sure what's that's got to do with it."

"My point is completely proven," Margie smiled at the other girls and they nodded in agreement.

Must be a matelot thing, I concluded and gave in gracefully.

After we had transferred the swag back to our abode, we planned a trip to the Marina. Margie had taken charge of logistics and was mainly concerned about the volume and weight of the sails and rope, even for the high-tech materials that were now available. "Easily managed with a car or a small van, but I'm not sure how we do it on foot," she concluded.

"Couldn't we sail it round?" I suggested, hesitantly.

Margie slapped herself on the brow. "Of course we could, there're loads of little sailing dinghies in

136

the lagoon. It won't be easy bringing one into the bay here, but it's certainly doable…"

"Steve and Alan could…" Lynn started.

"Okay, fuck it! If we happen to see the lads in the lagoon, we'll see if they'll help," Margie conceded, "but I reckon I could do it myself."

"I certainly could," Cecilia piped in, "but maybe we'd be better with something a little bigger than a dinghy, about twenty foot say, with an inflatable row boat. The bridges will probably be closed so we'll need to drop the mast to leave the lagoon and tow it out with the inflatable. We sail it round here to Cupecoy, anchor offshore and row in. The inflatable will be light enough that we can lift it out of the water and stow it in the tunnel – much safer than leaving it on the beach."

"You're going to steal a boat," Lynn seemed horrified by the idea.

"Not steal, just borrow. We'll need sheltered mooring, somewhere convenient for us in the short term, and we can return her to her original location when the power goes back on." There seemed to be no comeback to Cecilia's world view.

***

In a role reversal that I suspected was setting a pattern, the three girls set off to find a yacht while I was left to tidy up the house and wash accumulated dishes. *Typical, the bloody dishwasher was loaded up but not run before loss of power, so I've now three days' worth of dishes to sort out.* I used a bucket full of water from the terrace pool for washing, which reminded me of the larger swimming pool in the garden of the neighbouring resort. *Could be a useful resource until we get our rainwater collection sorted out.*

I normally had a cleaner who came by twice a week, but guessed that she would have other things on her mind at present. *Also, she lives in Marigot, so she won't be able to simply catch the bus over as usual.* I shrugged my shoulders and then started to sort out and store systematically all the goods from the supermarket as a prelude to tidying up and cleaning the house from top to bottom.

After my chores were finished, I wandered up to have a look around the main Sapphire Resort building. There was no sign of any staff, but a number of tourists – who mainly seemed to be American, retired and ranging from overweight to grossly obese – sat around the lobby in dejected-looking clusters.

One of a pair of huge, almost spherical women in matching, tent-like, tie-dye smocks shouted to me as soon as I appeared. "Sir, sir, are you staff here?"

"Afraid not," I replied rather curtly, with a feeling of foreboding.

"But, sir, our mobility scooters don't work and neither do the lifts, and we're on the third floor..."

"Move into anything free on the ground floor then," I suggested, trying to escape as quickly as possible and aware that the other guests were following this exchange with clear interest.

"But how do we get our luggage? The lift doesn't work."

"Use the stairs, that's how you got down here wasn't it." I headed for the corner of the lobby where the activities desk was located.

"We were stuck in our room for a full day, until there were no more drinks in the mini-bar," she wailed.

"Then we had to come downstairs on our bottoms," her companion added, "we couldn't get back up to the third floor again."

"And we only got some snacks and drinks from the pool bar, but these're almost finished and the door into the kitchen is locked." This was the characteristic whine of the first whale.

"Not my problem, I'm afraid," I raised my voice to address everyone in the lobby. "There's a little shop in the basement that has food and drinks. It has only a light wooden door, so I'm sure you'll be able to get in. There's probably more in the pool bar kitchen, but that's behind a heavy steel shutter, because it also has the storage room for alcoholic drinks. I'm sure that, between you, you could get in somehow." I was searching through a drawer of the desk while I spoke and smiled when I found what I was looking for, a small key labelled *bikes*.

I completely ignored the babble of voices and questions in my direction, but could feel the mood of discord. *I bet some of the younger, fitter members of the group have already found the shop in the basement, but not let on to the others. Now the fatties will be wanting them to fetch supplies and share them around. I bet this won't end well.*

I hurried to the bicycle rack in the underground car park, where a couple of dozen hire mountain bikes were chained together. I unlocked them and selected bikes for myself and my three housemates. I wheeled these to my villa, two by two, with one hooked up to a trailer clearly designed for carrying children, but which could function for more general transportation of goods.

***

I was just pondering what to do next when a distraught Lynn crashed through the door. "Fuckers, fucking bastards!" She looked like she was about to burst into tears.

I rushed over and put my arms around her. "What's up, it can't be that bad, can it?"

She pushed her face into my shoulder, continuing her tirade in a muffled voice.

"Come on, Lynn, tell me what it's all about." I led her towards the settee, grabbing a now lukewarm Carib from the fridge as I passed. "Here, sit down with me, have a mouthful of this and tell me what's up."

After a couple of deep swallows of beer, the blonde calmed down a little and, with lots of fits of swearing, told me what had happened. In order to get to the lagoon, the girls had to walk past the flat that they shared, in a cheap apartment block close to the Princess Juliana airport. Lynn had volunteered to collect a change of clothing while Margie and Cecilia went in search of a yacht. However, at the entrance to the building, a group of three young men had blocked her way.

"I even know the bastards; they also live in that block. I can't remember their fucking names, but I think two of them are Ozzies and the other is Canadian. They work the wave riders and paddle boards somewhere on Simpson Bay, big tough bastards they are. They said there was an entrance

140

fee for the building – a blow job each. I told them to fuck off, naturally, but when I tried to get past the two blond ones grabbed my arms while the other one pulled my shorts down and then stuck a finger right inside me, the fucker." Now she started to cry, shaking in my arms.

"The evil shite managed to pull my shorts off and I'm sure he would have raped me if I hadn't been so scared that I literally started to pee myself. They just threw me on the ground then one called me a dirty bitch. I managed to grab my shorts and run – they didn't even chase me; just said they'd get me next time I go back to the apartment."

I let her cry for a bit while I stroked her hair. By the time that she had calmed down, I knew exactly what I was going to do. "Okay, Lynn, why don't you just soak in the pool for a bit. Just drop your dirty clothes on the terrace, I'll wash them later. I'll get you a pair of my running shorts and a T-shirt – they'll do you till I get back with your change of clothes."

"Chris, you can't do that – they're really big, fit buggers. Three of them. They'll kill you."

"Big, fit and three of them: that's good, so I won't need to hold back."

"But you haven't got a chance, don't do it," she pleaded.

"Don't worry, they may be tough, but I'm trained to fight. I can assure you, it's not a problem," *As long of none of them have any combat training, that is.*

"Well, if you're so certain, then I'm coming with you!"

"That really isn't necessary…"

"I think it is," she interrupted. "If you really can give them a good kicking, then I want to watch."

One look in her eyes was enough to convince me that her mind was made up. *Now I've just got to put my money where my mouth has dropped me.*

***

Within 15 minutes we were ready, Lynn in my somewhat over-sized running kit and me with my usual shorts and T-shirt, but wearing an incongruent pair of heavy walking boots. As I passed the kitchen on the way to the door, I spotted the knife rack and selected the rough metal spike that served as a sharpener, shoving it into my belt. *I think I could sacrifice that for this bunch of yahoos.*

We cycled to the apartment block, with my bike hooked up to the baby trolley. It took little more than 10 minutes, during which time I noticed how deserted the road was. Apart from a few abandoned cars, there were only a couple of pedestrians and one other cyclist to be seen. When we pulled into the front parking lot, I immediately spotted Lynn's tormenters, sitting on a bench in the shade of a coconut palm beside the main door of the building.

I dismounted and propped my bike on a parked van. "Why don't you just wait here?"

"Are you really sure about this? Look at the size of those fuckers!"

About two metres for the blondes and a few centimetres less for the attempted rapist. Look ripped, but swagger like body-builders rather than

142

fighters. Should be okay. However, I was well aware that I had done no real training for a couple of years and competition level MMA was a few years before that, while I was at Uni.

"What the fuck you want man?" the dark-haired one demanded, evidently the ringleader.

"Well, if you apologise nicely to my friend here, I won't damage you quite as much. But you're going to get a severe kicking in any case."

"Look, it's the pissy-pants bitch," one of the blonds observed. "Her boyfriend here must be high on something, though. I wouldn't normally bother with a stoner like that, but I would call his behaviour threatening, don't you think guys?"

"Of course it's threatening, you fuck-wit. At least I don't need to worry about kicking you in the head as you're clearly feeble anyway. So, are you on first?"

"Watch this, guys, I give him thirty seconds before he's bleeding on the..."

He didn't manage to finish as, true to my word, I kicked him hard on the side of the head. In mixed martial arts we spar with bare feet and, even then, a kick that isn't blocked in any way can do a lot of damage. My heavy boots magnified this considerably. The idiot's eyes had already started to glaze over when I stepped forward and punched him in the throat, followed by a full power kick to the solar plexus: he was clearly out of the game even before he toppled silently onto the ground.

The speed and ferocity of my attack had taken the others completely by surprise, allowing me to step forward and stamp down on the left foot of the second blond. The sound of breaking bones was audible over his scream of pain. "You are also clearly one neurone short of the ability to form a synapse, you stupid cunt! If you're expecting to fight, don't wear fucking flip-flops!"

I feinted a move towards the screaming man, ducking inside the haymaker that his pal was trying to lay on me, probably thinking I hadn't spotted it. My elbow smashed the gang-leader's nose and, while he fell backwards with his hands automatically going to his damaged face, I kneed him in the groin, pulling a large hunting knife from a sheath on his belt and hurtling it into the shrubbery before returning my attention to the hopping blond. *Now I can take my time and make a job of this.*

"Now pay attention you cunts. At least, try to stay conscious for as long as possible, because you're going to learn an important lesson here," I was aware that I was speaking more for Lynn than my victims. "When three men, three large men, attack a young woman and sexually assault her, it's a sign that they have gone beyond the mores of civilised society." I kicked the right knee of the blond, eliciting another scream and causing him to fall backwards onto his back.

"In civilised society you'd be arrested and tried for your crimes, but outside society it's the law of the jungle," I dropped forward, my knees crushing his chest, hearing ribs break. "It goes like this," I started punching his face and head, methodically pulping him, "you hurt my friends or family and I hurt you worse, see what I mean?" I stopped before

144

he could escape into unconsciousness, not expecting a response to my rhetorical question.

Now it was back to the raven-haired man, who seemed to have recovered slightly, although tears of pain were coursing down his cheeks. "Now, you – you're the big boss here," I dummied a punch to his head, then kicked him in the gut, causing him to drop to his knees, "I believe called the leader-aff in Scotland, but I don't know what it is where you come from. Whatever, you obviously deserve most punishment." I got to work on his face, breaking both cheekbones and bursting his eardrums. "I hope that you spot that I'm first taking away your good looks. You weight-lifting types are very much into appearances. Frankenstein's monster will look like Mister Universe compared to you by the time that I'm finished."

Number one blond still wasn't stirring, but I stamped on his face for a bit, just for good measure, before going back to blond two. "The important thing about punishment, according to the law of the jungle, is that you have to make sure that it doesn't lead to a cycle of retaliation. The first punishment must be so severe, so far over the top, that the offenders want only to crawl into a hole in a ground and never come out again. They piss themselves at the very thought of another encounter – as I notice you already have, you dirty bastard." I caught hold of one of his hands, easily resisting his feeble attempts to wrench it free, and held it against the tarmac, using the heavy knife-sharpener to smash his fingers, the bones in the back of his hand and probably his wrist.

145

"It's all very biblical, actually, *eye for an eye* sort of a thing." I released the bloody wreckage and transferred my attention to his other hand, repeating the job. "You laid your hands on my friend, so I'm taking your use of them away, at least for the near future. You were assaulting her as a form of sexual gratification, so now you won't even be able to wank for months."

The man was now hovering on the brink of blacking out, so I addressed myself to the pack leader. "But I haven't forgotten making the punishment so awful that even the friends and family of those punished are scared to retaliate. You alpha male types think you've got big balls and your virility is very important to you. So, think hard about this..." I started kicking his groin and, even when he stopped moving, continued to stamp on his gonads.

As I moved over to repeat the entire process for blond one, I noticed that Lynn had moved over and was watching me with huge eyes. "You really don't need to watch this," I said to her while I worked. "Maybe you should just go up to your apartment and get the clothes."

"No way! I've been listening to what you've been saying and I realise that I agree 100%. When you started to smash those guys up, I wanted to stop you, but you're right, they wouldn't have learned a lesson and would either have tried the same thing somewhere else or rounded up a bunch of their pals to have a go at you."

"Okay, done here, now the tricky bit, the guy who stuck his finger into you and was going to rape you."

"Why's that tricky, he looks only semi-conscious at present."

"Yes, well I want him to be fully aware of what I'm doing to him: which is going to be excruciatingly painful, so I think I'll leave his hands until last." I casually kicked in a couple of his ribs and, while he was distracted by this, undid his belt and pulled his jeans and underpants down.

His hands moved to protect his groin and he rolled onto his belly, saving me the effort. I passed the knife sharpener to Lynn and then dropped my full weight onto the would-be rapist's back, spreading his butt-cheeks. "He penetrated you, so *eye for an eye*?"

Lynn hesitated and I wondered if this was a step too far for her, then she shrugged and sank the implement into his arsehole. "Three times he did it," she noted as the roughened spike was thrust in three times to the hilt. "I was screaming, but maybe not as much as him now."

Indeed, his high-pitched screams were deafening and I began to worry that we might attract unwelcome attention. Leaving the spike in place, I rolled him onto his side and started kicking his groin until well after he lapsed into silence.

"Okay, I'll get the clothes now," Lynn announced, "but remember to do his hands."

"Sure thing," I agreed, "but, as a matter of principle, the knife sharpener stays where it is. I just need to find a brick or a large stone."

"There are loads of stones around this little flower bed," she responded coolly, just before she disappeared into the building.

Mmm, a girl after my own heart. Just a shame she's a lesbian.

***

We cycled back in silence, both of us with large rucksacks and a third in my trolley. It was only when we were entering the house Lynn asked the question that she had evidently been brooding on. "Those guys, how badly did you hurt them?"

"Bad enough to put them in hospital for a very long time, but not life threatening, I don't think. Probably it'll be an extremely long time, if at all, before their sex lives get back to normal."

"But that's assuming that they can get to hospital and that treatment is possible under current conditions."

"Yes, they're now very dependent on their neighbours – as is the case in the jungle. If they treated those around them well…"

"Not a chance, they were a group of loud-mouthed tossers from the beginning, although it didn't occur to me that they could ever sink so low."

"In which case, it doesn't look very good for them. That is, of course, assuming that their attack on you was an isolated incident. There may well have been others. In fact, it'd be surprising if none of your neighbours saw the fight, but you saw that nobody appeared to help. Think about it – say you or your daughter had been raped by these fuckers and you then found them out cold on the ground. What would you do?"

"I would have taken the big rock that you left beside the bodies and caved their fucking heads in," her eyes flashed in fury. "Actually, if I could have found that big knife that you threw away, maybe I'd have cut off their dicks and balls first."

"Yes, I strongly suspect something like that's going to happen and it's why I'm not worried about having placed a burden on what must be an over-strained medical service. I'd bet money that they're not going to get that far. In fact, if someone – or a group – decide to finish them off, I'd guess the corpses will end up as fish food in the lagoon, so nobody has even to worry about burying them."

"Well, anyway, I don't think we should tell the others about this, just in case there's ever any comeback on it. I'm more than happy to be your accomplice here, but we shouldn't lay it on anyone else."

"I've no problem with that," I agreed, "but you have to think of some way of warning them, so they don't get caught out the way that you were. Anyway, I'll leave it up to you – I won't say a dicky bird."

"You do, however, need to get out of those clothes and wash all the blood off. Your boots as well, thinking about it. Anyway, let's go down to the loo and get that sorted out – I'll help you. After that you can help me unpack and store the stuff I picked up and then we can have a sun-downer while we wait for the sailor girls."

Something in her smile gave a hint that helping me wash might not be the only thing on offer. *I*

wonder if she really is 100% gay or more bi?
Maybe I'm going to find out?

* * *

Wild sex in the surf with the trim Lynn turned out to be nothing but wishful thinking on my part. She did, however, notice me wince as I tried to wash my back, and immediately offered to help. "Did one of those guys hurt you?" she enquired as she gently rubbed my neck. "As far as I could see, they didn't manage to touch you even once."

"Yes, that's the essence of the true fighting arts: hurt your opponents and don't let them hurt you. I'm not one for these sacrificial moves, where you let someone land a blow so that you can get in a better one. Okay in a ring, but not sensible in real life, where something like a concealed knife or brass knuckles may be involved."

"So, what's up?"

"Pulled muscles. I've hardly trained at all in recent years," I confessed. "I still know the moves, but the muscles aren't up to controlling them properly. I'm going to be sore now for a couple of days, so I hope that I don't have any more fights in that time."

"Well, I can certainly give you a massage, which should help. Cecilia's actually better at that sort of thing, although she's such a slut that it'll probably turn to sex before she's halfway through oiling you up."

Now that's something I should keep in mind, I grinned. "Okay, I'll take you up on your massage offer, even if it doesn't end up with wild oily sex.

150

It did, however, finish up with a very professional *happy ending*.

***

The sun was setting when the yacht sailed into the bay and we watched from the terrace while Cecilia and Margie struggled to push a concrete block overboard that would serve as a temporary mooring. Packages were then transferred to an inflatable dinghy and we moved down to the beach to help Cecilia manoeuvre it onto the sand. "This is just the first load," she explained. "Margie's organising the rest of our booty, but it'll take at least two more transfers to get it all ashore."

"Is this all just sails and ropes?" I enquired as I started to unload the boat.

"It is this time and maybe also the next load. But we've also got a couple of large barrels for storing water in, a little gas barbeque and a couple of cylinders of gas."

"Do you want me to take a turn rowing?" Lynn asked.

"No, it's fine, Margie and I can handle this. You two can just drag this stuff off the beach and store it somewhere suitable."

"The garage would probably be best, I guess," I decided while we got the last of the material from the inflatable and I pushed it out into the surf, grunting as pain shot up my back.

"Are you okay with this?" Lynn enquired when Cecilia was out of earshot. "I could do it by myself, you know."

"Don't worry, it's just muscles, so the work will probably do them good."

151

"Okay, then let's just get this done. Maybe when we're finished you could get Cecilia to give your back another work over."

"Well, I'll see how I feel after dinner," I smiled, remembering her comments on Cecilia's approach to massage.

***

Lynn and I prepared dinner while the others told us about their yacht hunting trip. This had been made a lot easier due to meeting a coastguard at the marina. He had been in the process of checking out boats to see if anyone was living on-board. His main purpose was to find yachts that were usable without electrical power and recruit sailors to crew them. He was thus very pleased to help the girls select a yacht and load it from a chandler in exchange for their promise to bring it back to Simpson Bay tomorrow to report for duty.

Lynn and I both offered to join them, but Cecilia emphasised that, currently, the coastguards wanted only expert crew with the brutal comment that we – especially me – would be more hindrance than help.

The other main news from the coastguard was that they seemed to have some limited contact with the outside world. Details were very vague, but the gist was that the chances of either a return of power or help from elsewhere were slim at present. The implication was that, although we had lots of problems, Sint Maarten was well off relative to other islands or the mainland. *Somehow, I'm not surprised about that.*

152

We had a couple of drinks after dinner, but the consensus was then for an early night.

Well, it's been a hard day, but we really do seem to be getting ourselves sorted out now.

PA+2 days, Mumbai, India

Rashmi Kapoor had just finished her lunch break, sneaking in a quick vape in the small staff room at the back of the Louis Vuitton store that was linked to the famous Taj Mahal Palace hotel. It had been raining for a couple of days now – which shouldn't happen at all at this time of year – so the sprawling megalopolis was already experiencing flooding in some areas. She was musing on how lucky she was to have a job as security guard in a part of the city rich enough to have proper flood defences; then the lights went out.

Although common enough in the slums, such a blackout was almost unknown in this area. She couldn't remember anything more than a local outage when road works cut a power cable. Typically for this time of day, there were no customers in the exclusive boutique. The store manager had left to eat lunch out and Rashmi's male security colleague was delivering an order somewhere in the hotel, so there were just three sales-girls keeping her company. All four women gathered in the bright area near the external windows, becoming increasingly worried by the prolonged absence of the two men. They also wondered what kind of power cut could possibly not only knock out lights, but leave cars stalled on the street and kill mobile phones and even their e-cigarettes.

With time, discussion gradually shifted onto how to they might get home, as the daylight gradually faded and greater numbers of clearly confused people wandered past. Police were very noticeable by their complete absence. Rashmi was glad to see that the rain had now stopped, but dreading a possible two-hour walk home, when crashing noises caused her to run to the door onto the street, where a group of young men were hammering against the armoured glass with metal poles. *Lucky that these doors are electric and default closed.* She had expected that her appearance would frighten the raiders off. However, apart from a couple of obscene gestures, she was completely ignored. Nevertheless, the doors proved too much for the thieves and, after ten minutes, they moved further along the street in search of easier targets. During the entire time, none of the passers-by had done anything to intervene.

There was a mechanical safety lever that would disable the door lock, but the staff agreed that they would be safer in the store than outside and settled down to wait for power to return.

By the next day, the staff were hungry and thirsty; water was not running, toilets not flushing and it was getting uncomfortably hot and humid in the absence of air conditioning. Crowds had been gradually filling the streets outside but, after a few half-hearted attempts, there seemed to be little interest in stealing any of the contents of this store. For Rashmi that was especially worrying – looters tended to focus on lightweight luxury items and the shop was packed with them.

By midday, the salesgirls had decided to leave. Now Rashmi had a tricky decision to make. She could open the door to let the others out, but there was no way, in the absence of power, that it could be re-locked from outside. As a guard, could she just walk away, leaving free access to all potential thieves and vandals? Pride in her job won out and she waited until it was relatively quiet outside, releasing the lock and shoving the sliding glass doors open just long enough for the women to rush out and then quickly locking herself back in.

Without company, time dragged. She found that there was still water in the large capsule coffee machine used for clients and, in a back cupboard in the manager's office, found a small box of biscuits: not really satisfying, but enough to ward off hunger pangs.

Rashmi slept poorly during her second night in the shop, woken several times by attempts to smash in the door. It was difficult to tell in darkness broken only by the few burning torches, but the mob looked less purposeful, almost as if they were trying to break into any premises, regardless of what it might contain.

By the next morning, Rashmi had had enough. At first light, while the street outside was still quiet, she unlocked the door and tried to slide it open – with no success. The attacks during the night must have damaged it. After straining for ten minutes, she remembered a toolbox that she had seen in the corner of the manager's office and headed there in search of a suitable tool. Five minutes later, she was back with a small crowbar and, after much cursing, managed to prise the door open. When the gap was wide enough, she slipped through and then used the

156

crowbar to force the door closed again. Without the lock, any determined looter would be able to force their way in, but there was nothing more she could do.

Rashmi walked along the street towards the waterfront, absent-mindedly tucking the crowbar into her belt. Despite the early hour, a large number of dazed-looking people sat in groups along the promenade or dozed in cars scattered about the road. Everywhere she looked there were signs of looting and vandalism, with plumes of smoke indicating a large number of fires burning throughout the city.

Slowly making her way along towards the Gateway of India, she came across Anushka, one of the Vuitton sales girls, in a group of about a dozen other women, several of whom she recognised as staff from other nearby shops. They were clearly glad to see her – or, at least, her uniform. It seemed that surrounding areas of the city were effectively impassable, due to fires, flooding, explosions and rioting mobs. There were areas where many people have died and things were getting worse by the hour as the survivors suffered more from thirst and hunger. Even in this up-market area, there were several gangs of men who, after an orgy of pillaging, were now increasingly fighting each other and anyone else in the vicinity.

The main focus for the looters was now the Taj Palace hotel, which was defended by a mixed group of hotel security, police and well-dressed men who were probably private guards of some of the rich and famous hotel residents. Although the defenders were outnumbered, their firearms were clearly holding the attackers back. From the amount of blood and the scattered bodies thereabouts, the guns had already been used. Being well aware of the dangers of stray bullets, Rashmi encouraged the others to move further into the plaza beside the Gateway, an area in which the proportion of women and children was notably greater.

Just after midday as determined by Anushka's automatic watch, a tricycle rickshaw approached which was guarded by two armed policemen. They were quickly mobbed when it was clear that they were selling bottled water. The prices were usurious, fifty-times higher than normal, but Rashmi's group were able to bring together enough cash to buy three bottles. Rashmi obtained a fourth bottle in exchange for her canister of Mace.

Mid-afternoon, sounds of shouts and screams neared as a group of five young men forced their way through the crowd, grabbing people at random and taking any of their possessions that met their fancy. Rashmi felt the other women moving behind her as they approached. Just before they reached her, however, a girl in her teens was grabbed and, with two of the thugs holding her arms, the others started to rip the clothes off the screeching girl.

No matter how bad things are, there are always animals like these that make things worse. The look of surprise on the face of the youth who was in the process of unbuttoning his trousers was almost comical as the crow bar smashed into the back of his head. As he staggered to the side, a second swing brought her weapon into the face of the man holding the girls left arm. Being attacked by a small, rather chubby woman was so unexpected that Rashmi was able to knee another of the would-be rapists in the groin before the others began to get themselves organised, with additional distraction as their semi-naked victim sunk her teeth into the wrist of the remaining man holding her.

Rashmi experienced a moment of cold fear when she saw the man whose groin she had kneed pull a knife from his belt, catching her eye with a feral stare. Then he screamed as a woman jumped onto his back and jammed a small pair of scissors into his right eye. Suddenly chaos erupted as dozens of women swarmed over the men – punching, biting, kicking, scratching... One of the yobs tried to escape towards Rashmi's group, waving a hatchet at head height. She ducked and swung the crowbar against one of his knees, causing him to crash to the ground before he was submerged by an irate group of sales assistants.

Rashmi backed away from the fray and looked down at the bloody tool in her hand. *Something's changed today. We women have had enough. The entire world may be falling apart, but maybe that's not a bad thing if it finally means that we stand up for ourselves.*

PA+2 days, Everest South Base Camp, Nepal

Willy Meier was in a really bad way now.

He had originally been very pleased with his decision to climb solo using basic equipment when the big expeditions reported loss of all communications and failure of their high tech heaters and refrigeration kit. He had none of this kind of stuff and his little gas cooker still functioned fine.

He was still acclimatising to the altitude and had been out walking when he noticed the strange daylight aurora and flashes of light that persisted even when he closed his eyes. It was like some kind of preliminary build up towards snow blindness and he began to worry that his dark sunglasses might not be up to spec. This persisted for about ten minutes, then gradually died away. To be on the safe side, he cut his planned trek short and headed back to camp.

The tent city was in an uproar when he arrived three hours later, with loss of contact to climbers on the mountain causing most concern and loss of cooking facilities causing most discomfort. Nevertheless, there was plenty of food that could be eaten cold and drinks in bottles and cans, so no serious worries beyond the bizarre simultaneous failure of all electronic equipment, which was assumed to be associated with the strange visual phenomena that had occurred at the same time. The consensus seemed to be that it was some kind of electrical storm but, without internet connection, there was no way that this could be checked.

Willy was in his tent having an afternoon snooze when he was aroused by the commotion outside. Scrambling out, he found out that two Sherpas had arrived from camp 1, almost 700 metres above at an altitude of 6 km above sea level, reporting that many of the climbers there had taken sick and were in need of assistance. The Sherpas themselves looked pretty ill, with traces of sunburn on their normally impervious skin and coughing blood. It looked like altitude sickness, so they were taken to the hospital tent and given oxygen while a messenger was sent off to Kathmandu to organise their evacuation in case electronic communication was not quickly re-established.

Feeling unusually tired, Willy ate an early meal and crawled into his sleeping bag, falling instantly asleep.

**

Next morning the camp was strangely silent. The two Sherpas had died during the night and many other climbers were also reporting symptoms of a similar nature, severe enough to confine them to their beds. Two of the largest commercial expeditions had been spooked by suggestions that this could be an infectious disease introduced by the sickened Sherpas, so had broken camp early and started the hike back to Kathmandu. Willy did not feel good himself, but felt reassured by the fact that his lethargy had been noticeable since he returned to camp the previous day and hence predated the arrival of the supposed plague carriers. In any case, to be on the safe side, he kept his distance from the others to the extent possible, which was aided by the location of his small tent on the periphery of the main camp.

As he had no mirror, he was unaware how sunburned his exposed skin looked or how bloodshot his eyes were. His vision was blurred, which he attributed to the consequences of poor quality sunglasses during bright, cloudless weather at such a high altitude. Coughing blood he accepted as part of the acclimatisation process, while blood in his stool passed unnoticed.

He dozed off just after brunch, which he had to force himself to eat. This was, for him, extremely unusual, but, before he could think about it further he fell into a sound sleep that lasted until he was woken up by the light of the rising sun on his tent.

***

He returned to consciousness only slowly, first aware of aches and pains that seemed to permeate his entire body and only afterwards aware of the stench that informed him that he had shit himself during the night. Without attempting to extricate himself from his sleeping bag, he struggled to unzip the entrance to the tent, noting blood on his fingers after rubbing his nose part way through this action. Sun poured into the tent when he finally opened the flap, sending a shock of pain through his watering eyes and causing him to close it again quickly.

Willy's thought processes were sluggish, but he was aware that something was seriously wrong, even for the range of symptoms that could result

162

from the bucket term *altitude sickness*. Although he worked as a ski instructor in the winter and mountain guide in the summer, during his military service he had been in an ABC unit, participating in exercises related to attacks by atomic, biological or chemical weapons. His symptoms were much more like Ebola or acute radiation poisoning than anything related to altitude. He strained to remember details, recalling that Ebola was transmitted by human contact, as was the case with many similar diseases. This should have decreased risks in his case, given the way that he had avoided contacts over the previous fortnight while he prepared himself mentally for his solo climb.

As far as radiation was concerned, he could not think of anywhere further from nuclear activities than this remote Nepalese valley. Nevertheless, his ailments matched well what would be expected after an extremely high radiation dose. *In fact, these symptoms occurring so quickly would be consistent with a lethal dose.*

Suddenly he retched and threw up a bloody mess, making the stench in his tent even worse. He tried to call out for help, but his hoarse whisper drew no response. Suddenly he remembered his strange experience when walking the previous morning. *Flashing lights even with his eyes closed: that could possibly also be caused by a high dose of radiation.*

He retched again, this time it seemed to be entirely blood. His body was wracked with pain and, when he rubbed sweat from his brow, he noticed that his hair was also falling out.

163

His eyesight seemed to be worsening by the moment, so that it was mostly by feel that he searched though his rucksack for his small first aid kit. He took out the syringe, knowing what it was even being unable to read the label. A dose of morphine high enough to take away all pain for at least twelve hours. As he struggled to inject it, he realised that he had only this one dose. However, deep down, he knew he was not going to need a second.

PA+7 days, Nagoya, Japan

Our DMRC team now numbered five, as we had been joined by one of the professors and a couple of students. The professor, Akira Takahashi, had cycled with his wife and young son from a residential suburb of Nagoya where he lived on the 15th floor of an apartment block, aiming initially to set up camp in his ground floor office of the Department. He was thus very happy to take up my offer to let him have my apartment on campus.

Takahashi-sensei's speciality was seismic monitoring, but he was reasonably familiar with the centre's communication network and took over responsibility for liaison between Tokyo and Nagoya's various disaster response groups. As both students were 1st year post-graduates, they were of little direct use and were assigned as general support for Akira, mainly transferring messages by bicycle when no other option was available. Nevertheless, Shoko and I talked them through our own operations whenever time allowed, aware that students such as these would play an important role in long-term Japanese national recovery.

Although localisation of most of its citizens in major urban agglomerations aided re-establishment of communications, the demographics of Japan's greying population meant that huge numbers of pensioners, many in their eighties, nineties and more, lived in upper floors of residential skyscrapers. Loss of power for elevators was thus a critical problem and finding those trapped in upper floors and relocating them, wherever possible to low-rise villages in the countryside, was a priority.

After a week, emergency supplies of food and water were becoming depleted in the bigger cities and lack of sanitation was also causing concerns. The former was being handled predominantly by the *self-defence force*, the Japanese equivalent of an army. It was tasked with clearing routes in key roads and waterways and establishing transportation of goods by any method available – ranging from horses and carts to vehicles recovered from museums and creative re-engineering of otherwise useless electric trucks. This was greatly aided by the coastal locations of, and rivers running through, most Japanese cities.

Re-establishing mains water and sewerage was a trickier problem; which was being initially managed in a patchwork manner using surviving portable generators and fuel cells to pump water and modifying waste water drainage networks to allow raw sewage release to waterways.

On the longer term, however, it was clear that modern Japan in its present form could only exist if supplied with electric power. Fundamentally, the generating capacity from nuclear and hydro plants could be brought on line as soon as transmission networks could be repaired, but this was a huge job for the surviving, localised power sources. Distributed solar and wind power had been less resilient to the EMP event and would need complete replacement in most cases.

The basic aim was to transform the mid-21st century power grid into one more like that of the mid-20th. This not only needed a lot of scavenging from junk yards and re-engineering of existing equipment, but required workers with experience that had not been used for several decades. In this regard demographics helped, the longevity and general good health of the Japanese meant that engineers with skills last used half a century ago could be found and recruited to work on this task, even if mainly in a teaching or guidance role. Priority was set on establishing mini-grids for key urban and strategic industrial areas. It was accepted that even this modest aim would take months and, even if progress was autocatalytic to some extent, rebuilding a functional national grid would take at least a decade.

I was gradually spending more of my time helping Shoko with the problem of rebuilding the trading network required to supply key imports – predominantly of food. Unfortunately, Japan's nearest neighbours had all been very badly hit, especially their mega-cities that were the bases for all government and commercial activities. South Korea, Malaysia, Indonesia, Vietnam, the Philippines, Laos, Cambodia and even the smaller East Asian countries were in complete chaos. There appeared to have been a military coup in North Korea and the scion of the Kim dynasty and all close relatives had been assassinated. China had gone completely silent, although spy satellites showed devastation of major cities and industrial complexes.

Australia showed the same general pattern, with Sydney, in particular, now a wasteland and

Canberra rendered impotent by its remoteness. Unfortunately, as a consequence of global warming, Australian agriculture was dependent on high technology, in particular in terms of water supply. Until a lot of critical infrastructure was recovered, potential sources of imports from here were limited. However, as highlighted in Shoko's summary, if Japanese resources allowed it, investment in supporting Oz could be highly beneficial.

As a typical case of Murphy's law, the most promising option in Asia – Oceania was one of the most distant, New Zealand. This was one of the few countries whose agriculture had generally benefited from global warming and had been inherently less vulnerable because of its relatively low population and smaller cities. Of course, in the Southern Hemisphere, it was now autumn and a major concern was harvesting of crops given the highly mechanised nature of many farms. *There's got to be a way of benefiting from this situation – we just have to work out how.*

***

Shoko had pointed out the fundamental problem in her now typically verbose manner. "It seems that our Deity has been particularly capricious here. We have this dichotomy: the Kiwis have lots of food and too few people to harvest it, while we have a surfeit of manpower but nothing growing at the present time. We both seem to be scuppered."

"That's one way of looking at it, the other is that it is exactly this kind of conflict of requirements that's solvable by a little lateral thinking. This is what we're supposed to be good at."

"I suppose you already have a solution, then, and I'm supposed to work it out."

I replied with my most irritating grin.

"Bugger! Mike, you're impossible! You think we can solve our problems in New Zealand, on the other side of the world!"

"Yes, of course, as you have already pointed out in your succinct analysis, that is exactly the advantage."

"It's bloody 9000 kilometres away! That's an advantage?"

"Well, it wouldn't be if it was east or west of us," I conceded, giving her a hint.

"So, it's because it's south of us..." she frowned. "Yes, as I noted, they're now in harvest time, so that is certainly an advantage for us in terms of getting food soon. But, still, it's so far away and our transportation system, especially shipping, is kaput."

"Is it?" I asked annoyingly.

"There's nothing big that's operational now or will be in the near future..."

"Exactly, so..."

"Mike, why can't you just tell me instead of this bloody mating dance every time?"

"It's good for your soul. Now stop faffing about and solve the problem. Think 1588."

"That's ancient history, I'm a scientist remember, how can you expect me..."

"...or maybe summer 1940, does that help?"

"Mike, stop it please! Give me a proper hint."

"I don't need to – you're sitting in front of one of the most powerful work stations left in Japan."

"But Google doesn't exist anymore, there's no internet!"

"So what? There's the knowledge base integrated into my assessment package."

"It contains history? I had no idea. Why on earth did you include anything like that?"

"It's the basis of heuristic analysis, assessment of present problems in terms of past solutions to comparable problems. By their very nature, the problems we study are rather unusual, so having as extensive a database as possible is useful."

"Okay, okay, smartarse, point made. So, what was that first date?"

"1588."

"Main thing recorded seems to be battles involving the Spanish Armada. Do you think we should invade New Zealand?" she added, sarcastically.

"And summer 1940, sometime around end May, start of June I think?"

"That was during the Second World War, I know that much. It seems that Germany was winning the war in Europe and Allied troops had to be evacuated from Dunkirk."

"That's the one – and the similarities are?"

"Wars – that's clear, but you didn't seem to think much of my invasion suggestion. Mmm," her brow furrowed, "there were lots of boats, ships, involved. By current standards, these were mainly quite small... The Armada managed to cram about 25,000 people onto 130 ships... And the evacuation

170

of Dunkirk involved lots of little ships to move over 300,000 soldiers. That's what you're getting at, isn't it? All of our large ships are useless, but Japan has thousands of small boats. Many of these will be needed for local fisheries, but we could probably find hundreds of sailing ships that'd be capable of making it to New Zealand."

"Coordination and finding crews will be the major challenge, then volunteers who'd be prepared to sail to New Zealand and work in the farms there," I added.

"Yes, well I'm sure lots of people would rather be working in the New Zealand countryside with lots of food available than stuck in a Japanese city with nothing to do, just watching supplies dwindle."

"Of course, such a long trip would be hazardous, some of the boats wouldn't make it."

"But that's the advantage of the Armada idea – they travel together in groups, so can help each other in case of problems. It also reduces our need for navigators who can manage without modern equipment. One or two would be enough for each flotilla, with the rest of the group just following their lead."

"Okay, so what do we need to do now?"

"I'll get on to Tokyo straight away, but I'm sure that they'll go for it. We'll also need to cut a deal with New Zealand somehow or other. There needs to be something in it for them in addition to a supply of labour. If they were stuck, they could probably get that from Australia."

"I'm not sure that Oz is a very good option for anyone at the moment, but we could make the case for Japan by promising that we would prioritise New Zealand for regional support as soon as we have the capability to do so. We would, in any case, give them access to our disaster management tools, but we could offer to help them make best use of their capabilities."

"You talk up a good case, Mike. I'll suggest to Tokyo that they nominate you as lead negotiator here."

"Wait a minute, Shoko, this's the job that you're supposed to do."

"But you promised to train me up. All you need to do is establish the links, I can do the donkey work thereafter. I promise that I'll make it worth your time," after quickly checking that nobody in the centre was looking in our direction, she rubbed her hands between my legs. "What do you think?"

"Hussy!" I whispered. "I'll do this only because I'm your teacher, not as a bargaining counter for your sexual favours."

Her smile showed me that she was more than happy with her manipulation of me. *As bloody usual. I'm three times her age, but that girl knows how to wrap me round her little finger.*

***

The two students had moved into the DMRC and we generally ate meals together, usually also with Akira's family. The boys, Yuki and Hiro, slept in one dormitory while Shoko and I shared the other. It was clear that both the students and Takahashi-sensei were a bit uncomfortable about this situation, but nobody actually commented on it, maybe due to Japanese politeness but probably due to the anomalous conditions that we were living under at present. Indeed, I thought that Shoko might have been more interested in one of the lads than a crumbly like me – or one of the boys might make a play for her – but there seemed to be no interest on either side. *Strange, but not atypical of Japanese students based on what Shoko told me previously.*

Another oddity as far as I was concerned was that neither of the boys drank alcohol. After they moved in, I sent them to the refectory to top up our supplies of their drinks of preference and they returned with a trolley-load of cans of coke, green tea, Oolong tea and Pocari Sweat. *I can't imagine that ever happening if Western students were allowed free pick of what they wanted in a booze shop.*

We had discussed the option of the post-grads bringing some of their friends to eat with us, but Akira, Shoko and I decided that this could be a slippery slope that could transform us into a glorified soup kitchen. As a compromise, after meals, the students and their friends used our facilities to cook food that they had collected and took this over to the student union to share with others. It thus got a bit hectic in the kitchen at times, but this had minimum impact on our work.

After the students and Takahashis left, I broke out a bottle of Dom Pérignon. "Well, lass, that's a week we've survived after a disaster of truly biblical proportions. It may seem strange that we're celebrating when so many have perished or are living under dire conditions, but what we're doing here has a real chance of saving lives and speeding up recovery. I know that you've been under a lot of strain, but I want to say that I'm extremely proud of all that you've achieved."

"I've achieved? I've done almost nothing – it's all been you!"

"Not at all, you've been doing most of the heavy lifting, I provide only the occasional guiding touch."

"Usually by being a complete pain in the arse," she smiled.

"Maybe so – so a toast to hard working underlings and pain-in-the-arse senseis."

We clinked glasses, more like water glasses than champagne flutes, and sipped the delectable wine. "I really haven't done too bad, have I?" she asked, giving me a demure look.

"You've done brilliantly."

"And I'm shit hot in bed, n'est ce pas?" Now she looked a bit less demure.

"Not terrible," I conceded.

"So, you ought to get your flabby ass into action asap, before the bloody students get back."

"You think that your screams of passion may disturb them?"

"Well, let's just see who screams the loudest. Come on and see what I've got lined up for you," she picked up the Champagne and led the way.

Well, no arguing with that! I lifted the glasses and followed her, with a noticeable frisson of anticipation.

174

PA+7 days, Cupecoy, Sint Maarten

It was now 3 days since I had been appointed a deputy of the KPSM, the Korps Politie Sint Maarten. I had a feeling of foreboding that morning, when I answered a knock to the door of my villa and found a tall, black policeman standing there. My first thought was that I was wrong in my assumption that the police forces had better things to do, which would prevent any comeback from my fight with Lynn's attackers. "Hello, my name is Sergeant Kilpatrick," he flashed a badge in my direction, "I take it that you are Mister Christian Herzog and you're a visitor to the island."

"Yes, that's me," I answered cautiously, very aware that I was wearing only a very small pair of swimming trunks that might be better classified as a posing pouch. "Is there something that I can do for you?"

"I'd just like to have a word with you, can I come in?"

"Sure, no problem. Lynn, we've got a visitor," I shouted, remembering that she had been sunbathing in the nude on the terrace. "It's a policeman," I added to make sure that she got the message.

I led the sergeant to the small table in a shaded part of the terrace, the coolest place in the house at this time of day. Lynn was now wrapped in a towel and perched on the edge of a sunbed. "I must say that I'm surprised that you know my name – is your computer database back in action?"

175

"I wish it was, sir," he smiled reassuringly. "If we could get any of our systems up and running again our lives would be a lot easier. Actually, I heard about you from your friends, the ones who're working for the coastguard now."

"Cecilia and Margie, that explains it. So, what can I do for you?"

"As you've probably heard, we've been having some problems with civil order, mainly in and around Simpson Bay. Many of the tourists there are American and Canadian, drawn by the casinos. Quite frankly, we would have problems maintaining control even without loss of our cars, radios, tasers and stuff. Even the handguns that we would consider for serious cases have electronic locks and are completely useless. The only protection we have are our batons and some cans of mace. So I'm looking for some volunteers that I can deputise – and I've heard a rumour that you can handle yourself in a fight, which is now a prime requirement," his grin widened.

"I used to compete in mixed martial arts in my student days," I conceded, "although I'm a bit rusty now."

"From what I've heard you're still in pretty good shape," his smile widened, "and that's what I'm looking for. Even in the current force, most of the older guys aren't up to hand-to-hand and trouble has been getting worse, day by day."

"Well, I'd certainly be prepared to help in any way I can. What do I need to do?"

"Most of the trouble is in the afternoon and evening, so you report in at midday. We're running out of the coastguard building, just beside the lift-bridge in Simpson Bay,"

That makes sense. In the absence of electronic communications, public services are more effective if physically located together – and the girls said the coastguards had some kind of contact with the outside word, so would be the obvious centre of activities.

"I can do that; I know where it is."

"I take it you've got a bicycle you can use, Christian"

"Please call me Chris. Yes, I've got a bike."

"I've got a bike too," Lynn interrupted. "Can I volunteer also?"

The tall black policeman looked her up and down in a sceptical manner. "Have you got some fighting experience?"

"I can help Chris out – and I have a baseball bat."

"A baseball bat?" he laughed. "Actually, thinking about it, that's maybe an ideal tool for the job. I've got to warn you that it's pretty dangerous out there and we've already had several guys hurt, one seriously. On the other hand, nobody is going to be suing for police brutality under present conditions. What do you think, Chris, would she be a help?"

I looked into the girl's eyes and saw her daring me to turn down her offer. "Actually, I think we'd make a pretty good team. Often the presence of a woman can help defuse situations and the key to successful combat is to avoid getting into fights in the first place. This is Lynn..." I suddenly realised that, after four days, I still didn't know her surname.

"...Sinclair, pleased to meet you. Anyway, just call me Lynn."

"Okay, that's all sorted out now. I've got another few calls to make, so I'd better get going."

We all shook hands, learning the policeman's name was Jim, and I led him to the door. *Well, who'd have thought that – get into a fight and end up in the police rather than being arrested by them.*

***

Lynn and I reported for duty and were first issued stab vests and baseball caps, both emblazoned with KPSM in dayglow yellow. We were also given utility belts containing a side-arm baton, a can of mace, a first aid pouch and a number of ziplock strips to act as handcuffs. Lynn modified a velcro loop to act as a holster for her baseball bat, to the amusement of the other police officers.

We were grouped with four other new recruits from visitors to the island, the others all being North American, but very much contrasting to most of their compatriots. Jim and George were policemen, the former a tall, wiry Texas Ranger and the latter a squat, heavily-built member of the RCMP. Tracy was a veritable blonde Amazon, who was a detective with NYPD, while the other without a police background was Benedict, a two metre ten brick shithouse who was a professional hockey player from Quebec. *I've no idea what Benny's fighting experience is, but he's, by far, the most intimidating looking of our small group.*

Sergeant Jim Kilpatrick paired us up – Jim with George, Benny with Tracy and, of course, Lynn with me – and gave us a short briefing. "On behalf of all in Saint Martin, I want to thank you all for volunteering to help out. I know that some of you are experienced police officers – probably more experienced than me – but you all must recognise that this isn't a normal policing job. We have to try to maintain order, but we don't have the equipment that we're used to. In particular, we don't have the luxury of a jail. Even if we could find somewhere to lock people up, we don't have the resources to look after them. What we have to do, therefore, is to punish anyone needing it in an appropriate manner, discouraging repeat offences."

The three police officers looked at each other and Tracy spoke up for them. "You realise that we're thus acting like vigilantes. We could be hung out to dry when the power comes back on."

Sergeant Kilpatrick looked grim. "I'm well aware of that and the KPSM formally assumes all responsibilities for your actions. In effect, we've declared martial law. From what we hear, the chances of getting power back in the foreseeable future are slim and it'll take extreme measures to prevent total system collapse before then. Getting through the next few weeks will be the hardest, especially for all of the tourists who're far from home. It's also hard due to the huge quantity of booze available at present, which is fuelling most of our problems."

Tracy still looked uncomfortable. "There have been a few murders, I've heard. What do we do then, if we have no prisons?"

"In most of the cases so far, the perpetrator has been easy to unambiguously identify. We would like it to be otherwise, but we've had no alternative to summary execution. We've put up notices to that effect in the main trouble hotspots, so people can't say that they haven't been warned."

George seemed to have problems accepting this. "I'm not sure that I could do that, kill someone unless my life was actually threatened."

"You don't need to, bring them back here and I'll handle it."

"And you've actually done this, killed someone?"

"We've sentenced over twenty in the last two days, since martial law was declared," the black policeman looked incredibly sad, "including two women. There've been over thirty deaths resisting arrest. I've heard this called the law of the jungle," he gave me a meaningful glance, "and that's what it is. Rule number one, don't let anyone hurt you or your partner: if in doubt, over-react. Rule two, if you don't think you can handle things, get out fast and come back here for reinforcements – no heroics. Rule three, don't hesitate to mete out any punishment you think applicable and don't bring anyone back in cuffs if you can possibly avoid it."

I scanned the faces of the other recruits, they all looked unhappy, but I noted a determination. The briefing had served its purpose, making it clear to us all how serious the situation was. *And I thought that being a policeman in an island paradise must be a cushy number. We're getting sent out like bloody Judge Dredd – only without the high-tech weaponry.*

***

The first two days went by quickly, following a similar pattern. During early afternoon, things were relatively quiet. We cycled our assigned beat, which extended from the causeway along the lagoon side of the airport to Maho and Cupecoy. We were regularly flagged down by both residents and tourists, the former mainly wanting to know when the power would return and the latter when they would be evacuated or how they could contact friends and family back home. Lynn usually handled these enquiries, bending the truth to make things seem as positive as possible. We also provided advice about where food and drink could be obtained and directions to assembly points where those wanting to volunteer to work or who had other special needs were being handled. As the day wore on, more people emerged from the resorts seeking shade and relief from the climbing temperatures in their no longer air-conditioned abodes.

Many of the tourists congregated in the bars and restaurants, which had all been broken into by now. Warm beer, wine and spirits gradually led to loss of inhibitions and bellicose drunkenness; then the first fights would begin to break out. These were usually inherently constrained by the unfitness of those involved and could be stopped by our appearance. Lynn would give those involved a good tongue-lashing and warn them of the punishment to

181

be expected in the case of a repeat, emphasising the conditions resulting from martial law.

If fights did not break up immediately, I went into Rambo mode and waded in savagely, using my baton to inflict painful, but not crippling, injuries. While this happened, Lynn would go through her spiel, with more emphasis on the fact that there was no comeback in case anyone was seriously injured. Occasionally wives or girlfriends of the combatants would attempt to intervene, but a poke in the gut from Lynn's baseball bat was usually enough to stop that in its tracks.

As it got nearer to sunset, larger fights occurred. If there were more than about half a dozen involved and it was simple fisticuffs, we generally just let them work it out of their system. In the case of weapons appearing or groups attacking individuals, my blows resulted in broken bones or concussion and Lynn's bat smashed the faces of aggressive camp-followers. If we considered it appropriate, Lynn always having the casting vote, we added smashed hands to the punishment of the worst offenders. Our crippled or unconscious victims were simply left where they fell,

After the sun went down, the darkness acted to drive the gangs off the streets and drunks out of the pitch-black bars, so things quietened down. By about eight o'clock we went off duty, leaving policing to the local professionals. The tumbrils also came out then for the nightly collection of bodies for disposal.

During the first night we came upon our first murder, a fat husband who had knifed his even fatter wife. He was standing over her body, crying. When he saw us approach, he turned as if to run, then realised that this was pointless. "I'm sorry, I didn't mean it. She kept on going on about how this trip was all my fault, when it was her who wanted a Caribbean holiday. It's not my fault."

I borrowed Lynn's bat and swung at his head with all my might. He had time for a look of surprise, before the blow broke his neck and he dropped like a sack. "Unambiguous offender and the punishment fits the crime, don't you think?"

Lynn looked shocked, then shrugged her shoulders. "I almost felt sorry for him, but you're right. There wasn't any other option."

That evening we also encountered our first rape, one young Hispanic-looking man holding down a middle-aged black woman in an alleyway while his compatriot thrust into her. This time I used my baton to cave-in the rapist's face before kicking his accomplice in the side of the head. While Lynn ministered to the woman, I systematically broke bones and destroyed internal organs.

I could see a group of men and woman at the end of the alley and raised my voice for their benefit. "This is what no tolerance policing looks like. I'm going to cripple and castrate these bastards and leave them to die in unbelievable pain. Tell everyone you know about this and behave yourselves from now on. You really don't want to get on the wrong side of me."

I turned to see that the rape victim was sitting up, watching the horror in the eyes of her now helpless attackers while Lynn pulled down their trousers. "Or on the wrong side of her," I added as Lynn's baseball bat slammed down into a groin with a squelch that made me wince.

On our second shift, there were three murders, two serious assaults with weapons and four rapes. We did not return any of the perps to base in cuffs.

***

It was mid-afternoon on our third shift when things went badly wrong, which I attribute to my over-confidence. We were dealing with punters generally carrying too much weight, with little or no real fighting experience. For the few exceptions, we had the benefit of surprise and growing familiarity with the weapons we carried. In dozens of actions, neither of us needed to use our mace sprays. After our first shift, Lynn had managed to replace her trainers with a pair of combat boots, which she now used to good effect during mopping-up operations.

We were cycling past a new resort close to our home in Cupecoy, when we were waved down by a harrowed black woman. "Officers, help, they's raping ma daughta!" Her incongruent accent sounded as if it came from somewhere in the deep south of the US.

We leapt from our bikes. "Where are they?" Lynn asked.

"They's in dare, by de pool. But you's gonna need moa men. They's eight o' them."

"Eight, are you sure?" Lynn checked.

"Shoo I know, ma stupid daughta's been ravin' about them fo' a week. They's some boy band muthafuckas as fa' as I know. Ma' girls not de first,

184

neither, they been rapin' boys and gals and we all too frightened to do a ting 'bout it. They's a bunch o' mean mothas!"

"A boy band, eight of them, I think we can handle that," I smiled confidently in Lynn's direction.

"There's a bunch of ho's with them 'n'all, maybe five o' so."

"Yes, well my partner here is very good with showing such types the error of their ways. So it's through the lobby here?"

"So'n'uff, but they's eight…"

"Okay, madam, please follow us and, when you get the chance, grab your girl and get out of the way."

The boy band's eight members seemed chosen for their diversity, but all were extremely handsome, tanned and muscular. All but one had black hair cut in diversity of styles, the exception having a polished, bald head. A guy with a pony tail was easily holding a screaming, diminutive, teenage girl, while one with dreadlocks was buggering her, to the apparent amusement of the rest of the group, and being egged-on by four pretty blonde girls, who were all naked.

Apart from the rapist, who was clad only in tattoos, the other boys sported a range of designer shorts and were either bare chested or wore lurid muscle shirts. *These guys are ripped, but a fucking boy band – how tough are they going to be?"*

"Right, you bunch of evil fucks, get well away from that wee girl and prepare for a serious kicking.

Haven't you stupid shits heard about no tolerance policing?"

The tableau froze for a second that was almost comical, then I was met by a wall of laughter and ribald comments in French. Very deliberately, dreadlock guy looked directly at me and then started thrusting again into the squirming girl's bum.

I put my hand behind my back and felt the handle of the baseball bat placed into it. I half turned away, obviously seen as a sign of retreat from the increasing barrage of French, while I wound up and unleashed a blow right into dreadlock's face, which exploded in a cloud of blood and perfect teeth. I continued moving forward to punch ponytail in the ribs, certainly breaking many of them. I pulled his victim from his shocked grasp and passed her to Lynn, while I stomped on a bare foot and rammed the handle of my bat into his throat, crushing his larynx.

I tossed the bat back to Lynn, who had now shooed the girl and her mother off and turned to the shocked group of the remaining band members. "As far as I'm concerned, you cunts are all accessory to rape of an underage girl and you'll be punished on that basis. That includes you stupid fucking sluts," I turned to address the girls. "My partner here will handle you. You can surrender now and lie face down with your fingers locked behind your back. It won't stop you getting a good beating, but it might be marginally less painful."

I had drawn my baton and was unsurprised that nobody had taken up my offer to surrender. The six guys fanned out in front of me, although I noted that one, a rather effete type with a half-shaven head and hair that flopped over his eyes was showing some reluctance. Holding the side arm of my baton, I punched the end straight between his eyes and he dropped, poleaxed. *And then there were five.* I grinned when I saw uncertainty in the eyes of the two facing me, but was also aware of two others curving around to my side, while the bald-headed one moved backwards, watching me with an amused sneer.

Short back and sides and shorts riding so low that they looked about to fall down at any time, you're next. My selected victim was moving to my right side, so I fainted to the left and let loose with a side kick that smashed his nose. My baton then drove into his stomach and I jumped around him to avoid a fountain of vomit. His staggering body was now between me and the others, so I used this opportunity to pulp his kidneys. *And then there were four.*

As short back and sides collapsed, a boy with a muscle shirt that proudly sported the text *wifebeater ...it's what they're there for* rushed me and managed to land a punch on my shoulder. The bastard was strong and this knocked me off balance, so that I struggled to block a kick aimed at my groin. My uppercut landed below his jaw and resulted in a satisfying crunching noise and a spray of blood, indicating that he'd bitten off the end of his tongue.

Two others now came at me, one with hair cut in stripes and the other with a type of Mohican. I blocked a high kick and caught his ankle, causing

Mohican guy to fall on his back, but stripey managed to land a couple of punches into my side, possibly cracking a rib. I ignored the shock of pain and moved in to knee him in the groin before using my baton to smash him on the back of the head. Mohican guy had struggled to his knees so I started to rapidly punch his face with knuckles and the end of my baton. Seconds later he was also out of the game.

To my surprise, I then heard a slow hand cap and saw that bald guy had moved back and was grinning in my direction. "You know, Monsieur Policeman, you fight quite well for an old man." His English was strongly accented, leaving no doubt that he was a native French speaker. "But those guys," he waved his hands at the bodies around me, "they are chosen to be pretty, to make the young girls wet – and lots of the young boys also. They don't know how to fight. But I do."

He slowly walked towards me, moving like a cat. I then realised that I was in very big trouble. He had been studying me and letting me tire myself on the cannon fodder. *If he does really know how to fight, I fucking hope it's sport fighting, giving me a chance to cheat and use every dirty trick I know.*

Holding my baton by the side arm in right hand, I used my left to pull the canister of mace from my belt. Baldy blurred in a back roundhouse kick that was so fast that the mace was flying from my hand before I realised what was happening. His grin widened as he stood facing me, right shoulder forward in a classic combat stance. *Fuck, even in my prime, I'm not sure that I could take someone as fast as that. And I'm far from my prime now.*

"Are you scared yet, Monsieur?" he goaded me, certainly reading the uncertainty in my posture.

"Kill him, Marcel, kick his fucking..." the female voice behind me cut off in a gurgle of pain. *Baseball bat to bitch's mouth.* I grinned despite my hopeless situation.

"You think I'm funny?" Marcel slid forward, landed a one-two combination to my gut and bounced back to position. "You feel that don't you, old man?"

Once upon a time, I'd stomach muscles like rock, but now they're more like rubber. I fought to control the vomit response caused by the shock of pain. *This bastard's fucking playing with me, he could take me down any time he wants, but he wants cat and mouse, death of a thousand cuts.*

I saw the next back roundhouse only at the last moment and, although my block saved my head, it just about broke both arms and threw me backwards to the edge of the pool. Again, I managed to block a kick to my groin, but the force of it propelled me into the pool.

The water was chest deep when I came spluttering to my feet. Marcel was standing at the side of the pool, completely relaxed. "So, Monsieur Punchbag, you want to come out and play or you want that I finish you off in the water? I think drowning is a good way to die, no?"

"Okay, you baldy cunt, no more mister nice guy," I waved him forward, "come on in and get your fucking arse kicked."

A look of annoyance flashed over his face, to then be replaced by a feral grin. "You have a very big mouth for such a shitty fighter, I think I must teach you a lesson."

When he jumped into the pool, I moved forward and sent a wave of water into his face. This unexpected move gave me only a split second of advantage, but I managed to grab one of his arms and slam on a wrist lock that forced his head under water. Punches slammed into my side, but were slowed by the water and, although they hurt, the damage they inflicted was limited. I seemed to have the whip hand now, but the young man was incredibly strong and managed to wrestle his head up so that he could catch a breath. I clamped my legs around his waist to increase my leverage, but he was now using his elbows and knees, relentlessly weakening me.

In desperation, I head-butted him in the ear, causing a grunt of pain before he managed to wrench his arm free and catch me in a strangle hold. He could have made it worse by holding me below water, but he was evidently enjoying the process of slowly choking the life out of me. I wriggled like an eel and tried to force his arms apart, but I knew I had no chance. Gradually my vision was blurring and I started the slow slide towards unconsciousness. *I just hope Lynn has run for it,* was my last thought.

***

I was completely disorientated when I slowly came to, realising that I was sprawled on the side of the pool. I closed my eyes and groaned, feeling the

190

myriad aches and pains that wracked my body. I slowed my breathing and tried to relax, forcing pain into the background. I then reopened my eyes and found that I was staring into Lynn's face.

"Are you okay, Chris?" she whispered. "That was a bit of a beating that you took, can you move?"

I checked this by slowly turning my head to the side, amazed to see Marcel's body floating face down in the pool, within a cloud of scarlet. "Fuck, what happened to baldy?"

"He forgot about me, didn't he? He was so focused on strangling you that he didn't even see me swing the bat. Caved in the entire side of his head. I don't know if he was still alive or not, but I turned him over, face down, when I got in the pool to get you out."

"How long have I been unconscious?"

"Only a couple of minutes. I sorted out the slags..." I painfully turned my head to see where she was pointing, the pile of bloody girls lying in a corner of the pool bar," but I need to finish up with the guys. Three are dead, but the rest are just handcuffed at present, not in very good shape though."

"I need a few more minutes here, so maybe you need to do the honours."

"There're a bunch of victims and their families who seem more than happy to do that for me. What do you think?"

"Law of the jungle: I say let them do what they want to these bastards. The pool is polluted anyway, so they can throw the bodies in there. We can get them picked up this evening."

"This pool terrace backs onto a cliff above Cupecoy beach. They suggested turfing them off that."

"Whatever, saves the body collection guys some effort, I suppose. Anyway, I think I'll be able to walk in a bit. Lucky that we're so close to home, not sure I could manage the bike.

Okay, that's a serious mistake that I was lucky to live through. As soon as I can, I'm starting serious training again – and treating myself to a more extensive set of fighting tools. Can't just depend on Lynn to get me out of trouble every time. God, I really love that woman!

192

PA+7 days, Rio de Janeiro, Brazil

Ruy Freya told everyone that he had one of the best jobs in Rio. As an engineer working on the cable car to the top of Pao a Sucre – Sugar Loaf Mountain – he certainly worked with a view second to none. At the top station, the panorama was breath-taking and, even after two decades, it still retained its power to awe. Ruy had been taking a coffee break a week ago when the impossible happened, the sea of lights below him suddenly vanished. *It's as if the entire city of Rio de Janeiro has been teleported to another planet, leaving only a void in its place.*

It was several minutes before Ruy realised that the lights on Sugar Loaf had also gone out and that it must be a power cut, of the type that occasionally happened in the favelas. He could not, however, recall the entire city ever being blacked out, so realised that something must be seriously wrong. By then the first pinpricks of light were appearing in the distance, in the direction of the airport and with time, more generally throughout the city. After a while, he guessed that these must be fires and was glad to be well away from whatever was happening at ground level.

Without power there was no way that he could run his checks, so he stumbled his way towards the area of bars, restaurants and gift shops that was so busy during the day but, at night, populated only by a squad of cleaners. In total there were four men, including himself, and eight women. *As I'm an engineer, the others seem to think that, somehow, I can get things sorted out. As if it was only a case of changing a fuse.* He tried to disabuse them of this idea and, as the hours of darkness drew on, hide the fear that was building in line with the fires spreading below.

With daylight the pall of smoke over the city indicated the scale of the fires, which was particularly bad in the distant area where Ruy knew the oil terminal and LPG storage tanks lay. Around midday, the first of a series of huge explosions from that area showed that his worst fears had been realised. The cryogenic containment of the liquid petroleum gas had been lost and the tanks were exploding in series, like falling dominos. The wide avenues of the city were black with crowds of people and he was sure that this represented a riot of previously unparalleled proportion. The complete absence of traffic was a mystery, but indicated that the city had been abandoned by the authorities. The boutiques of Copacabana and Ipanema would be plundered and the luxury hotels along the Avenida Atlântica raided.

By the end of the first day, the stranded Brazilians on the Sugar Loaf had done a bit of plundering themselves; hunger leading them to help themselves to snack food and boredom, combined with worry, resulting in forced entry to a bar so that they had access also to alcohol. During the first night, two of the cleaners, Phillipe and Ronaldo, got into a fight about Consuella, the youngest and prettiest of the woman. Ruy managed to break it up,

194

but how will things develop if power doesn't return soon?

Ruy liberated a pair of extremely expensive binoculars from the duty-free tourist shop, costing the equivalent of about 3 months of his salary, and settled to watch the developing apocalypse. Day by day Rio burned, both architectural masterpieces and dire slums being reduced to blackened, smoking ruins. The crowds gradually thinned as abandonment of the city centre progressed, but the binoculars revealed the bodies left scattered in the streets and pools of blood from pitched battles between rioters that were so large as to be observable from this height.

Ruy didn't see the second fight, but ran to respond to screaming during the fourth day when two of the women discovered Philippe's body hidden in a dumpster. He confronted Ronaldo, but he simply denied all knowledge of the crime. *In any case, what can I do? I'm not Polizia, it isn't my job.*

That night, further screaming brought him running to the restaurant where the women slept. A drunken Ronaldo was trying to pull Consuella away, while the other women attempted to fight him off. He approached the man from behind and drew a large wrench from the work belt that he wore at nights, when he considered himself on duty. One hard blow was enough to down the man, but then he was suddenly scared. *How can I defend myself against retaliation? I've got to sleep sometime and I'm sure that Ronaldo is a murderer, who's well capable of doing it again.*

The women were equally worried and, after extensive discussion it was decided that there was only one solution, removing this threat permanently. They dragged the unconscious man to an inspection deck at the bottom of the cable car, which extended out into thin air and was lit by a three-quarters moon. He removed the barrier chains and pushed Ronaldo off. A couple of the woman screamed while the body dropped into the void.

On the way back, Ruy suddenly remembered the fourth male member of the team, Jesus. As expected, he was found blind drunk, lying in the bar beside two empty rum bottles. He certainly was not a witness and no threat to anyone. *More of a threat to himself, really, as he'll certainly drink himself to death if we're not able to escape soon.*

Instead of sleeping in the cable car control room, as he had previously, Ruy allowed the women to talk him into sleeping in the lounge attached to the restaurant. That night Maria, who was Consuella's aunt, sneaked into his bed and, although they were both married, they made long, slow gentle love in an attempt to forget their fears.

Now, after a week, we're all resigned to our captivity on the mountain. The woman seem to have worked out a rota and I now sleep with a different one each night. I've also noticed that the ladies no longer sleep alone, but mix in pairs and trios. How much is sexual and how much is just physical contact I have no idea, but our little community seems stable. We take food each day to Jesus, but he's completely uninterested; any time awake is just a race to return to oblivion in the bottom of a bottle.

196

It rained heavily last night and finally the fires below seem to be dying. The streets were, however, deserted, and although it was discussed every night, nobody was keen to fight down the dangerous emergency escape route to the surface. *We all know that we'll have to do it sometime, but we'll postpone a return to reality as long as we can, marooned in our oasis of calm above the skeleton of what was once a jewel of South America.*

PA+30 days, Nagoya, Japan

Day thirty had been selected as a checkpoint for a review of recovery progress in Japan and an evaluation of the overall global context – with our DMRC tasked with the latter job. I now had an established routine that involved rising about six am and jogging for an hour around the empty campus before breakfast. Occasionally Shoko would join me, but she really was not keen on running – preferring to get her exercise between the sheets. In fact, since our celebration of day 7, our time between the sheets was mostly spent sleeping. That was when my nymphet lover discovered the functionality of the operating table in the medical room within the centre, which then became the base for her sexual explorations.

The operating table and associated equipment had been designed with tele-operation in mind but, unfortunately, the links to university hospitals scattered around Japan had not been hard and hence it was now usable in stand-alone mode only. Among the standard setting options was one that transformed the table into a conformation for gynaecological inspection – something that appeared to have featured regularly in Shoko's porn video collection. *That first experience was an eye-opener for me and the very thought of it was enough to give me an erection. Nevertheless, Shoko continued to explore variants, reflecting either the extent of her imagination or the perversity of her video collection.*

198

I had to force my mind back to the task in hand, preparing a succinct summary of international communication resources. Since *the Incident*, as it was now euphemistically termed, a major expansion of the NATO and allies' military hardnet had been incorporation of the nodes provided by submarines – both nuclear and conventional. These were playing a key role, especially in the US, as they were now located at harbours around the coastline, providing essential links to surrounding communities. The nuclear subs were particularly valuable as these could also supply power and provide medical and workshop services.

It was notable that warships had proven to be less robust. Although fitted with hardened communication and weapons control systems, the rest of the complex electronics standard to a high-tech fighting ship could be considered *semi-hard* at best. These had been wiped out completely by the solar EMP. *Semi-hard is a bit like being a semi-virgin – it's all or nothing.* Although still components of the hardnet, with the exception of those that had been in harbour, these ships were now mainly powerless, drifting hulks with negligible value. This even applied to the huge, nuclear-powered aircraft carriers.

Limited links with Russia and the Confederation of Independent States had also been established, although China still refused to respond to all approaches made. Australian submarines formed the main link to Oz, but internal communication was still extremely limited due to the abandonment of Canberra, the large-scale destruction of Sydney and extensive damage to other major cities.

Communication to and within Africa, South America and the Indian sub-continent was almost non-existent, with the notable exception of Argentina, which possessed both a military hardnet and a number of submarine nodes. *I guess that, for sake of completeness, I should note that we have had no contact with Antarctica, even contact to a hardnet station at the US polar base was lost and, basically, the entire continent has been written off.*

For Japan the key link was to New Zealand and the original military hardlink to Wellington was complemented by one provided by an invaluable Japanese submarine that was now docked there. This sign of commitment to strengthening collaboration between the two countries was well received and had greatly aided my negotiation of trade links.

It was my original contact with the NZ disaster management team that made them aware of their relatively privileged position and led to a direct discussion with their Cabinet. My tools would help them organise redistribution of their population, mainly away from the bigger cities, and maintain their production of an excess of food from their agricultural and fisheries industries. In the near future, Japan would largely replace traditional export markets in the UK, the rest of Europe and the US and support rebuilding their technological infrastructure. This synergistic relationship would benefit both countries and put them in a very strong position in whatever new world order emerged from the ashes.

The armada heading for New Zealand now amounted to over 1200 ships, with flotillas of between 10 and 50 vessels forming a chain between the two countries and Okinawa acting as a key staging point before the long ocean voyage. Although predominantly sailing ships, an increasing number of steam ships recovered from museums were being added, along with a few fuel-cell powered vessels in which electronic controls were replaced by simple mechanical, electrical or manual systems.

The main aim was to transport 100,000 Japanese labourers to New Zealand, distributed between ports closest to where their assistance in the harvest or other farming activities would be of greatest benefit. The ships would return with agricultural exports that would otherwise go to waste. Although it broke my oenophile heart, a mass market for wine no longer existed and hence a major job would be ripping out the highly successful vineyards and replacing them with crops more suitable for slow ocean transport – root crops like potatoes and fruit like apples. Facilities for preserving meat for transportation in the absence of refrigeration, such as drying and smoking, would also need to be constructed.

I completed my summary and dispatched it to Tokyo, with a copy to Wellington, just before Shoko kissed me on the cheek and informed me that it was time for lunch.

***

During lunch the team summarised output from their original tasks. We now had two further professors – Toyota and Sasaki. Also, three post-docs – another Hiro, Ken and a blonde Swedish girl called Helga. There were also about eight post-grad students, but these were constantly changing as they were transferred in and out of the DMRC and I lost track of their names.

Takahashi-sensei started with an overview of the current status in Japan. The latest estimate of total loss of life was about 2 million – a gigantic number in absolute terms but, as around 2% of the total, an extremely low fraction by global standards. The SDF was now charged with national logistics – redistributing both populations and supplies, which involved working closely with teams from the Ministries of Transport, Agriculture and Fisheries, together with their associated research organisations. Medical infrastructure was still problematic, although portable generators had been supplied to regional medical centres. Industrial infrastructure was almost non-existent, awaiting re-establishment of a national electrical power grid. Experimental micro-grids were being tested around the nuclear power plants and the speed of their expansion would be the rate determining step for national recovery.

I then gave my summary, followed by Toyota-sensei, who overviewed global damage assessment. Due to the constraints on communication highlighted by my analysis, this assessment was selective and highly uncertain. One clear conclusion, however, was that the US had been hit hard. Death toll so far was estimated as at least 10%, the centres of most cities were burnt-out shells and large areas were extensively polluted from nuclear melt-downs and fires at chemical plants. Millions of evacuees were starving: freezing in the north without heating or roasting in the south in the absence of air-conditioning. Police, fire and medical services had collapsed and only in areas with an original military presence was martial law effective. Although the potential to feed its populace from domestic resources still existed, the highly industrial nature of farming, and the distances between agricultural centres and needy populations, indicated that this could turn into an even greater catastrophe if preventative measures were not implemented.

In Europe, the situation was generally better, but varied significantly from country to country. Damage and death rates were higher in the big cities, especially those like Paris and Berlin where ethnic tensions were already high. A wide-bodied airbus had achieved what Guy Fawkes had failed to do, completely destroying the House of Commons in London. Although it was so early in the morning that deaths were limited, this wiped out some key English hardnet infrastructure. The Mediterranean countries were better positioned in terms of food resources, but general lack of disaster management infrastructure made their effective utilisation unlikely. In any case, without effective EU communication or guidance, responses were generally ad hoc on a national or regional basis.

The situation in Russia and the CIS was remarkably similar to the US, with only a bit less civil disorder but also less effective integration of military support. With the single exception of Israel, information elsewhere had to be derived from satellite images. Deaths were guessed to be up to 10% or more, but complete destruction of industrial and transport infrastructure and loss of any form of policing would result in a value much higher as starvation, illness and conflicts took their toll.

The nuclear attack of India on Pakistan had, indeed, resulted in retaliation with a biological weapon – some form of gen-engineered plague. Conditions were so dire that the guess of about 20% death toll could well be a considerable underestimate.

Sasaki-sensei took over to cover East Asia in more detail. Most information was available from the countries with closest links to the US military hardnet, South Korea, Singapore and Taiwan, while, for many others like Vietnam, Cambodia, Laos, Malaysia and Indonesia, again it was mainly satellite image analysis. It was a picture that was now becoming familiar, initial deaths concentrated in the big cities, but potential for widespread famine and disease if infrastructure not recovered. "It is very obvious that the huge global population of around 10 billion is sustainable only with a sophisticated network of technical infrastructure," he concluded. "Without this, the carrying capacity is, at a maximum, about half of this. Thus, even if we guess that deaths so far are maybe as high as a billion, there are a lot more to go. An awful lot, unless we can bring back power and communication within months.

And there is absolutely no way that's going to happen. From the sombre faces around the table, everyone was evidently thinking the same thing.

Finally, Shoko reviewed Oceania, with emphasis on Australia and New Zealand. She didn't bother giving details of disaster impacts that would simply repeat what we had already heard, but concentrated instead on potential to support Japanese national recovery. The short-term focus on the kiwis would allow us to re-establish Pacific Rim trade and, all being well, would be autocatalytic. A Japan-NZ alliance would be well placed to incorporate Australia, when it rebuilds at least regional coordination. If links were also established with Argentina, this could form the basis of a powerful international trading bloc. "With the collapse of the super-powers – the US, China and Russia – and probable disintegration of the EU, something like JANA: Japan-Argentina-New Zealand-Australia, could become the major global economic and political power," she concluded.

Suddenly a shiver ran up my spine. *I've been focusing so much on short term; I'd forgotten about long term. Bugger, we could be in deep shit! I've got to have a confab with Shoko pdq.*

***

As soon as lunch was finished, I took Shoko to one side and whispered that we had a serious problem to discuss, which couldn't be done in front of the others. The young researcher was clearly surprised at by this, but agreed to go with me to one

205

of the seminar rooms on the fourth floor, next to my old office.

The seminar room was musty from having been unused for a month, but was well lit by the windows along one wall. The table that dominated the room was surrounded by 10 chairs; we sat together by a defunct whiteboard that normally served as a computer display.

"I think we've a problem, a serious one," I started.

"Of course we have problems, lots of them, but there now seems to be light at the end of the tunnel, don't you think? Maybe even, at least for Japan, the trace of a silver-lined cloud."

"That's exactly the problem!"

"But how can good news be a problem?" she scowled when I didn't answer immediately. "Is this another one of your bloody tests?"

"It's so important, that we need to run it through together – but why not have it contribute to your education?" I forced a grin that I was sure looked false.

"So, things are developing well, going a bit better and faster than we originally expected – and that's a problem."

"In a nutshell."

"Wait a minute, you started looking funny at the end of my presentation today."

"Exactly, it was your summary that made me realise that I had missed something, something that could be very important."

"Mmm, what did I say... something about JANA wasn't it?"

206

"That's it. It's a good acronym by the way."

"So, JANA is bad news for us?"

"No, JANA is extremely good news – but for us."

"Well, more than just us, really, as we recover the benefits will trickle down to the rest of East Asia – Oceania. Who isn't that good news for?"

"You mentioned them explicitly in your summary."

"What, the super-powers? But this development won't harm them. Basically, they're all so buggered-up that they're beyond help at present. In a few years, when they've got themselves sorted out, even they would benefit if we already have the working basis of a global economy. Why would it be bad news for them?" she scowled in concentration.

When I refused to provide any further hints, she continued somewhat reluctantly. "Well, the old super-powers wouldn't be so super any more. But that's now fait accompli, there's nothing that they can do about it."

"Isn't there?"

"Mike, stop being a pain in the bum! If the US and Russia are knackered, then they're screwed and that's it. Nothing that we do influences that."

"Are you sure?"

"Shit! Will you please stop – there's no way…" Shoko ground to a halt as some new thought dawned on her. "Although, I suppose, it depends if you consider super to be an absolute or relative characteristic…"

I clapped my hands. "That's it, in a nutshell."

"But, wait a minute," she now looked distressed as the implications dawned on her, "the only way that they can prevent being side-lined, assuming that their rate of recovery is constrained, would be to hold us back. Surely, under present circumstances, nobody would even consider that?"

"These are the super-powers that came up with the doctrine of mutually assured destruction – would you like to bet on that? And if it came to an all-out nuclear exchange, do you think that they would target only their opponents, leaving the rest of the world untouched?"

We sat together in silence, while Shoko assessed the implications of this revelation. "If any country attempted to sabotage recovery at the present time, they'd have to do it surreptitiously. We're all interdependent and something like this could backfire badly. Even the US, which has the lion's share of hardnet capacity, would lose out if something like this came to light. They'd be a pariah, abandoned by all their current allies."

"Yes, that's what occurred to me as a result of your presentation. Something like this would never be considered by the guys that we regularly deal with – the disaster management teams. It's the kind of thing that the dark side of the CIA cooks up, possibly a small clique operating without the president or senior military being aware of them."

"And you think it's possible, that a few nutters would have the capabilities to block our plans?"

"Well, of course they'd need to have the required resources already in place…"

"But, surely that's not very likely?" Shoko interrupted.

I gazed at her in silence and then she finally blushed. "Like me, you mean?"

"Yes, I was admiring you while you gave your presentation when the connection finally clicked. The events of the last month have been so far beyond anything ever considered in strategic plans, they'll be flying blind – but it is very probable that they'll have intelligence sources in place. Hell, if the EU had you, you can be 100% certain that the US, China and Russia have people throughout our control centres. It'll take a while before the threat to their dominance becomes obvious, but we're actually providing the background that they need – like your presentation."

"Shit, maybe I should have been a bit more careful about what I said."

"No, your presentation was perfect," I patted her on the shoulder. "We need to discuss things openly within our teams and can't afford to block our effectiveness with unnecessary secrecy. What we need to do, however, is to implement counter-measures in terms of both decreasing our vulnerability and providing some kind of deterrence."

"How can we deter the USA, Mike? As you already pointed out, their heartland may be buggered, but they still have military infrastructure second to none."

"So, we just need to be sneakier than them. Our advantage is that I'm sure that we've seen this as a risk before our opponents have identified it as an opportunity. You need to summarise our discussion to the very top guys in Tokyo security, but it must be kept as secret as possible. If they will wear it, they should leave the counter-measures to me – which not only reduces risks of leaks, but also allows deniability in case I screw up. All blame can be piled on the head of the crazy gaijin."

"Are you sure you can do that? I thought counter-espionage was supposed to be a job for professionals, James Bond types with a license to kill," she grinned.

"Well, we don't have any handsome young Englishmen to hand, so we will just have to make do with a crumbly old Scot," I grinned back. *And I just hope she never finds out that I am quite capable of killing, even without a license.*

***

Just before dinner that evening, I was surprised to see all the rest of the DMRC team head off, the post-grads giving strange looks in my direction. Before I could ask, Shoko explained. "It's now one month since the Incident, so I thought we'd celebrate – a bit like we did after the first week."

"Well, I guess it won't surprise you that I have already looked out a bottle of Champagne. I originally thought of retreating to the clinic with it after dinner, just like before." I raised my eyebrows suggestively. "But now, I guess we can have it with dinner, if it's just the two of us."

"Well, actually, it's not just the two of us, I've got a friend joining us for dinner. But we can certainly drink the sparkly then."

I felt slightly disappointed, but realised that it would be nice to see someone different. The team tended to work on top of each other and I had little chance to meet new people. "Okay, but we can then spend some special time together, just the two of us."

"Well, I don't know about that either," she smiled at me in a cryptic manner and refused to comment further while she prepared dinner.

In view of our visitor – and our 1-month anniversary – I showered before dinner and dressed in a loose linen shirt and trousers, rather my usual coveralls. *What on earth is that girl up to? I can tell from her sphinx-like smile that she's got some kind of mischief planned, but I can't for the life of me think what.*

***

The mysterious friend, Nomura-sensei, appeared about forty minutes later. Akiko was a pretty, middle aged Japanese woman with paged black, silky hair. She was dressed in a white blouse, short black skirt, white knee socks and black pumps reminiscent of a school uniform. Elsewhere this rig-out might have appeared strange, but I had seen that this look was very popular with Japanese women of all ages.

After I shook hands with her and the ladies kissed each other on the cheeks, we sat around the table with glasses of chilled Chablis while Akiko and I got to know each other a bit better. Aki, as she preferred to be known, was a professor in the geography department, so I immediately assumed that Shoko had recruited her to help in our project. I

211

was thus surprised when I realised that this information was new to my young lover and that Aki had clearly no idea at all about what we did.

Over dinner, conversation slowly drifted towards our projects and it was evident that Aki could be a useful member of our team. Shoko was delighted. "Well, this is really serendipitous, we meet on a contact notice board and it turns out that you fit in perfectly with our work profile. How cool is that?"

Notice board, what's that? However, before I could enquire further, Aki started talking about a project of hers on population demographics in North Korea, leading to a discussion of how the events of the last month may have impacted the already fragile stability of that country.

After desert, cheesecake accompanied by the Champagne, there was some conspiratorial whispering in Japanese between the women that made me instantly suspicious. *It's clear that, although they seem to get on like a house on fire, Shoko and Aki hardly knew each other before tonight. So why was Nomura-sensei invited to our little celebration?*

I was even more bemused when the woman each took one of my hands and I was pulled to my feet and Shoko led us to our medical room cum boudoir. There I was seated on a chair in the corner while the ladies started to kiss and fondle each other, slowly peeling each other's clothes off. The action varied from rather serious through sensual to comical – the last in particular when they struggled together to remove Shoko's tight jeans. I was completely transfixed, *probably looking like a stunned mullet,* baffled by this development. This foreplay lasted for about ten minutes, played out in almost complete silence, the women only occasionally giggling or whispering to each other while I goggled wordlessly, afraid to break the spell.

When down to panties only, Aki wearing little white, semi-transparent schoolgirl knickers and Shoko a minute black tanga, I was dragged to my feet and together they started to caress and undress me. Initially I felt embarrassed by my substantial erection, given that I had first met Aki only a couple of hours previously, but this was soon replaced by a tide of lust as I got more actively involved. After I was completely naked, I removed the ladies' panties, gasping at the sight of Aki's shaven mons and the glint of gold revealing an intimate piercing.

Following Shoko's instructions, we bound Aki to the table – set in some kind of gynaecological format, although more prone than the usual chair – using silk scarfs that my nymphet often used for our role-playing games. While I worked between the legs of our captive with fingers and tongue, Shoko was squeezing and biting her nipples. I had no idea how this was choreographed, but Aki's groans and screams – together with the wetness of her vagina – indicated that it was having the desired effect.

"Now, fuck her," Shoko commanded as she climbed onto the table and positioned her groin above the other woman's face, still savagely pinching her nipples.

Thank Christ for that, I don't think I could have held on much longer. I did as ordered, thrusting hard into the soaking orifice with all my might. *Just as well Aki was also right on the edge.* Her orgasm started immediately and she screamed and writhed like an eel, causing me to come simultaneously although, for me, it was a less drawn out and much less noisy event.

When I withdrew, Shoko slid forward so that the ladies were now in soixante-neuf position. I sagged back into my chair with a sigh, moving it nearer to get a better view of what my lover was up to, watching her alternate between sticking her tongue deep into Aki's vagina and toying with the gold ring through her clitoral hood with her teeth. At the same time, she was almost absentmindedly sliding her finger in and out of the woman's rosebud arsehole.

Why did this never happen to me when I was young enough to take full advantage of it? Nevertheless, this show would bring life to the dead. Indeed, after a relatively short time, I felt capable of renewing active participation in the ménage a trois.

I moved to the other end of the table and was waved forward by Aki. She took control of my now rigid member and guided it to complement the actions of her tongue and fingers. I used my hands to spread Shoko's tight cheeks and better view the action as I started work on her vagina, before being transferred to Aki's mouth and an eventual finale in my lover's bum.

I staggered back to my chair and collapsed into it; this time being joined by the women after they

214

slowly prised themselves from each other. Aki spread my legs and then they each straddled one of my thighs, nuzzling my neck while stroking their hands over both me and each other.

"Well," Shoko whispered huskily, "how was that? Were you disappointed that we didn't have the evening to ourselves?"

"I think I can honestly say that, despite my great age, I've never experienced anything remotely like that" I sighed. "But I'm still a bit baffled about how this all came about. How did you two meet? Did you really plan for this to happen?"

The ladies giggled like schoolgirls, a somewhat disconcerting experience under the conditions. "Well, Mike, I wanted something special for your birthday..."

Shit, my birthday, it is right enough – I suppose it's easy enough to forget trivial like that when you're looking at the end of the world. "How did you know it's my birthday? I'd completely forgotten about it."

"The staff and students had been planning a party for you – it's your sixtieth and that is very important in Japan – the beginning of your second life. A beer party downtown is, of course, no longer on the cards, but I thought that this would be a reasonable substitute."

Wild decadent sex with two beautiful women as a replacement for a beer party! I mused on this, flabbergasted. "But, where does Aki come into the picture?" I turned to the naked woman. "If you're my birthday present, then a sixtieth must indeed be a very big deal in Japan."

"No, Mike-san," she giggled, "I didn't know it was your birthday – I just arranged this via the contact board in the students' union."

The contact board thing again. "Oh, how does that work?"

The two girls looked at each other as if amazed by my ignorance, then Aki continued. "Well, I'm not married but I like to have sex every now and again. I'm too busy for dating and, anyway, the contact boards are more interesting. Of course, before it was online and I used to go into Tokyo for meets. I'm really pleased that this meet worked out so well – it was so convenient."

"And you usually organise sex with couples?" I enquired, amazed at the open attitude to sex displayed by the woman who, during dinner, had looked so demure.

"I think I now prefer couples," she seemed to be amused by the question, "although, of course, I do meet singles – male and female – sometimes."

"Have you ever tried two men?" Shoko enquired.

"A couple of times, but the guys were gay. It was fun, but I think the boys were really much more interested in each other than in me."

"What was it like – what was the best fun bit?" My lover's fascination with this topic was evident.

"Well, double penetration, I suppose. With couples you need a strap-on, which isn't as good as the real thing. The gay guys are good, they take their time and the sensation is incredible – but I feel that they are doing it for each other, not for me."

I was rather worried by the gleam in Shoko's eyes. *Thank God it's a year until my next birthday! Christ knows what kind of ideas this has put in her head.*

While the ladies further discussed the pros and cons of different variations of double penetration, I could feel my eyes grow heavy. *Old age certainly doesn't come alone. I'm here with two red-hot women who are openly discussing wild sex and I'm ready for a snooze.*

I was shocked awake by a nip to my chest. "Come on, sleepyhead, we've got to take advantage of the time before the students get back. Aki and I have some ideas for round three, but we need your equipment for it," she playfully slapped my dick.

"I'd have as much chance screwing you with a bit of spaghetti," I moaned. "I think I should just head for bed and leave you two youngsters to it."

"No way," I received another slap, "you'll perform and like it! We don't have a strap on, although Aki'll bring one next time, but I do have a dildo so we have the makings of some double penetration scenarios."

"And don't worry about this," Aki added as she slipped off my knee and started massaging my willy, "I'm sure I can get this back into working order."

"Definitely," Shoko joined her friend between my legs, "we'll lick you into shape."

They certainly did.

217

PA+30 days, Cupecoy, Sint Maarten

I awoke and stretched, careful not to disturb the woman sleeping at my side. *Lynn, who'd have thunk it?* After weeks of claiming to be straight gay with a solid partnership to Margie, two days ago she and Cecilia announced that they were changing bedrooms. *Maybe there'd been signs but, apart from Lynn teamed with me for police duties and the other pair working together for the coastguard, I hadn't noticed any indications that a change of this magnitude was in the wind.* It was true that Cecilia's lovemaking had been less manic, but I had attributed this to her markedly decreased alcohol intake. To the relief of us all, the responsibilities of her new job seemed to have sobered her up – both literally and metaphorically.

I pulled the single sheet covering us lower to expose the girl's tanned, muscular body. *Maybe not as spectacular as my previous bedmate, but very nice indeed. Sex with Lynn was also a bit less athletic, but maybe in this case a change was as good as a holiday – Cecilia could be exhausting.* I gently caressed the sleeping woman's bum and closed my eyes, going over the transformation of my life caused by the *Incident*.

After a month, the need for vigilante policing had declined considerably, so Lynn and I no longer did regular duty, but were on call as and when needed. It seemed to be the case that, although large numbers had been involved in disruptive behaviour, serious problems had been caused by a few ringleaders and, with them out of action or scared off, things had cooled down considerably. In addition, although there were still large quantities of booze on the island, these were being stockpiled as people began to realise that it might be a long time before resupply could be expected.

My encounter with the boy band had put me out of action for a couple of days, but I was back on patrol, with ribs strapped up, as soon as I could manage it. However, I had learned my lesson and was a lot less gung-ho than previously. I also started rigorous training to get my level of fitness up to scratch. I thus felt a bit sorry to ramp down my activities just at the time I was best prepared to carry them out.

With more free time, Lynn and I had looked around for other volunteer opportunities, finding labouring work to support the agricultural development team. Our first job involved digging up the Cupecoy golf course to prepare for planting with sweet potato and plantain, which was considered as a prelude to the bigger job of clearing the forested centre of the island – which would both provide wood and charcoal and greatly extend the land area for growing food. Although the environmental impact would be significant, this was considered less of an issue than assuring a suitable diet for the island's population. This would complement the fisheries, which were already quite well re-established following refitting some of the large number of yachts anchored in the central lagoon and in marinas and sheltered coves around the island.

A significant number of the tourists on the island at this time of year were sailors. Most of the yachts with Americans on board that were set up for manual operation – or which could be readily modified to do so – sailed off over the first couple of weeks, in some cases with additional crew or passengers who were prepared to offer huge sums to escape from the island. From the rumours I had heard from the coastguard, I was fairly sure that the situation would be, if anything, worse on the mainland and I seriously doubted that electronic money transfer, the basis of well over 99.9% of previous transactions, would be functional. As those leaving tended to be a younger, fitter cohort than the average tourist, this could also be a factor contributing to decreased trouble on the island.

Sailors from further afield, mainly from Europe, had been generally less willing to venture out of sight of land without the electronic navigational aids that they were so accustomed to. An increasing number were being incorporated into the fleet organised by the coastguard for fishery, goods transport or messenger duties.

My musing was interrupted by a sharp bite on my left buttock. "Fuck!" I spluttered, turning to see a grinning Cecilia crouched by my side. "Christ, this is my bedroom – couldn't you at least knock?"

"Well it used to be our bedroom, although it seems that you're adjusting okay to my absence."

"Yes, fuck off, Cecilia, you slut," a voice behind me added. My sudden movement had evidently woken Lynn. "At the very least you could put some clothes on if you're intruding into our bedroom."

"But I never wear clothes around the house," Cecilia's grin widened.

"Yes, because you're a slut!"

"But neither does anyone else," she pointed out.

"Yes, but we don't flaunt it the way that you do, crouching there with your legs wide open."

"You can't see me with your face buried in Chris's back."

"But she is, isn't she, Chris?"

"She is actually, I could just about make out what she had for breakfast," I admitted, awareness of the view causing a first physical reaction.

"Your knowledge of anatomy is somewhat limited," Cecilia laughed. She then stood up, turned, bent over and spread her bum cheeks. "How about this, can you see what I had for breakfast yet?"

"Fuck off, Cecelia!" Lynn and I said as one, myself aware that my growing erection was unmistakable.

"Okay, already, just remember that I'm supposed to take you to the coastguard commander this morning," she flounced from the room, deliberately leaving the door wide open. "You've got time for a quickie before breakfast, so get a move on."

A brown hand snaked around my waist and took hold of my rigid cock. "I knew she would get you hard, she really is a slut, isn't she?"

"Mmm, I suppose so, but she certainly has a very dirty body."

"Yes, filthy. And bangs like a shithouse door in a high wind," Lynn pushed me onto my back and climbed on top. "Margie and I certainly had a few very wild threesomes with her."

"I thought that was only while she was drunk," I noticed that my partner was very wet already.

"Also, in the last couple of weeks when she was sober. It was actually much better then."

"So, there's been lesbo ménage a trois in the last fortnight – I'd no idea…"

"You never have," she started to bounce energetically on top of me. "Anyway, you can watch next time, how about that?"

With images of that in my mind, this was going to be a very quick quickie.

***

Over breakfast we speculated about what the commander could have in mind for us. Although not of the level of the other pair, Lynn had a fair bit of sailing experience, so she could be drafted as sailing ship crew, for which there was growing demand as more yachts were refitted. All three girls agreed, however, that the coastguard would have to be very desperate to want me for such a job. In any case, drumming up crew was carried out at a much lower level and would not merit an interview with the commander.

Cecilia was remarkably quiet during the discussion, implying that she maybe knew more than the rest of us but, in typically annoying fashion, she refused to say anything.

We cycled together to Simpson Bay, Cecilia and Margie heading off to report for duty while Lynn and I were directed to a corner office at the back of the Coastguard HQ. The commander was a woman who I guessed to be in her early forties, seeming to be a bit young for such a position. In any case, her crisp white uniform and demeanour radiated an air of confidence that was appropriate for the job. I became suddenly aware that my working shorts, T-shirt and stained walking boots were very scruffy by comparison.

Commander Konig stood to shake hands as we entered and introduced Captain de Witt of KPSM, a man that I knew of and had seen occasionally, but had not previously spoken to. Konig came straight to the point. "Chris, Lynn, the Politie were very impressed at the help that you provided when they needed support for crowd control, so I wondered if you'd be interested in joining a special unit that we're now forming. This is a cooperative effort between Coastguards on Dutch and French sides, the KPSM and the Gendarmerie."

"That's a strange combination," I smiled. "What are you hunting, pirates?"

My grin vanished as de Witt gave a startled cough. "How did you know?"

"Oops, sorry, that was supposed to be a facetious comment. Although, now I think about it, maybe not so surprising."

"How do you come to that conclusion?" Konig leaned forward, evidently very curious about my reasoning.

"Well, piracy has a long history in the Caribbean, although I'd guess that, in recent decades, it has been largely replaced by smuggling."

"You can say that again! Anyway, go on."

"Since the Incident, I imagine that smuggling is fairly pointless. We've lost money as a component of our society and, until that's replaced by something, avoiding payment of duty is a non-issue. We now have a barter economy and trade by ships around and between the Caribbean islands is expanding rapidly. I guess that, for existing criminal networks, piracy of trading ships would be expected."

I waited for a moment to see how Konig would respond, but is was de Witt who spoke up. "Yes, I'd heard that you were some kind of risk analyst back in the real world, so it's not so surprising that you've worked this out."

My two interrogators seemed to be expecting more, so I continued. "I guess you're setting up a team now because you want to nip this in the bud. The criminal gangs involved are likely to be well organised – so completely different to the rioters that we had to deal with on the island. If they get established, they could become a plague that'd threaten the entire recovery process."

The commanded nodded. "Yes, that's also our conclusion. There is some good news though – we know where most of the smugglers' bases are due to our previous investigations. At that time, however, we were hampered by the law, such as the need to provide hard evidence to support searches, limitations on invasion of privacy, and other nonsense like that. With martial law, our hands are now free to act."

I see where this is going now. "So, I guess you want a team to put these gangs out of business, permanently. No arrests or anything like that."

De Witt looked unhappy. "If it was at all possible, I would take another approach, but I can't see an alternative. In the past pirates terrorised the entire Caribbean, ruled entire islands. We can't let that happen again."

"But I see a problem here," Lynn spoke up for the first time. "These guys will have firearms, won't they?"

"During smuggling operations, they generally avoid having guns on board," de Witt answered, "as this increases the severity of the sentence if they're caught. The gangs do, however, also clash with each other and then guns often appear – usually pistols and shotguns. Things get a lot rougher up around Jamaica, where machine guns are common, but there's not much of that locally."

"So will we be armed then?" Lynn enquired.

"We've got a bit of a problem there," de Witt looked uncomfortable, "as most of our firearms are electronically locked. They're now useless."

"What? You want us to go up against armed gangs with our batons and pepper sprays?" Lynn glanced at me with a look of amazement.

"Well, initially…" de Witt's discomfort seemed to increase. "Our plan was that you would confiscate any weapons that you find and can then use them in later operations."

"But, initially, we have to take out an armed band of criminals," Lynn persisted.

"Yes, well that's why we wanted to talk to you today. We think there is a good chance for you to do just that."

"And when would that be?" I asked, suspiciously.

"This evening, actually, over on Saba."

Given my musing of the morning, I was unsure whether to be happy or terrified about this.

***

The reason for this rushed initiation of what seemed to have been an action only in the first stages of planning was the audacious boarding yesterday of a schooner out of Oranjestad en route to Sint Maarten. This was not only a very valuable boat, but its crew of ten women were experienced ocean racers and it was carrying a cargo of canned food. The piracy had been witnessed by a couple of other yachts and the schooner was now blatantly moored in the harbour at Fort Bay in southern Saba.

The coastguard investigators were convinced that this was the action of Rene Hassell and his gang. "A really bad bastard with a gang that includes more lawyers than hired guns," as the commander put it. "We know that they've been smuggling booze and tobacco for decades and more recently moved up to drugs and girls, illegal immigrants sold into prostitution in the US. They were very high tech, in terms of surveillance counter-measures, but often used small sailing boats for the smuggling as these blended more into the inter-island tourist traffic."

"How big a gang does he have?" I asked.

"The core is mainly family, with probably about ten of them on Saba at present. They live together in three large villas on the outskirts of Saint Johns, just above the harbour. These're the ones most likely to have firearms. There are maybe another dozen or so gang members who're boat crew. Probably carry knifes or brass knuckles, but unlikely to have much real fighting experience beyond the occasional bar brawl."

Konig began to sketch with chalk on a blackboard with a colourful frame advertising Red Stripe beer, which had clearly been requisitioned from a beach bar. "They have a covered dock, workshops and a warehouse for their camouflage business of top-end rum export located at Fort Bay: basically, they control this harbour completely. Even a dive shop, a bar and a restaurant there are owned by Hassell."

"Our key aim has got to be protecting the girls that he has kidnapped," Lynn pointed out. "Where will they be?"

"My guess would be the warehouse, as they have cages there for storing rum," de Witt answered. "In the past, Hassell ran everything from his villa via a secure intranet, but I guess he now needs to use a more hands-on approach. This wouldn't worry him if he knows that we've lost all of our remote surveillance capacity, which I'm sure he does. It has been claimed that he often *sampled the goods* when smuggling prostitutes, so I wouldn't be surprised if he wasn't spending some time with the kidnapped girls."

"You really think that he'd enslave those women?" Lynn was plainly horrified.

"Under the present circumstances, I'm pretty sure of it," the policeman answered with a shake of his head. "Those women can identify their kidnappers, so he'll either use them on island to service his men or sell them on somewhere they'll disappear, probably Jamaica. I think the women were all Caucasian – young and fit to boot. They're valuable goods."

"Okay, you've sold us on this," Lynn responded for us both, her frown in my direction daring me to contradict her.

"Yes, fine," I shrugged my shoulders. "So how many of us are there in the team?"

"For this operation, you're it," Konig answered, almost apologetically. "We're certain that Hassell has informers in the KPSM, the coastguard and equivalents in other islands where he operates, so we can't use any of our forces without risking tipping him off. Other foreign volunteers will simultaneously hit his satellite operations run out of Saint Eustatius, Saint Barts, Anguilla and Saint Kits – we aim to completely destroy this operation in one fell swoop."

"But, by the sound of it, we've got the headquarters, the hardest target."

"Well, you're our best team," de Witt smiled encouragingly.

I'm not sure if that's a complement or a death sentence.

***

228

Shortly later we were joined by a rather bemused-looking Cecilia and Margie. Again with the aim of assuring no leaks of our plans, they would use our yacht to take us over to Saba. While they dropped lobster pots along the west coast, Lynn and I would slip into kayaks and paddle along to Fort Bay harbour, arriving there about two hours before sunset. We then had an hour before Konig would assemble a *recovery team* to sail to Saba. By the time that she reached Fort Bay, we should be able to confirm the way was clear for mopping up operations by using a green flare. No flare and the coastguard would simply sail back to base.

All went smoothly until we approached Fort Bay harbour and were immediately spotted by three youths who were sitting on the breakwater, fishing and drinking beer. *Thank God that I'd realised that this was a possibility and all our police kit was stored in the waterproof compartments at the back of the large, plastic kayaks.* I was thus wearing only swimming trunks and Lynn a bikini bottom, her pierced nipples clearly being the focus of the lads' attention.

"Hey, guys, is this Saint Martin?" I shouted. "I think we're lost."

This statement of the obvious caused the boys to crack up, although jokes at our expense were in such a thick accent as to be completely incomprehensible. As we approached the shore, the smallest of the pack waved us off. "No, man, you no can land hea'," he shouted. "This private property, you know."

"I'm really sorry," I called back, "but I just can't paddle any further. And my girlfriend's been a bit sea sick, she can't go on until we've rested a bit. We can just have a seat on the beach here and drink some water then we'll go on. Where can we land around here? Or can we just dump the kayaks and walk?"

I had already run my kayak up on a little patch of sand and jumped out with a theatrical stagger to pull it higher. I then caught Lynn's bow and pulled her canoe onto the beach beside mine. The young men were now rushing towards us – *probably aiming to get a better view of Lynn's tits as she slumped back in her seat.*

"Hey, man we told you, you can no land, this beach like private owna'," the smallest of the three, who was in the lead, seemed to be the nominated spokesman.

I had now opened the compartment at the back of my kayak, taking out a baseball bat that I leant on heavily. "Come on guys, I hurt my leg and I can hardly stand. Give me a break."

The small guy, who still must have been 170 centimetres, very wiry and deeply tanned, was now standing directly in front of me. I now noticed that the lurid T-shirt that he wore over cut-down jeans had a Spiderman motif. He also had a holstered pistol on his belt. "You like Spidey, do you? I've got a Doc Oc T that I'll give you if you let us rest up for a bit."

The bloke seemed baffled by my offer, *probably not up on his Marvel mythology.*

"A dunno what you talkin' about man, but that's a fine bat you got, you gonna give me that?"

Out of the corner of my eye I could see that the other two blokes, both black with dreads and stripped to the waist, again with cut down jeans, were approaching Lynn. "That a mighty fine honey, you know. I could use some of that," one commented.

"Yah, sweet, just like them saila' gal bitches. This one can stay!"

Spidey turned to glance at the merchandise being discussed and I faked stumbling forward, swinging the bat with all my strength. The loud crack as it contacted with the side of his head almost certainly indicated a broken neck and caused the other pair to turn in alarm, allowing Lynn to scythe the blade of her paddle into the throat of the nearest one, who fell choking into the surf. The other was fumbling to remove a large sheath knife from his belt, then changed his mind when he realised that I would be on him before he drew it. His raised arms blocked my blow, although at the cost of a smashed elbow, while Lynn's paddle walloped him in the kidneys. He crouched in pain, screaming something unintelligible, before my punch crushed his larynx.

"Shit, sorry, I should have taken that guy down faster, before he could shout out. Anyway, I'll quickly check to see if anyone heard while you finish these three fuckers off." I ran up the side of the breakwater and peered over. There seemed to be a couple of people hanging about in front of the warehouse at the other end of the harbour, but no sign of any alarm. Any sound that we had made was probably well masked by the waves that crashed against the harbour wall.

I scrambled back to the kayaks and saw that Lynn had already done her job, three bodies were bobbing face-down in the surf, and she had already started getting kitted up. "Fuck, I hate sandy beaches," she muttered under her breath, sitting on a rock and trying to wash her feet before donning her combat boots.

"Looks all clear," I reported, "so we can move off as soon as I get my stuff sorted out."

"Okay, but I take point," Lynn waved the pistol that had previously belonged to spider-thug. "Unless, of course, you've learned how to use one of these. *Teasing, as she knows I've never fired a gun in my life.*

"Whatever you say, boss. The tricky bit's going to be getting round to the warehouse as there's a lot of open ground between here and there. There's presently a couple of guys hanging around outside and the large truck access doors are wide open, so we could even be spotted by folk inside."

"Is there a view from the warehouse door into the harbour?"

"Only bits of it," I tried to visualise the scene in detail, "we could paddle in if we were careful. There's a lower covered dock area and I don't know if there's anyone there. The masts of the schooner were clearly too high for it to be brought in, so we'll have cover if we stay behind it."

"Did de Witt mention if there was access from the lower dock to the main warehouse?"

"Not that I can remember, but it'd seem logical. The entire point is to be able to move smuggled cargo out of sight of any aerial monitoring."

"Well, I say that we go for entry at the dock and work our way up. We just need to hope that there aren't any bad guys on watch."

"If there was anyone on watch, it'd be the guys floating in the shallows there," I tried to put myself in the shoes of the smuggler patriarch. "Even under normal circumstances, the coastguard never raided this place. The way things are now, I'd guess it's an option that's completely ignored – especially if they have moles inside the police organisations like Konig assumed."

"Right, let's do it. If the worst comes to the worst, we can always try the lost tourist ploy," she pulled a baggy T-shirt advertising a Saint Martin bar over her SMKP stab vest."

Real flying by the seat of our pants here – not that, under the circumstances, there's any other way to handle an operation like this.

***

We took care to paddle as quietly as possible while we followed the breakwater along to the harbour entrance, despite the fact that breaking waves would probably drown any sounds we made. We then took a course that kept the elegant schooner between us and the dock, until we were under the bow of the ship. Peering out from cover, I could see camouflage netting along the front of the dock – no doubt intended to further shield activities therein from view. *Now, however, it helps us, making it less likely that we'll be spotted.*

"There's a little jetty just to the side of the main dock," I pointed out in a whisper. "If we tie up there, we can follow that catwalk into the main dock."

Lynn nodded her agreement and led the way. A couple of minutes later we were creeping along the steel walkway and slipping under the camouflage curtain. The secret dock was cavernous, but very dim, lit only by the light that penetrated through the netting separating it from the harbour. We waited for our eyes to adjust after the bright sunshine outside, listening for the sounds of any workers who may be present. To my surprise, the faint noise that came from the far end of the dock seemed more like crying than anything else.

Now on a wide concrete roadway that bordered the harbour, we could see four sleek power-boats and three small cruising yachts that were tied up within the dock. Along the harbour edge, piles of boxes, crates and drums provided cover for us as we moved towards the source of the noise. The crying could now be heard to be accompanied by grunting, making me suddenly aware of what was happening in the darkness ahead.

Clearly Lynn had also worked this out as she pushed the pistol into her belt, drew her trusty baseball bat and hurried ahead, worrying less now about making a noise. We approached a back area, partitioned off by a sliding door that was left slightly ajar, and immediately encountered a faint smell of sweat, sewage and unwashed bodies. The cries and grunts were now more distinct.

Edging through the door we encountered a tableau lit by a couple of oil lamps. A large mesh cage in the centre of the storeroom enclosed a huddle of naked women. Outside it, another was being held down by two naked men while being raped by a third – a huge, flabby, bald-headed man. As we ran towards them all three turned towards us, gaping in surprise that was almost comical.

By instinct forged by our time on patrol together, Lynn targeted the rapist while I focused on his two accomplices, remembering to concentrate on silencing them although aware that screams from this location would probably go unnoticed.

When there is space to swing it, a baseball bat is a fearsome weapon. Wielded with full force against an unprotected head it is lethal in most cases, but otherwise results in concussion and damage to the neck and skull that is treatable only in an intensive care ward. *As there are no such facilities now available, if these bastards are not dead immediately, they soon will be.*

The fight was a complete anti-climax: within ten seconds our victims were down and out, lying in pools of blood. The girl who had been raped was still screaming, but the accompanying cries and shouts from the pen containing the other women had gone silent. Lynn started talking to the girls in a low voice while I searched through discarded clothing until I found the key that opened a padlock on the gate and allowed them to file out. A statuesque redhead and a small raven-haired woman immediately rushed to the side of the girl who was still crying, unable to move from the spot where she had been abused.

"Alright, ladies, please keep as quiet as possible. We're here to get you out, but we're going to need your help. Now, for starters, are your clothes somewhere around?" Lynn asked.

"No, we were forced to strip on board, immediately after we were boarded by these fuckers." A tall brunette replied. "They've been raping us one by one, although focusing on the blondes so far." She moved towards the fat rapist who was unconscious but still breathing. "Can anyone see a pair of bolt-cutters or anything similar?"

I spotted a table holding a pistol, a small machine gun – maybe an Uzi – and a sheath containing what proved to be a wicked looking machete. I handed the knife to the woman. "How about this?"

The tall girl turned to Lynn. "You okay with this, you're police after all."

"Not real police, just folk who take out bastards like these. Please be my guest."

We watched in silence while the brunette helped three different blonds geld the bodies on the floor.

"Okay, girls, can any of you use a gun?"

The brunette spoke up immediately. "I'm in the territorials and have also done a bit of competition shooting. My name's Pat, I'm the captain of Living Waters," she added.

I remembered the name of the sailing ship painted on the bow as we sheltered behind it only shortly before. *Makes sense that she's the spokeswoman.*

Lynn handed Pat a pistol, while another three women came forward. They gave their names as May, Alice and Alison and were, respectively, Canadian biathlete, Bermudian coastguard and US marine. May received a pistol, Alice Lynn's baseball bat and Alison the machete.

"Right, they're probably disgusting, but the clothes that these fuckers were wearing are better than nothing. Just distribute them as best you can. You can also have these…" she pulled off the baggy t-shirt and began to struggle out of her shorts.

I started to do likewise, offering also the wife-beater that I wore under my stab-vest. *I've heard of getting dressed to kill, but undressing to go into battle is something I've never even considered before.*

Lynn and Pat were now whispering to each other, plainly disagreeing about something but not wanting the other women to hear. I moved to my partner's side to listen in.

"…better here, look after the others until we get finished upstairs," Lynn said.

"What's the point of that? We clearly need to take out this entire nest of vipers to give us a chance of escaping and the best chance would be if we focus all our efforts in a surprise attack."

I gently patted Lynn on the back. "She's right, you know, the unarmed girls should stay back, but these others are probably better trained than we are.

At the very least, the women with the guns could team with you to nail down whoever is in the main warehouse, while Alice and Alison lay in wait down here to ambush anyone who comes down the stairs who isn't us. I can then focus on the guys outside."

"That's it? We're just going to gun down everyone we see upstairs?" Pat asked.

"You got a problem with that?" Lynn addressed her question to both Pat and May, who had now joined us.

"Not a one, just checking," Pat grinned ferociously. "Just let us know what we need to do."

"Chris goes first. If possible, he'll remove anyone outside the building. I go next and check the distribution of bad guys. If it looks doable, I'll take out groups with this," she waved the Uzi at them, "while you pick off outliers – Pat take my left, May my right."

While Lynn sorted out logistics, I cautiously climbed the dark stairwell, lit only by a candle on a halfway landing and the little light coming from an open door above. As I neared the door, I could hear a babble of voices, all in broad local dialect. I peered round the jam and saw about a dozen men and half a dozen women, most of whom were sitting at a long bench, checking the content of boxes and shouting out to a couple of girls who stood at what looked like ancient school blackboards, making ticks on some kind of table. None of these workers seemed to be armed beyond the odd sheath knife.

The main problem would be a group of five, three men and two women, who were playing cards beside a rack that contained a diverse range of rifles, shotguns and pistols. At least one of the men also had a pistol holstered at his side. I quickly withdrew and crept back to the dock to update Lynn.

I had to really focus on the logistics of the operation, while Lynn confirmed her original plan, with the refinement that the card-players would be her main target. It was difficult to accept that the three women were going to do the heavy lifting while I had only a support role. *Got to lose this chauvinistic crap – a little girl with a pistol is a lot more effective for this job than a big, muscular street-fighter armed only with a stick.*

I returned to the upper door and peeped out again. No sign that anyone was looking in my direction. I crawled on my belly to a waist-high stack of packages which could well be some kind of drug – heroin or cocaine, possibly. Then I was able to move behind a wall of cases of rum and make my way to the side of the open door facing the harbour. Peering through it, I counted three older guys who were smoking while they played dominoes in the shade of a breadfruit tree.

At that moment the three women poured out of the stairwell and Lynn immediately opened fire on full-automatic, hosing the card-players and then spraying those sitting at the long table. I had time to note that the Pat and May were standing in matching double-handed shooting poses, coolly popping off shots while Lynn ripped off a spare taped to her gun and changed magazines.

The sound of the firefight had caused chaos outside, one of the guys literally falling backwards off his chair, kicking the table and dominoes into the air. The other two jumped to their feet and raced towards the warehouse, drawing pistols as they came. Coming from bright sunlight into the gloom of the warehouse, they hadn't even seen me before my baseball bat had crashed into the face of one, using the momentum to keep turning and deliver a back-roundhouse kick to the other. Both flew backwards out of the door, surprising the third man who cautiously climbed to his feet and picked up a huge machete that had been propped against the trunk of the tree.

Machete man was at least two metres tall and well built, his bare chest showing bronzed skin covered by intricate tattoos. He shook back his long blond hair which was caught up in a ponytail, and cautiously sidled forward. *Reminds me of baldy boy-band guy, the way he moves. I'm fucking not going to get caught like that again.* Discretion the better part of valour, I retreated back into the warehouse, waiting for him to make the move that would force his eyes to adjust to the difference in illumination. That would give me an advantage, but I looked again at the gigantic knife and compared it to my baseball bat. *I need something more.*

It seemed an age before the big guy made the decision to enter, although I could still hear the sound of gunfire, so it could only be seconds. He sidled in, close to the left-hand side of the door, waving his machete in front of him. The instant that his head came into shadow, I threw my bat at his stomach and hefted a large package above my head. He had managed to divert my bat with a blow of his knife and automatically also cut at the package that I hurtled towards his head. He was instantly enveloped in a cloud of white powder and I quickly retreated out of its way while he started coughing, choking and retching.

I risked a glance back towards the ladies and saw that they had gained the gun rack and were all now in possession of what looked like Kalashnikovs. Most of the gang were lying in pools of blood, guts and brain fragments, but a couple had managed to find cover behind a stack of cases of rum and were blindly throwing bottles in the general direction of the women who were stalking them. *Well, that's not going to last long.* Just then, out of the corner of my eye, I saw that one of the card-players had managed to sneak his way along to a side fire exit and I spotted him just as he disappeared through it.

"Fuck!" I muttered as I carefully ran to recover my bat, both holding my breath and covering my mouth and nose with my hand. The powder seemed to have mainly blown out of the building, but my victim was writhing and foaming at the mouth, evidently in a very bad way.

Club in hand I sprinted for the fire door, but emerged carefully, realising that I would be at a momentary disadvantage in the bright sun outside. I relaxed when I saw that my target was quickly peddling a bike uphill, away from the harbour. Three more mountain bikes sat against the wall of the warehouse, so I grabbed one and set off in pursuit.

The road from the harbour was steep and I was soon panting, drenched with sweat. I was aware, however, that I was gaining ground and I should soon overtake the runaway. I was actually no more than about ten metres behind him when he turned into a driveway, the heavy gate protecting it lying open, and sprinted with a final burst of energy for the central and most grandiose of the three villas therein. Again, a heavy front door was lying ajar, allowing him to drop his bike on the porch and run straight in, with me close on his heels.

Yet another step change in light level when I entered the dim hallway, so I stopped to let my eyes adjust and make sure that I didn't run into any surprises. I could hear my breathless prey shout something, but could only make out a couple of words. Unfortunately, these included *guns* and *kill the bastards*.

The long hallway led into a bright courtyard, where I could see a middle-aged man panting, bent over with his hands on his knees. He raised his eyes to glare at me. "Just who the fuck're you, you murdering cunt?" His accent was very confusing, some strange mixture of Caribbean and Brit English.

"Doctor Hassell, I presume," suddenly remembering our briefing; the leader of the smuggling gang had studied law in London. "If you're not totally blind, you'll see from my vest that I'm KPSM, so not a murderer, more of an executioner. Under martial law you and your gang of evil bastards are sentenced to death. I'm here to carry out that sentence."

"So that's what the Politie are wearing now, budgie smugglers?" he sneered at me. "But I don't really care. You've invaded my house, where my family live, so you're going to die for this."

"You don't understand the new reality," I sneered back. "We know that your entire family are knee deep in all this shit, from your mother to your wife to your kids – plus your pack of incestuous relatives. You're all going to die: everyone aged over fifteen. Younger kids will just be abandoned here: maybe the local villagers will look after them. On the other hand, given how this community has lived in fear of you over the years, maybe they won't."

I was happy extending this dialogue, giving me a chance to catch my breath and get my bearings. In particular, I was listening for sounds of anyone else in the house who might come to Hassell's aid. The large open courtyard contained a central fountain and was surrounded by a roofed walkway which was probably intended the allow access to the surrounding rooms during rain. Plants and bushes in pots were scattered around, together with a number of chairs and benches, giving the area a cluttered feel – *not really the ideal arena for combat.*

The sound of running feet on a wooden floor came from an open door to my left and I moved towards it while Hassell shouted out a warning. This was evidently ignored by the two men, both carrying pistols, who burst into the courtyard, actually running past me in their rush to come to their boss's defence. The clutter of hanging flower pots, standard lamps, sofas and coffee tables made

243

movement difficult and I could not get a proper swing with my bat. Nevertheless, I managed a solid two-handed jab into the ribs of one, a tall fair-haired man, and a side kick that smashed the knee of the other, who actually looked to be little more than a boy.

As the tall guy span to face me he got off a couple of wild shots before my weapon made contact, smashing his right wrist. The boy had actually dropped his gun when he fell to the ground, crying and clutching his knee, before another side kick landed on the back of his head and took him out of the game. The man was scrabbling to pick up his pistol with his left hand when my baseball bat crushed that also. He was moaning in pain as he turned to me, his hands hanging uselessly at his side and a pitiful look on his face. "Please, please don't…" My uppercut had all the force of my now well-trained body behind it when it landed below his chin, lifting him off his feet as he flew backward to crash through a glass coffee table and end motionless on the ground.

Although probably unnecessary, I broke the necks of my two victims. *No way I'm leaving any possible threats behind me.*

Hassell had taken advantage of my distraction to run off and I could hear his footsteps through a door opposite. I raced after him, coming into an airy library with three walls lined with floor to ceiling bookshelves and other display cases. The facing wall of glass doors, now partially open, looked onto a sun deck and a swimming pool. My target was rummaging in the drawer of a large mahogany writing desk, pulling out a large automatic and struggling in his haste to switch off the safety.

Without thinking I hurtled the baseball bat at him and, although it caught him only a glancing blow, it was enough distraction to allow me to close in and grab his gun hand, forcing it into the air. This did, however, leave me exposed and he head-butted me, breaking my nose and bringing tears to my eyes while blood spurted down my face. Still holding his wrist, I blindly slammed my elbow repeatedly into his face and throat until he dropped the gun and wrenched himself loose.

We stood for a moment, glaring at each other with the width of the desk between us, before he darted to the side and used his elbow to smash a display case, allowing him to grab a gleaming sword.

"A pirate with a fucking cutlass," I groaned, "you've got to be kidding me!" I then dived to the side as the blade whistled towards my head, grabbing my bat before my breakfall took me back onto my feet at the other side of the room.

I held the bat with my right hand and drew my baton with my left, holding it by its side-arm. Hassell slowly moved towards me, his stance indicating that he had fencing experience. He jabbed at my shoulder, which I twisted to avoid, then sliced at my neck. I blocked this with my bat, but was horrified to see the chip cut out of it by his blade. *That bloody thing looks like an antique, but it's fucking razor sharp.*

I moved back to avoid another jab to my torso, but then stepped inside the thrust to wallop his sword-hand with my baton. There was a clang as it bounced off the basket-shaped guard and I grunted as a fist slammed into my stomach. Here my regular training was paying off, letting me slip back out of sword range, uninjured by the blow.

Hassell had a gleam in his eye. "You attack my business; I'll get my revenge. But attack my house and I'll make you really fucking suffer: you, your family, your friends, the entire fucking KPSM!" he shouted. "This starts with you. I'm going to fucking cut you to ribbons."

I quickly glanced behind me to make sure that it was clear, then retreated back into the cluttered courtyard, taking cover behind an ornamental shrub of some kind.

"Hiding isn't going to help, you know," he taunted me. "The cutlass was designed for close-in fighting on ships. You'd best run away now, although I'll hunt you down and there's no chance of you leaving Saba alive."

I dodged around the shrub, keeping it between me and him while he thrust and slashed at me without success, foliage flying in all directions.

"You know, for someone who claims to know swords, you can't fence for shit," I laughed at him, goading him into wilder attacks. "You wave that pig-sticker around like a magic wand, you fucking fairy." I noticed that this last comment seemed to particularly annoy him so I followed up on it. "Yes, you certainly noticed my trunks, didn't you? Spend a lot of time looking at young lads' groins I suppose, you poof. Hanging around toilets with your tiny dick hanging out?"

Obviously type A gang bosses don't like their manliness being questioned. I grinned as his anger grew and he started cursing under his breath, this time in incomprehensible broad dialect.

"Come on you shirt-lifting wanker, you scared of my little sticks or just my really big willy?" I stepped out of cover, my weapons by my sides, only two paces away from him. He leapt forward, swinging down at my head. *He's sure that I can't evade him this time.*

He had an instant to register shock when, instead of attempting to duck the blow, I moved forward to block it with crossed bat and baton. The sword cut deeply into them and the shock ran down both my arms, but my forward momentum allowed me to drive my right knee deep into his gut. His body sagged while he gasped for air, allowing me a second blow with my knee into his side, which cracked ribs. Dropping the bat, I grabbed his sword arm just above the wrist and then, dropping the baton, grabbed his elbow to apply an arm lock that threw him against the low wall around the fountain, probably breaking a few more ribs in the process and driving him onto his knees. Keeping hold of his wrist, I pushed it on top of the wall before I dropped down on his arm with both knees, rupturing his elbow and leaving bits of bone protruding from the gory wound.

His first scream of pain altered to a whimper as he hovered on the edge of unconsciousness. Although one hand was still trapped in the guard of the cutlass, the man was clearly finished. I kicked him onto his back and splashed water from the fountain onto his face. "Don't want you missing out on any of this pain, you bastard. You need to stay awake, at least until the girls cut your balls off, you rapist cunt."

"Let him be, you fucker. Move away or I'll blow yo' fucking ass off!"

I jumped in surprise, then slowly turned to look at the thin girl, clad only in a bikini, who stood in the library doorway, Hassell's automatic held in her shaking hands.

"You don't want to do that, I'm police..." I started, mesmerised as her finger tightened on the trigger, just before her head exploded in a red mist.

"Fuck!" I gasped, aware that I had literally pissed myself. I closed my eyes and tried to slow my racing heart. Then I looked around and spotted Lynn at the entrance of the courtyard, a Kalashnikov in her arms, still held ready for action as she scanned the area for further threats. "Christ you cut that tight. I fucking wet myself!"

"I can see that," she grinned. "Anyway, I'm sure we can find something dry for you in this fucking palace." At that point Pat came up beside her, carrying an identical rifle. "You can check through this place and make sure it's clear. It looks like all the other baddies are in the left-hand villa, as we're drawing some fire from it."

"Aren't you going to just wait for the cavalry?" I asked as I stepped over the wall into the fountain and crouched down to rinse my legs and swimming trunks.

"I've already sent up the green flare and de Witt's lads should be here shortly. We've got a few

248

more of the girls armed, though, so we thought that we'd do a bit of mopping up ourselves. It's just a shame that you can't shoot – otherwise you'd be able to help."

I guess the size of the KPSM armoury will've increased significantly as a result of this action, so learning to shoot might not be such a bad idea. "Okay, I'll tidy up here and then check on you," I climbed out of the pond, feeling much better.

"Fine, but also clean up your face when you get a chance, you've got blood everywhere." With that, Lynn led Pat back outside.

I wonder if Lynn realised that this is my blood for a change. Anyway, let's see where the first aid kit is.

I quickly went from room to room and confirmed that the villa was, indeed, empty. One room was clearly set up for massage, but seemed to have a secondary function as a medical centre. I washed my face there, cleared some clotted blood from my nose and then, very cautiously, packed both nostrils with cotton wool to stop remnant bleeding. A glance in a mirror showed that I would likely end up with a couple of black eyes.

Back in the courtyard, I prized the cutlass loose from Hassell's hand and zip-locked his wrists together behind his back, ignoring his whimpers of pain. I then rolled him onto his back, pulled his trousers down to prepare him for the girls' attention, and then, to make double-sure he wasn't going anywhere, smashed both kneecaps with my bat, which snapped on the second blow as a result of the damage that his sword had done.

I threw the useless bat away and strode back into the library, finding a scabbard in the display case that had held the cutlass and attaching it to my belt. *Fair exchange is no robbery!* I returned to Hassell's groaning form and placed the blade in the scabbard before heading off in search of my partner.

I was just in time to see the final stages of the battle. Although it was clear that the fugitives in the villa had no shortage of guns and ammunition, they evidently had little or no combat experience. Whenever one of them exposed themselves to shoot, our biathlete markswoman would nail them. *She would make the perfect sniper in another life.* This attrition had been enough to cause the trapped criminals to attempt a breakout from the back of the villa, using a group of children as a living shield. They walked straight into an ambush set by Lynn and Pat, who had mown them down, firing at head height regardless of the risks to anyone shorter. As Lynn later put it: "Anyone who would hide behind their own children deserves to have their genes taken out of the pool. It's Darwinism in action."

It transpired that our markswoman was one of those raped by Hassell and she did the honours, after we had drugged him with adrenaline to keep him conscious while his penis was hacked off. We left him to bleed out while Lynn and I walked back to the harbour, arriving just in time to see the coastguard ship tie up.

Our yacht was also in harbour, with our worried looking friends standing on a bollard to catch first sight of our approach. We had time to give them quick hugs before going over to report to

Commander Konig. Lynn did most of the talking, keeping it brief and highlighting only main points of the action. It was agreed that we would have a full debriefing the next day, so could escape quickly to join Margie and Cecilia.

The sun was setting as we set sail for Cupecoy and it was dark by the time we moored in our bay. We decided to sleep the night on board and so, after a dinner of stale sandwiches and warm beer, Lynn and I dragged our weary bodies down from the galley to the cabin, which contained a small double bed. We allowed the others to undress us by candlelight, wash us down with sponges and applying antiseptic cream to the various cuts and scrapes that we had accumulated. This slowly evolved into relaxed four-way oral sex that worked wonders to help me ignore my assorted aches and pains. *What a way to end a day, I could take a lot of this!* Of course, I couldn't and was fast asleep within ten minutes.

PA+30 days, Dumbarton, Republic of Scotland

Jimmy Kemp peered into the warehouse, which seemed to stretch to infinity in the gloom – huge wooden barrels at the side of the alleyway extending as far as he could see in the light of the oil lamp that he carried. The rest of his team were scattered over the square kilometres of bonded warehouses that surrounded this otherwise nondescript town, working with pencil and paper to estimate the inventory of whisky and other spirits contained within.

One month ago, he had been a senior lecturer in Chemical Engineering at Glasgow University, heading a research group that specialised in adapting fuel cell technology for the third world. "Well, I guess that's what we are now," he muttered under his breath, remembering the complete chaos of the first week after the Incident, effectively a prisoner in his flat near the Uni, just off Byres Road, trapped by the rioting that enveloped the entire West End of Glasgow. He had almost completely run out of provisions that could be consumed without electrical power when his partner, Alan, a detective with the serious crimes squad who had been on duty when the lights went out, finally made it home.

All policemen available had been struggling to maintain some semblance of order for the entire time, sleeping in cells whenever they were too exhausted to go on. The centre of the city had been like one of the lower circles of Dante's Hell for days until it was a burnt-out wreck with everything that could be looted already cleared out. Action was now slowly moving out to the huge supermarkets and shopping centres of the commuter belt, leaving the old, sick and lame abandoned in their yuppified multi-story flats while the bodies of the dead and the completely inebriated were left where they fell.

After a tearful – and then passionate – reunion, Jimmy learned that Alan had not returned to stay, or even passed by to provide reassurance, but was actually there to pick him up and take him over to George Square where he had been summoned for discussions with a team of bigwigs who were charged with recovery from the loss of electric power. Of course, he had not realised then how serious things were and had still been regularly flipping switches to check if power was back on.

Alan was part of the police coordination and logistics part of the team, but it had actually been Sir Frederick, the head of the Engineering faculty, who had requested him to lead a fuel cell team charged with implementing local power sources as soon as possible. Although high efficiency fuel cells were sophisticated and required complex catalysts and fuels like liquid hydrogen, very basic cells could be cobbled together that effectively *burned* alcohol in air. His speciality had been developing designs that used the crude alcohol found in the backwoods where the poorest of the third world population lived. It was strange but, no matter what the limitations of local technology were, means could always be found to ferment fruit and grain and then distil it to higher strength liquor. That's what his cells ran on.

So, instead of helping some African backwater, his technology was being applied to speed Scotland on its way to recovery, aided by the vast volumes of high strength spirit stored in locations like this. It seemed almost obscene to consider using whisky, Scotland's most valuable export, as a basic fuel, but he now knew that international trade could be forgotten about for the near future and hence this was a sensible option. But somewhere within his Scottish soul he felt that this was wrong in so many ways.

Of course, access to alcohol had been a driving force for my week of terror and is still a major blockage to restoring social discipline and starting recovery. This is another benefit – burn the stuff before the mob can break in and drink it: this concern explaining the soldiers deployed here in contrast to complete abandonment of other areas where pillage continued. "I can't believe these stupid fucks are still stealing mega holo TV sets, rather than useful things like bicycles," he muttered, casting his eyes towards a rather gloomy heaven.

Finally, this approach had the benefit that, even after the existing stores were used up, Scotland needed only anything fermentable and some peat to allow alcohol production to recommence throughout the land, with or without electricity.

Of course, with electricity, I'd have found out the volume of spirits in all these warehouses within seconds. As it is, it'll take weeks and then a continuous effort of keeping inventories updated when fuel cell production and use ramped up. "Anyway, it has its advantages," he addressed the empty building while he selected a bottle of single malt from a case beside the door, "nobody'd grudge me a few wee keepsakes, to help keep warm now the central heating's gone the way of all flesh."

He had a smile on his face as he continued his Sisyphean task.

PA+6 months, Nagoya, Japan

After five months as spy-catcher, it's time to drop the hammer. Now I really have to put my money where my mouth is.

I had initiated my investigations with the help of Shoko's contact network of younger disaster response guys in Tokyo. The key move was installing smart monitors to identify anomalies in the work profiles of all staff associated in any way with the Japanese hardnet and the disaster response centres. This identified five potential links to the US embassy, one to the Chinese, one to the Russian, one to the UK and two to the French embassies in Tokyo. The filter was set at a 75% confidence level: on a quick check I noticed that, if I had dropped it to 40%, it would also have fingered Shoko. In any case, this was enough to get me Yoshi, my co-worker from cyber-warfare.

Focused searches then identified a number of suspicious code blocks that had been input by three of the possible US moles, coming up blank with all others. According to Yoshi these were components of a Trojan, parts of which showing relationships to ancient ransom-ware. "My best guess is that the plan is to scatter building blocks throughout the system that're innocent enough not to set off any alarms but, in the future, could be assembled into something that would crash our entire hardnet – maybe permanently. We'd never have found this stuff if we weren't explicitly looking for it in the first place."

Typically, the Japanese were horrified to discover that their allies, the Americans, were setting up a move to sabotage our efforts to facilitate recovery around the Pacific Rim. In the face of such a dire threat, however, the kid gloves came off and we were authorised to take any defensive action required. *Given that attack is the best form of defence, this carte blanche was I needed.* In fact, we had already carried out all the work required to build our own stealthed Trojan into the monthly updates of my response tool and the associated knowledge base that I provided via the international hardnet. This was sent individually to the disaster response centres that we dealt with, the Trojan being in a viable form only in the versions sent to lands with suspected spies in our system. I then activated the Trojan only in the US.

Although it had never occurred to me when I was developing it, my disaster management tool turned out to be the ideal vector for installing and servicing spyware. In its original incarnation, it was widely known in the technical community and had been installed in sensitive systems after comprehensive review by cyber-security teams. All I was doing now was responding to the automatic systems in place that check back with me for tool upgrades, the autonomically managed updates of the supporting knowledge base, answering queries or providing support for specific simulations.

The key factor that provided us with a window was the fact that, even in the US, cyber-warfare was managed completely independently from the military hardnet. The main threat to the former was remote access by an enemy and so all key activities were run on an intranet, physically isolated from the internet and with ultra-secure management of any data input or output nodes, to the extent of physically printing out and scanning data rather than transfer in any electronic format. Key components of the cyber-war intranet were isolated within Faraday Cages to prevent EM eavesdropping, but the system as a whole was not nuclear hard and hence was destroyed completely by the Incident. Some cyber-war functionality still remained within the hardnet computers, but rigorous vetting of all communication over the net was impossible.

After initiation of the Trojan, we had access to all internal US communication over their secure national hardnet. Communication was hidden within the constant flow of data between myself and the US disaster centres, which I expanded by offering to make more of my time available for them – an offer which was gratefully accepted. Shoko was less happy about this as it meant that I had less time for her, but recognised how critical this task was.

Considering bandwidth constraints, Yoshi and I concentrated on mining the CIA East Asia office and the CIA operations in the Tokyo embassy. Yoshi was a born hacker who delighted in this work, using cut and stick from decades of malware to build assessment and attack routines within the CIA's own sub-net. In effect, we were using the CIA's own approach against them, trusting that, unlike us, they would never suspect that they had been compromised.

Within a month we had identified all the key players – a half-dozen top CIA operatives, spread between Tokyo and Langley, and an army liaison officer in the Pentagon. This then allowed us to focus more on their activities, monitoring developments in real time and running back-traces to document the historical development of their actions.

Now I had everything I needed and the Tokyo security head, Hitoshi Mano, had briefed his opposites in the other JANA countries. This had included a full description of the tools that we used, which implicitly allowed our partners to confirm our claim that these had not also been used against them. I had passively observed this teleconference, seeing the outrage that was especially evident in the cases of Australia and New Zealand. Mano-san had informed his colleagues also of our retaliation capabilities and had to work hard to deflect calls to implement them immediately. After a couple of hours of hard negotiation, my originally proposed action was accepted – with the one caveat that I would manage the contact to the US in the name of JANA as a whole rather than the Japanese government when doing this. I was caught out by this development, but spotted that Mano-san seemed very relieved and wondered if I had been out-manoeuvred in some way. *Regardless, it's been my play all along and so I suppose it's reasonable that I finish it off. Limitations on communication and travel are now a silver lining, given that I'm likely to end up at the top of the CIA's hit list.*

***

I was now ready to rock and roll, Yoshi and Shoko beside me but out of view of the camera that I faced. Despite my extensive academic lecturing experience, my palms were sweaty and I was acutely aware of the number of JANA top brass who would be monitoring this conversation.

I nodded to Yoshi and the screen in front of me briefly showed the POTUS seal before being replaced by the face of the president sitting at his desk in the Oval Office. He was casually dressed in a polo shirt, unshaven and looked very tired. He jerked in a startled manner, certainly in response to seeing me on his screen.

"Hey, what the hell's going on here? This is supposed to be a conference call with Kowalski at Langley. Who the hell're you?"

"I'm sorry to disturb you Mister President. My name's Mitchell and I represent the JANA bloc of nations."

"I've heard of JANA, but still have no idea who you are," he seemed to be working on a keyboard off-screen, "but you seem to be on an encrypted CIA link and I don't know how that can be possible unless you're at Langley."

"I'm presently in Nagoya, Japan and this transmission is being monitored by senior representatives of the JANA nations, so it clearly is possible. In fact, it is the need for this *impossibility* that I want to talk to you about."

"Hell, I'm the President, you can't just hack into my network whenever you want to chat. The US of A may be in a bad way at present and JANA may be an important organisation, but there're

260

channels that you need to go through. Goodbye!"
There was a click but the image of the president
remained, looking even more confused.

"I'm afraid that we have complete control of
your entire communication network," this was a
gross exaggeration, as all my JANA observers
would know, but I had a point to make. "I can
switch on your TV..." I nodded at Yoshi and the
president jumped back, startled, "...but, of course
there's nothing on, so let's switch it off again,"
another nod to Yoshi and the president's face went
pale.

"You've hacked the fucking White House!" he
was losing his cool rapidly. "I don't care who you
are, but I'll do all in my power..."

"What we've done is in retaliation for a cyberattack by the US on Japan and our allies," I broke
in, something the president was clearly unused to, if
his glare was any indication. "We actually have the
capability to do to you what you intended to do to
us, but instead are contacting you to sort this out
amicably."

"I don't know what you think we've done, but I
can assure you that there has been no attack on
Japan, cyber or otherwise."

"We are aware that you don't know about it,
which is why you were our chosen contact. This is a
CIA conspiracy. I believe you call this stuff black
ops, assured deniability."

"But an attack, against Japan, at the present
time. I'm the fucking president! There's no way that
something like this can go on without me having the
slightest clue about it." He was now going red in the

face but, somehow, I sensed that his anger was covering a dread that we might be correct.

"Yes, that's why we're now downloading all details onto your computer, with copies to all members of your Cabinet and Joint Chiefs of Staff. The evidence is overwhelming and completely unambiguous, but I guess you can confirm this by interrogation of those named. This is clearly a case of treason which, under your present martial law, is subject to the death penalty. We expect you to check our material and provide assurance that the perpetrators will be adequately punished within twelve hours. We will call you again then, although you can use the attached link to contact us sooner if you prefer."

"This sounds like an ultimatum. You can't just order the President and the US government about like this…"

"We can and we are. Remember, we have the capability to carry out what your conspirators planned for Japan."

"And just what is that?" He sounded belligerent, but looked even greyer.

"Wipe out your entire national hardnet. This will cripple both your military and all civilian disaster response and recovery work. At the present time, the impact would be devastating."

"But that's barbaric! Nobody could condone such an action!"

"It is exactly what your CIA bastards were trying to do to us!" I shouted, the anger that I first experienced when this action was confirmed boiling up within me. "You have twelve hours, so I propose

262

that you use it well." I slumped back in my seat, realising that my hands were shaking and I was drenched with sweat. *Not often you get a chance to give the most powerful man in the world a tongue-lashing. Or maybe it's now the man that used to be the most powerful in the world – and it certainly will be if we have to take down their hardnet.*

I was suddenly aware of the babble of voices over the JANA link and words of congratulations from my Nagoya team, but I let them wash over me, taking a few minutes to get my head together before we started the inevitable post-mortem analysis and discussions of how we go further.

***

Shoko, Akiko, Yoshi and I were having an early dinner together, having driven all the rubberneckers out of the DMRC, when the alarm buzzer indicated a call from the White House over our dedicated hotline. I could just imagine the chaos in the JANA corridors of power as the great and the good scrambled to eavesdrop on this surprisingly early contact.

After checking that the others were out of line of sight, I opened the video link to the POTUS, noting immediately that he was more formally dressed and, even if somewhat drawn, had a sparkle in his eyes that suggested chemical stimulation. "Well, Mister President, this is an unexpectedly early contact. What can I do for you?"

There was a slight pause, as if the man had to force himself to speak, but his voice was steady. "On behalf of the United States of America, I would like to formally apologise for the actions of a rabid,

263

lunatic group of staff within our security apparatus who were responsible for planning, unbeknownst to the administration, a cyberattack on our respected and critically important ally Japan, together with the other countries that comprise the JANA alliance." *It's clear that the stilted phraseology has been drafted by lawyers, but poor old POTUS looks like he's accepted that the buck stops with him.*

"This is clearly contrary to both our own and international laws and we have immediately identified and punished those responsible in a manner appropriate to their heinous crimes." *All very good, except that I did all the identification work involved.*

"The attached file records these actions fully, in the spirit of the open exchange of information that was implemented after the Incident. We trust that this will not only demonstrate our commitment to actively participating in the global rebuilding process, but also the seriousness in our response to anyone within our programme who hinders this in any way."

He paused, evidently expecting some response from our side. In our previous discussions a rapid response from the US was one of the scenarios considered, but this was much faster than we had anticipated, so I would need to ad lib a bit. I could see that Yoshi and Shoko were rapidly scanning through the linked video files – as would be many others in our Tokyo team. "Thank you, Mister President, we greatly appreciate the rapidity of your response, which I should emphasise we have not been monitoring, although we have the capacity to do so." *I'm sure they're now doing everything possible to set up completely secure communications for POTUS and his top team, but we don't want to let them know exactly what functionality we have in place. It pays to keep them guessing.*

The president hesitated for a moment, then accepted that he had to take my statement on trust. "I appreciate that, Professor Mitchell." *Adding my honorific shows he's been doing his homework, even though Doctor would be closer to the mark anywhere other than Japan.* "The key question is, where we go from here?"

"We are reviewing the material that you sent us at the present moment, but I think we can assume that you have done everything possible to right this wrong," I added this to my agreed outline presentation to show a reciprocity of trust. "We will thus immediately de-activate all tools within your hardnet and restore complete privacy to your operations."

"So you will remove the bugs in place?" his tone indicated that he had little expectation of a positive response to this formal request.

"This is the tricky bit," I smiled, "involving a lot of trust on both sides. We need to believe that there is no chance of a similar conspiracy ever occurring again, while you need to accept any assurance that we make about complete removal of tools from your system. We thus propose a compromise." I saw a look of surprise on Shoko's face. *I'm going completely off script here – I should be proposing staged removal of our bugs linked to verifiable constraints placed on the activities of the CIA.*

"Our national military infrastructure served well during the response to this unpredictable global catastrophe. The role of the military – and the associated security agencies – has to be redefined, however. Our priority is facilitating regional and global recovery, rather than assuring the security of individual states and defending national interests. Would you agree so far?"

Two messages appeared on a side prompter screen.

> Yoshi: files show interrogation and execution of all identified lead conspirators and arrest of those with more peripheral roles
>
> Shoko: JANA brass going apeshit – what're you up to?

The president frowned, clearly surprised by this question. "Well I don't think anyone would disagree with that, in general terms anyway, under the present circumstances." *Ever the politician, weasel-words and arm-waving, but he's nailed down here and he knows it.*

"Fine, so I propose – just a suggestion, the details of which need to be discussed by you and the JANA decision-makers – that all active incursion functions that allow us to access your net are de-activated and details are provided to allow you to remove them and validate that this doesn't leave any backdoors open. We will, however, leave a passive, automatous system in place that monitors for signs of suspicious activity and, in case anything is found, posts a message on the international hardnet, visible to all users including yourself."

"I'm not sure that my Chiefs of Staff could accept this," he responded, cleverly passing the buck. "This could put the US at an incredible disadvantage in terms of national security…"

"But, as you previously agreed, this is no longer very important. It may be difficult for some of your more senior and inflexible staff to accept this reality – which is the root source of our current problem. This is why we need to have a system like this, which captures any actions going on under the radar, which even you might know nothing about."

The president squirmed as the CIA conspiracy precluded any argument against this point. "You may be right," he eventually responded, choosing his words carefully, "but gaining acceptance by my administration would be very difficult."

"Yes, that's clear, so we need a more symmetrical concept that would be more palatable," I smiled as Shoko's look of confusion was slowly morphing into worry; *she clearly thinks I'm off my rocker*. "What about if the same automatous expert system was put in place within all national sub-nets linked to the international hardnet. We are all at risk from groups of jingoistic nutters who would put inappropriate, nationalistic fantasies before the realities of rebuilding a broken planet. It should be a win-win case for all participants."

I could see that POTUS was stunned by this concept, frantically trying to work though possible responses, which would undoubtedly be streaming down his prompt screen. "Of course, in an ideal world, we'd form some kind of global government, but that's not going to happen – we're too busy just getting by, solving urgent local and regional problems. In any case, a bureaucratic monstrosity like the UN shows only how not to proceed. So, we need to foster cooperation and collaboration between our present nations in some way. The basis of this must be trust and the approach that I'm suggesting might help build this."

"I need to think about this, discuss it with my administration," he did seem marginally happier on the basis of this possible light at the end of the tunnel. "The big problem I see, though, is getting all the other countries to accept it. It's fait accompli for the USA, you've already got your tool in place. But do you really think that Russia, China, the EU – even Japan for that matter – would actually allow you to compromise their internal security like this?"

"Actually, it's a fait accompli in all those cases also, the tool is already in place and needs only to be activated." The wide eyes of the president seemed to fit with Shoko's gasp and Yoshi's delighted giggle.

*****

After I finished with the president, I had a hard hour with the JANA coordination team to explain my move and confirm that I had misled the president by implication: the tools for net monitoring were not actually in place anywhere,

268

except for the cases where spying on Japan had been identified. I did, however, strongly recommend some type of global adoption of the system, starting with the JANA members. It was clear that they needed to discuss this between themselves before they got back to me to consider the practicality of implementation if my proposal was accepted. A first teleconference was scheduled in 2 days.

My team returned to the table to finish our disrupted dinner – cheese and wine for Shoko, Akiko and me and cheese cake paired with a disgusting looking chocolate milk drink for Yoshi. Conversation focused on the American response and the possibility that my radical proposal for global monitoring would be accepted.

Although I had yet to look at them, the US files were apparently rather disturbing. These not only showed the initial confrontations and interrogation of the key conspirators, but also graphic videos of their torture in a few cases and final execution – in all cases by firing squad. Although clearly implicated by the material that we supplied and confessions of his co-conspirators, the Pentagon coordinator repeatedly denied all involvement, claiming the evidence was faked – this supporting his position that JANA was a danger to the US. Interrogation methods became tougher until he finally broke under water-boarding, reduced to tears while he begged continuously for mercy during the entire period of his subsequent sentencing and execution.

Yoshi was keen to start with the next phase of hacking, but I insisted that, from now on, this would be managed directly by the new JANA security coordination team. In some ways it was a shame, as I had enjoyed working with the enthusiastic young man, but the transfer of the Japanese side of such operations to Tokyo was a sign of a return to some kind of normality. *If anything post-Incident could really be considered normal*

Shoko had reservations about openly presenting any anomalies spotted in our internal hardnet by an automatous expert system which, by its very nature, was inherently unpredictable and uncontrollable. "It's fundamentally a low-level AI, a neural net with intrinsic learning capabilities, can we really put our trust in it?" as she put it.

I wonder if, in the back of her mind, she realises that such a system might have spotted her role gathering intelligence for a foreign government.

"You're right," I answered, "but I can't see a credible alternative. It's the classic *Quis custodiet ipsos custodes?*"

"*Who watches the watchmen?*" Shoko translated for Akiko and Yoshi. "It's the inherent dichotomy of any security system, but I'm not convinced that it can be solved by smart software. I can see two problems – it will certainly make mistakes so we lose trust in it, or we trust it too much and fail to control other threats to security that are external to the hardnet."

"Both good points," I conceded, "which is why this can't be considered as a stand-alone system, it needs to be complemented by tools external to national networks that look for anomalies in the

270

expanding global knowledge base. I've already discussed this with Yoshi and he's convinced it's feasible. We could run it as an open service within the international hardnet."

"It really is essential to have this kind of tool, Mike-sensei," added the normally reticent Yoshi. "When we ran our tools within the US net, there was little chance of their presence being noticed. Now, however, the cyber-defence guys know the functionality of what we have in place and can root it out. I think I've done a good job with booby traps to prevent it being subverted or defused, but, given enough time and effort it can be done. Using meta-analysis of national monitoring output in the context of knowledge base evolution, however, we'd spot any such interference and could intervene as required."

"I have not a clue what that means, but it sounds very impressive," Akiko laughed. "It's now six months since the Incident and we have a special reason to celebrate due to the success of Mike's plan to defeat the Americans..."

"It wasn't my plan alone – Shoko helped and Yoshi did all the heavy lifting to implement it," I interrupted. "And we didn't really defeat them, more bring them to heel."

"Anyway, whatever," Akiko waved her arms dismissively, "the main thing is, Champagne! I assume that you have some?"

"Of course we have," Shoko grinned mischievously, "it's the normal prelude to celebratory sex."

"You don't need to shout about it," I whispered in her ear, "Yoshi's still here."

"Yes, wild ménage à quatre sex," she goaded me aloud, "with Yoshi as the key participant." The young man blushed when Shoko leaned to put her arm around his shoulders while Akiko kissed him on the cheek.

I pulled Shoko to my side and glared at her. "I have no idea what's going on, but Yoshi's de facto my student at present, so I can't do that," I whispered.

The annoying girl simply nuzzled my neck. "That's just an excuse because you're a boring old conservative. I'm your real student and you fuck me, Yoshi's more a collaborator and, in any case, will be back to Tokyo soon."

"But I..." Shoko cut me off with a deep kiss, allowing me to notice that Akiko was now kissing Yoshi on the mouth. *Fuck it, go with the flow; the women will have their own way regardless of what I say, so may as well enjoy it.*

***

Of course, I should have known that a special celebration planned by Shoko and Akiko was never going to be a simple two-pair ménage à quatre. While we sipped Champagne and the ladies sorted out our play-room, I learned that Yoshi was not the shy young lad that he seemed, but actually pre-op female-male trans-gen.

Although he said little himself, Shoko summarised his background for me when he and Akiko left together to refill our glasses, explaining that Yoko, as he was then known, had always been

272

aware of a difference between the way he saw himself and his physical appearance. *I've always been baffled by trans-gender pronouns, so it's good that Shoko refers to Yoshi the way I think of him.* This crystallised after puberty, when he started dressing as a boy and changed his name. He initially had a number of lesbian relationships with girls, usually also cross-dressers driven by yaoi fantasies.

"He's now living with a gay boy in Tokyo. Initially it was just a platonic friendship, but they've been lovers for a couple of years now. He started hormone treatment for gender reassignment, which should have been followed by surgery. I don't know when that'll be possible again, but he really doesn't seem to mind."

"I don't know if I find that kinkier than the case of him being an honest-to-God boy or not," I groaned.

"You're such a boring old fart," she punched me on the arm in a playful manner. "But it's certainly kinkier. Just remember he doesn't like vaginal insertion – but anything oral or anal is fine."

"Wait a minute, have you already had sex with him?" The others returned at that point, so Shoko changed the topic of conversation, but her smug smile was enough of an answer for me.

During the foreplay, when the ladies first stripped each other and then started work on Yoshi and me, I was distracted while I tried to mentally prepare myself for what I was about to see. Nevertheless, I could not restrain a gasp when Yoshi was backed onto the table and the girls slowly teased down the boy's boxer-shorts to reveal

273

a gaping vagina and a very large clitoris. "Surprise!" Akiko announced and the three of them burst into laughter. *No idea what the look on my face is like, but it must be very funny.*

Thereafter, my discomfort slowly evaporated within the miasma of the choreographed sex, coordinated by the two wild nymphomaniacs and with the enthusiastic participation of Yoshi. Within an hour I was completely exhausted and retreated back to my usual chair to watch the ongoing floorshow.

During an intermission in the action, with the three of them cuddled together in a pile chatting in a mixture of Japanese and English, I was roused from a light doze by the mention of my name. I had to concentrate to make out what they were saying.

"…but he doesn't seem so comfortable," Yoshi was concluding.

"He's just an old wimp, he'll get used to it." *Clearly my lover sticking up for me!*

"But he's very straight," Akiko added, "remember that first time with the two of us, I thought he was going to wet himself."

"But getting him to wet himself will take a bit more work," Shoko added, causing a burst of laughter. "Anyway, we can just label him as bi-curious."

"Is he really?" Yoshi sounded surprised.

"Of course," Shoko answered, "it's just that he doesn't know it yet." Another burst of laughter.

"So how far do you think he'd go?" Akiko seemed to be goading Shoko. "What about those

274

gay boys that I met recently, should we try with them?"

"I'd be in for that," Yoshi responded immediately.

"A pair of big boys reaming that tight little bum of yours, you'd certainly like that," Shoko laughed and Yoshi squeaked in surprise, letting me guess how she had made her point. "Anyway, that might be a step too far for monastic Mike at the moment, but we should set that as a goal to cure him of his puritanical ways." More giggles.

Monastic? Puritanical? How the hell can she use such terms given the debauchery that we've gotten up to over the last six months? On the other hand, if she really considers such kinky sex mundane, what might she and Akiko have planned for me in the future? I was struggling to answer these questions when I drifted off to sleep.

PA+6 months, Cupecoy, Sint Maarten

I awoke to another beautiful day in Sint Maarten, feeling happy for an instant before memories of the previous weeks came flooding back, bringing with them a sadness that brought tears to my eyes. I involuntarily squeezed Lynn, who was cradled in my arms, relieved to see that this was not enough to wake her.

We'd been lulled into a false sense of security. After the trauma of the first couple of months, we were settling down to a routine, a life very different to that pre-Incident, but with well-established roles in a process of very slow but continuous recovery.

After three months, Lynn had been appointed regional group leader for inter-island policing, supporting Commander Konig in planning and implementing responses to raiders and pirates, a scourge that seemed impossible to completely eliminate although the frequency of incidents was gradually declining. The local nests of criminals had been eradicated, but there was an apparently unlimited source of replacements from our bigger neighbours to the west: Cuba, Haiti, Dominican Republic, Puerto Rico and, especially, Jamaica, where social collapse had been much more severe.

I was part of Lynn's team, providing muscle as required in police actions, but our continually expanding arsenal of firearms, especially after taking down a Haitian gun-running operation, meant that marksmanship was more important than martial arts. *I'm now trained to fire a gun, but I know how shit I am. Lynn knows too, so I get a big stick while the others get Uzis.* On the positive side, I was now also unarmed combat instructor for new recruits – training coastguards and police from both sides of the island. This really was the job I enjoyed most.

Within a couple of months, Cecilia and Margie had completely mastered their yacht, which now sported its new name, *Sapphic Dreams*, proudly painted on its bow. They were in constant demand; net and line fishing in coastal and deeper waters, often with a small support crew, lifting lobster pots, transporting goods around and between islands. They were a pair of bronze goddesses, fit as fiddles.

Although we were fundamentally two couples, there was a bit of coming and going, usually initiated by Cecilia. Indeed, we often had other visitors stay over, especially after two coastguard colleagues moved into an empty villa next door. Margie thus sometimes ended up sleeping with Lynn and me when Cecilia was going through a hetero phase, rutting with one – or both – of our neighbours. *Of course, she could have just as easily gone to their place, but I'm sure that her preference for noisy monkey sex in my villa was just part of her inherently annoying character. Apart from such peccadillos, we were just like members of an aging commune who had grown to live amicably with each other.*

Cecilia and Margie often disappeared for several days on longer trips, living on board over that time. A fortnight ago they had set off for Saint Barts, where a huge container ship had blown ashore and was stranded on a reef off the east coast of the island. A hurricane warning was in effect, but updates came only in the form of text notices posted daily on the hardnet – the Coastguard system included nothing as sophisticated as a video interface to the remnants of the US navy typhoon and hurricane warning centre. The challenge was to check the ship out for anything of potential use and ferry it ashore before the hurricane hit and afterwards, if possible, moving the wreck and sinking it in deeper waters.

It was a completely clear day when they set off, the Category 2 storm expected in three days and tracked to just clip Saint Martin. The size, speed of movement and the storm track all proved to be tragically incorrect. The Category 5 hurricane hit us full on next day, with wind speeds gusting to about 250 km/h. The high winds had been noticeable when we awoke and we had struggled to strip down our rain collection system and close storm shutters while it got constantly wilder. Finally, Lynn and I were driven inside and cowered for hours in the lower room while the hurricane roared over us.

Approaching from the east, Cupecoy was relatively sheltered but, even here, the destruction was extensive. When we finally emerged in late afternoon it was to find a transformed landscape – trees uprooted or stripped of foliage, defenestrated houses with roofs blown off, cars scattered about like toys and, most incongruous of all, small boats that had been lifted from the lagoon and dropped randomly on roads, gardens and even, in one case, embedded in the wall of a hotel three stories above ground.

Despite the now-established short-cut through over the abandoned airport runway, it took us two hours to struggle our way to the coastguard headquarters, stopping regularly to help people trapped in damaged buildings and to join groups moving debris to open the path to Simpson Bay. It was complete chaos when we reported in, due to extensive damage to all lagoon-side buildings, caused to a large extent by larger ships that had been ripped from their moorings and driven onto and over the dockside. I hoped that all those living on boats had been evacuated prior to landfall of the storm, as there appeared to be no vessel left undamaged in the entire lagoon.

Lynn briefly talked to a harrowed Commander Konig, confirming that the fleet of sailing ships that had been so painfully assembled had been almost wiped out: most of those in harbour sunk or seriously damaged and all contact lost to those at sea. Despite our growing concerns about the safety of Cecilia and Margie, there was clearly nothing we could do for the coastguard and hence headed for the KPSM to volunteer for duty.

Reports were slowly filtering in of massive destruction to the settlements on the north and east of the island such as Marigot, Grand Case and Orient Bay. Nevertheless, Lynn and I were assigned to our old beat in Cupecoy, with the primary task of organising search and rescue, starting from Maho Bay and working our way towards Terres Basses.

Light was fading by the time we reached Maho and we were forced to give up after an hour, returning to the villa to reflect on how lucky we had been – and worry about our friends.

Over the next three days, rescue transformed into recovery of bodies, clearing up worst of the damage and setting up rainwater collection systems, as clean drinking water was a priority. Indeed, the hardest hit areas, roughly corresponding to the French part of the island, were now quarantined due to an outbreak of dysentery and what was suspected to be cholera, due to widespread pollution by raw sewage.

If I had been a believer, I would have cursed God. It seemed incredibly perverse, after the chaos caused by the Incident, for a deity to inflict a disaster of this magnitude on us just at the point when we saw signs of recovery.

The picture grew clearer, day by day, while the litany of devastation lengthened. The deluge of rain accompanying the storm had caused massive landslides, particularly in the cleared forest areas that were the basis of our expanded agricultural projects. This not only wiped out hillside settlements and closed roads, but also destroyed the crops that had been planted with such effort. The death toll was already greater than that directly resulting from the Incident and climbing steadily as diseases spread through the worst-hit populations.

It was a week before my personal nightmares were confirmed and we learned that the container ship off Saint Barts had vanished along with the four coastguard yachts that had been working to offload it. Although it was possible that they could have ridden out the storm or be shipwrecked on some island, we knew the chances of Cecilia and Margie surviving were slim. *If they haven't made it, there's little chance that we'll ever know for sure and, even worse, absolutely nothing we can do about it.*

Now I had been summoned again to meet this morning with Commander Konig – this time without Lynn. With the entire area of the Lesser Antilles having been hammered by the hurricane and the coastguard largely impotent at present, I wondered what this could possibly involve.

***

Konig looked like she had aged 10 years in the last fortnight. I could not imagine how it must feel after achieving so much, building up the key role of the coastguard in the form of a recovery fleet, to have it gutted by capricious fate, losing so many ships and their crews.

The commander got straight to the point. "Hi Chris, thanks for coming in. I know you've been busy since the hurricane with clean-up operations, but I wonder if you could take on another task?"

"Certainly, Commander, whatever I can do to help."

"Well, we'll be working together on this, so just call me Maria," she forced a wan smile, that was more like a grimace of pain. "You may have heard, we lost most of Grand Case," I nodded cautiously, uncertain what this had to do with me. "It was a storm surge that we reckon must have been about five metres high. Everything on the bay front is gone completely and it's just a debris field between the beach and the airport terminal building, which seems to be the only structure of any size left standing."

"Do you want me to put a recovery team together?"

"No, that's in hand – all we can do is evacuate survivors to sheltered settlements on higher ground. The problem for me, personally," she wiped a hand over her face, as if to wash away traces of emotion, "is that I had a team up there specifically assessing risks from the storm – based, of course, on the initial warnings.

"A coastguard team?"

"Not really. Just over three weeks ago we decided to set up a team to move forward on natural hazard risk assessment and response planning. I was nominated to head it and I put the group together from guys in the KPSM and Gendarmerie with relevant experience. There were six of them, the best that we had, given that most of this expertise exists off island. They've all been confirmed dead – along with about 70% of the populace in that part of the island."

"I'm really sorry to hear this, it's truly awful. I think it's clear from the events of the last fortnight that this kind of group is essential, as the island is now even more vulnerable to natural hazards…"

"Fuck, we were doing exactly the right stuff – we were just a few weeks too late. And not helped at all by that crap hurricane forecast," she shook her head in annoyance. "Sorry about that, Chris, this all gets to me sometimes."

282

"Not a problem. I can't imagine how you're holding it together so well. Anyway, what can I do to help?"

"I need to replace that hazard team and I need it up and running asap. I've heard that you've got some kind of experience here and hence I'd like you to take over this task."

"Replace the entire team, just me?" I was flabbergasted. "I do have training in risk assessment, but I worked in re-insurance, focusing more on financial aspects."

"But you do know what's involved and you've worked for years in the Caribbean…"

"Working out of Bermuda," I noted. "I've spent only holiday time in the Caribbean proper."

"Can you do the job, that's the question?" there was a hint of pleading in her voice.

There is no way that I can possibly refuse, no matter how far out of my depth I'm going to be. "I guess so, if you don't have anyone else. I'll need to start with a briefing on the current position, however, as most of my understanding of it is based on rumours and hearsay."

"That'll be my job, to form an interface between you and all the services that actually implement recovery operations. Do you want to start now? I've got a couple of hours before I need to meet with de Witt."

"Okay, let's do it." *What on earth am I letting myself in for? This is a job that comes with huge responsibilities and, after the next catastrophe, I'm the one who'll be blamed if everything goes tits-up.*

***

Before going into details, Maria let me know that the rush to find a victim to fill this position was also linked to a need to select someone to represent Saint Martin in a pan-Caribbean recovery planning team that focused on risks from natural hazards. Naturally, a special focus was on hurricanes, as the season had been getting longer with a greater number of more severe storms over recent decades – an inevitable consequence of global warming. From this perspective, a large hurricane hitting the Lesser Antilles was to be expected at some point; it was just bad luck that it impacted Saint Martin at such a sensitive stage of recovery and the storm was so severe. In any case, we needed accept this as a fact of life and incorporate it into recovery planning on a regional basis.

I sensed that this digression served to give her a chance to steel herself before outlining the current state of things in and around Saint Martin. Storm surges at coastal locations in the north east and landslides inland had caused the greatest immediate loss of life, although deaths and injuries due to falling or flying objects during peak winds were widespread. In some areas up to 80% of buildings were damaged, many completely destroyed. All roads were initially impassable, but now had been cleared although, especially in the French part and between Simpson Bay and Phillipsburg, these were reduced to footpaths in places.

Almost 50% of our sailing fleet was damaged beyond repair or had been lost without trace. It was notable that the huge powered yachts and cruisers – the floating gin-palaces of the mega-rich – had survived much better due to being moored in the most sheltered locations. Given that such vessels were effectively useless as modes of transport, they were being towed to locations within the lagoon where they could serve as residences for those now homeless, while the most valuable sailing ships were allocated their moorings.

I already knew that illness was a problem, but was horrified to learn its extent. Difficulty of access and limited medical resources meant that there was extensive infection of even minor injuries resulting in sepsis, tetanus and gangrene. Even before the hurricane, malaria and dengue fever – previously eliminated from the island – had begun to reappear and displaced populations camping out in squalid conditions were particularly vulnerable to such mosquito-borne diseases.

Finally, food was a concern due to loss of a large fraction of crops of fruit and vegetables. This was, indeed, the main driver of inter-island collaboration as badly hit areas could be supported by their neighbours.

"So, this is where we are now," she concluded. "It's mainly guesswork, but we estimated that we had a total of population of about 120,000 at the time of the Incident – including residents and visitors. Immediate effects thereafter led to between five and ten thousand deaths – our aim was to bury bodies as quickly as possible rather than count them. It depends on how effective our quarantine and medical responses will be, but I think the hurricane death toll will be at least twice as high. In a nutshell, this is now your job – reduce our vulnerability so that, when the next disaster emerges, its impact is less and we can recover better."

I was wordless as I struggled to take this in.

"Anyway, I have to go now – I'll be back in a couple of hours. There's a desk in the room next door with a notebook and a pencil for you to jot down ideas."

I sat down at what was now my desk and stared into space. *Where on earth do I even start?*

***

A notebook and a fucking pencil! This is what I've got, when I normally use expert systems that do all the heavy lifting and let me make decisions based on the input presented in a 3D, colour-coded argumentation network. And now, I don't even have coloured pencils – it's 2D black and white, or nothing. Fuck!

I stared into space for a while, then was overcome by a feeling of disgrace. *What the fuck am I complaining about? Two of my closest friends have probably lost their lives trying to bring all of this shit together and I'm moaning about no software crutches. Just got to man-up here. I know all the fundamentals required to do this job – but just need to get my lazy arse in gear. Probably the best way to start would be an argumentation model. I don't have holographic displays, so I need a fucking huge piece of paper. This little notebook isn't going to hack it!*

A little later I had requisitioned a paper tablecloth from the canteen and augmented my pencil with blue and black biros – *not my 3D*

286

preference, but going in the right direction. It's actually bizarre that this knowledge management tool was developed to work a way through the vast inventories of information that was made available by advanced science and technology. Now that the knowledge base had vanished into an inaccessible ether, maybe it could help us muddle through.

Getting started on the AM was straightforward, defining the aim of the exercise: *Saint Martin can develop resilient infrastructure.* But I had to write it onto paper rather than type or dictate it into a smart interface that produced a legible product. *How long has it been since I actually hand-wrote anything significant? I've just written this shit and I can hardly make out what it says!*

Anyway, small text, so that I've got lots of space to develop ideas, and pencil so that I can rub out and start again if it all looks like crap! The next step was also relatively easy – listing the questions that needed to be answered to confirm that I could reach my goal.

What are the key infrastructure components required?

What are the most important threats?

How are threats categorised in term of probability and consequence?

What are the scenarios that we need to consider?

How can we improve resilience?

What resources would be involved?

In terms of cost-benefit, how do we move forward most effectively?

I looked over this for over half an hour, but there did not seem to be anything that I could add or improve upon. *OK, that's the easy bit over, now I just need to answer all of these questions and the job's done!*

PA+6 months, Rotorua, New Zealand

Peter Savage's masseuse, Patty, was just getting starting to work on the knotted muscles in his back when he received a sudden slap on his bum.

"Sorry, boss, but your presence is requested back at base."

My assistant-slash-coordinator, Maggie, I just can't escape the bloody woman! "I hope you realise that I could have you done for sexual harassment!"

"Don't be such a poofter," there was merriment in her voice. "You shouldn't be lying about with a bare arse anyway, I thought you're supposed to keep your smalls on in these places."

"I've been getting massages from Patty here for a decade, so there's nothing I need to hide from her, ain't that true?"

"Sure thing, Pete, I've seen every part of your lovely bare bod." Patty helped him off the table and handed over a basket containing his clothes.

"Lovely? Lovely? You've got to be joking! Wait a minute, you're not a blind masseuse like I've read about, are you?"

"Ignore Maggie, she's just jealous that you get to play with my body while she doesn't. Anyway, I'll sign the chit for this massage, even though you were only getting started – with the usual tip."

"That's very generous, but we can sort it all out next week anyway."

289

"OK, Maggie, what's so important that you've got to interrupt one of the few opportunities that I have to relax?" Peter asked over his shoulder while clambering quickly into his clothes.

"It's the Japanese, they've arrived."

"About time! It seemed that none of them were getting past the coast. We're getting towards planting for an expanded range of crops to complement all the ranch land we have hereabouts and our manpower resources of stranded backpackers and unemployed tourist guides need to be strengthened by some real farmers."

"But they won't have the local knowledge…"

Now we go round the houses again. Maggie takes her role as Maori coordinator so seriously that it tends to swamp out everything else. She's a stunningly beautiful young woman with certainly a lot of Maori blood in her exotic genealogy. She's fluent in the Maori language, but was stranded in Rotorua while on holiday from her job as a management consultant in Auckland. In terms of the culture of the local indigenous people, as Rotorua born and bred, I'm sure I know a hell of a lot more than she does. Then again, I'm now in a management job despite not having any background in this – I'm a bloody geothermal engineer for fuck's sake!

"Okay, I now nominate you coordinator for links to the local tribes."

"But I'm already Maori coordinator…"

"No, you're now *everybody* coordinator. This is especially for the Japanese farmers that we're going to have to integrate in to our community. It

290

also goes beyond the Maori: this also includes all the other tribes – redneck cattle ranchers, Masons, lost-in-translation foreigners and the rest."

"Get stuffed, Pete! That's a poisoned chalice if ever there was one. I'll do the Maori but…"

"Nope, not the way it works – you ruin my day, I ruin yours." He nodded to Patty and the Thai woman who ran the business and set off for the short walk to the office on Fenton Street – his dejected underling dragging along behind.

***

Their office was, in fact, a corner on the top floor of the police HQ. After the Incident, it was important to physically bring all key emergency response and recovery coordination teams into close physical proximity after the entire internet, cell phones and even the few remaining landlines failed. *In the last six months, we've moved forward a lot with some basic walky-talkies, but this face-to-face link between all those involved has certainly been a key to getting things sorted out.*

Of course, we're blessed with a setting where the bounties of nature compensate for our lack of technological infrastructure. The Incident happened in Southern Hemisphere autumn, so that heating over the winter was a major challenge for many communities – in New Zealand and elsewhere. With the amount of geothermal activity in this region, the problem was only making better use of this resource using the low technology tools that we had available. *Much of the hardware was already in place – we just needed to strip out all of the smart controllers and monitors and replace them with physical valves and analogue meters. A lot more manpower-intensive – but it works just fine.*

Funnily enough, the lack of science throughout our community even had benefits when the lights went out. We had all these new age types producing organic candles and bio-oils, so that we had the knowledge base to allow a move back to the Middle Ages. Confirmation of established prejudices for those involved but, importantly, a way to move rapidly into a sustainable lifestyle – at least sustainable to the extent that we could keep everyone alive. But we're far from the 21st century and we need to cash in on our potential to export foodstuffs in order to get priority access to recovering technology. And that's what the Japanese are offering us.

Peter had only five minutes to scan through some messages left on his desk before Maggie led two members of the Japanese group into their office – a mismatched pair with the man towering over a petit woman who appeared as if she could be in her teens. The tall, thin man, apparently in his late thirties, introduced himself in perfect, if somewhat stilted, English. "Good day, sir, my name is Hiroyasu Nakamura, but you can call me Hiro. My colleague is Michiko Kato. I believe that we will work together to optimise the benefits that my compatriots and I can bring to your community."

Peter shook his offered hand. "Pete, Pete McClean, great to meet you Hiro – and you also Michiko. I must say, your English is excellent."

"Thanks, Pete. Our group members were selected on the basis of having at least reasonable

English, but I've been a Kiwi fan all my life. I played soccer at school, but always preferred watching rugby. I actually travelled to New Zealand for my honeymoon. This was in a magical place in the rain forest: Wairua Lodge nearby Whitianga on the Coromandel Peninsula. Do you know it?"

"I think I may have passed through Whitianga a couple of times, but I've never been into the rain forest – I'm more of a sailing and surfing type," Peter responded. *Actually, his accent does have a bit of a twang to it.* "Was that the only time that you visited us?"

"My honeymoon was the second time," he smiled, "but I've had a total of eleven visits to your country, before this one. My wife and I thought about emigrating, but we didn't have the courage to make this big step. Now, however, it's a lot easier."

"So, you are actually thinking of staying, not just helping us for a year or two?"

"I would certainly stay, given the chance. I'm not sure about the rest of the team, but I suspect that, after a couple of years, few will want to return to Japan." I noticed that his companion was nodding agreement, although she had yet to say a word.

"Now, how many are you and what capabilities do you have in your group?"

"Including myself and my wife, we're a total of twenty-three." He clearly noticed my face fall. "I know it isn't as many as you may have requested, but we were carefully selected with the aim of trying to help you recover your former agricultural productivity."

"You're all farmers then?"

"Oh, no, we're engineers."

This time Peter couldn't hide a sigh. *Engineers might be nice to have to help rebuild infrastructure, but our critical need is to get the farms back in operation and widen our range of agricultural produce.*

"...well, with a couple of scientists too," Hiro rushed on, as if to reassure him. "I am actually an agricultural engineer, specialising in no-till crop management and my wife is a bio-technologist, who has worked mainly on using grafting to diversify fruit production for specific climatic zones."

Okay, this does seem a bit better. Maybe these are the guys that we need after all.

"But the real gem is Michiko here, she's a knowledge engineer." The small woman blushed prettily, looking even younger.

Christ on a bike, a knowledge engineer! I don't even know what that is, much less how she can help us, cute though she is.

Michiko coughed before timidly speaking up. "Yes, I am Michiko Miyamoto, the KM engineer. But Nakamura-san is being too kind, I am not so important. This is..." She carefully drew a device that looked like an ancient ipad from a pouch strapped to her waist. "This is the agri-KB, the knowledge base, that will help us manage regional recovery and coordinate it with other national efforts."

Maggie squeezed to his side as they stared at the device. "So that's a functioning computer, with a communication link also? That must be worth a fortune!" Peter shook his head in amazement.

294

"Yes, it's a stand-alone unit with a pre-loaded database that includes generic agricultural knowledge plus the latest regional update for New Zealand prior to the Incident." Michiko was gaining confidence as she moved into her specialist area. "It runs off a solar charging unit, but I can upgrade to a fuel cell when I source one locally. I need to build some hardware, but we will then be able to hook up to the military hardnet satellites and this will serve as your local communication node."

"This will be essential for our team to have maximum impact," Hiro added. "In coastal areas we have many Japanese farmers and fishermen, who will provide manpower support. Inland, we need to rebuild your industrial agriculture and transport infrastructure. Our engineers, working with yours, will identify the key problems and implement the solutions developed with the KB."

"This is far beyond anything I expected," Peter was still gazing hungrily at the computer. "I would imagine that tools like that could be invaluable for aiding recovery in Japan. And you're just loaning it to us?"

"No, not a loan, it's a gift," Michiko smiled and set it down on my desk. "I will go through its functions with you both later, but it has a natural language interface in both English and Japanese, so you can start playing with it now. It is the Japanese team who are on loan. Unless we decide to stay permanently, assuming you want to have us," she added with a smile.

"This is incredible! I know New Zealand has a collaboration agreement with Japan, but this seems over-generous…" Peter forced himself to stop, realising that he must seem to be looking a gift horse in the mouth.

"No, it's actually completely in our own interest," Hiro smiled at his confusion. "For us Japanese, your agricultural exports are critical to assuring that we can feed our large urban populations. But, of course, we are not the only ones with these needs – the demand for assured supplies of food exists around the entire Pacific Rim and is a key to recovery of the entire region." This sounded as if it might have been a pre-prepared speech.

"Wow, it really sounds as if you're ready to jump start things," Maggie contributed while her boss struggled to grasp the full implications of this unexpected development. "So, what do we need to do?"

Michiko was clearly pleased at this enthusiasm. "Our KB has all the explicit knowledge that we need, but this is not sufficient for real-life application. It needs to be combined with tacit knowledge – the experience gained over generations by those who lived and farmed here. If we put all this together with an inventory of the resources you have to hand, we can develop an optimised plan to go further."

"My boss here had already put me in charge with organising your contacts with the locals – Maori, farmers and the like, so you can certainly count me in." Maggie smirked at her chief, no doubt aware that he wouldn't have minded spending more time with pretty little Michiko himself. "It's a bit

296

cramped in here, but we'll find spaces for a few desks somehow. We've got temporary accommodation for your entire team sorted out at the Millennium, an old hotel in the middle of town, with a meeting room set up for you to work in. We'll get proper houses for anyone who is interested after we sort out your requirements."

"Yes, we left the others at the hotel, getting themselves sorted out," Hiro responded. "I guess that, other than Miyamoto-san, we will spend most of our time working at the farms. We might eventually need a workshop, but that can get sorted out later. The single members of the team might be happy to stay in the hotel, but it would be nice for the couples to have some kind of apartment, maybe a bit further away from the sulphur pool."

"Yes, the smell of sulphur can be quite strong near the hotel, but I can assure you that you won't notice it at all after a few days," Peter smiled, remembering the few occasions when he actually noticed this omnipresent background to Rotorua – when returning after long spells living elsewhere.

After a few more pleasantries and promises to have a proper coordination meeting with the entire Japanese team after they had settled down, Maggie summoned one of her young assistants to accompany Hiro and Michiko on the short walk back to the Millennium and check if any further assistance was needed.

After the door closed behind them, the Kiwis stood for a few moments in silence – both of them trying to get their heads around this change in their fortunes.

"Is this really as good as it sounds?" Maggie finally asked.

"She looks about twelve, but little Michiko seems to know what she's doing. I hadn't ever thought about getting back to being a major agricultural exporter, more thinking about keeping everyone fed on a regional – or maybe national – level. But the Japs seem to have been planning in a much more sophisticated level, with a global perspective. Maybe a bunch of engineers is exactly what we need."

"Maybe you're thinking more in terms of a cute little knowledge engineer," his underling grinned in a most annoying manner.

Actually, little Michiko is so childlike that I'd be uncomfortable with any kind of romantic relationship with her and I just couldn't imagine having sex with anyone so petite. A strapping, big-breasted lass like Maggie, however, would be a different matter – not that I'd ever admit it.

"Maybe I am…" he grinned, "…but this is the future hitting us in the face. I'd written it off in my lifetime, but maybe we won't just get recovery – we could actually be better off before this fucking sun-thing hit us."

"A bit of schoolgirl knowledge management and everything'll be hunky-dory – you really think so?"

"I've been firefighting for the last six months – spending my time trying to ensure that things get less fucked-up. This couple have just breezed in and given us – for free – a tool that will, at the very least, make us the local centre for all recovery

298

actions and, with a bit of luck, the chance to become a key national player. Don't you see it?"

"I think you've been combining your massage with other pleasures from the mysterious East and that your brain is mince, boss. There's twenty-three Nips, with not one a farmer. You really think our problems are solved?"

"Weirdly enough, I've a feeling in my water that they are. Can't nail it down as yet, but I can see light at the end of the tunnel."

Maggie looked at the strange look in his face, completely new and maybe an indication of the stress that he had been working under and the impact of a possible end to it.

"Pete, boss, I've wondered for a while if maybe…" Maggie's voice had dropped to a whisper. "Well, maybe, if you fancied, we could perhaps…"

"Move in together!" Maggie's eyes widened at the response of new, dynamic, optimistic Pete. "I thought you'd never ask!"

As her solid body thumped into his and she started to sob against his chest, Peter felt strangely content. *I'm a fucking engineer – I build things. It's been a long hard drag just stopping things going to shit, but now I can get together with these Japanese engineers and rebuild this bloody country.* A bit of hyperbole, sure, but now he had recovered a missing drive and had a woman by his side.

PA+1 Year, Nagoya, Japan

I might well have lost track of time on a day-to-day basis, but there was no way that the 1-year anniversary of the Incident was going to go unmarked. For me, the bizarre steampunk existence in Japan had faded into the background to the point that I no longer noticed it. We had horses and carts together with stream trains and fuel-cell powered vehicles, but the system functioned smoothly enough and progress could be seen in terms of stepwise establishment of something approaching normal lifestyles, even if without the pre-Incident luxuries.

I had moved back to my flat on campus after a micro-net was established for the Uni, linked to a local power grid driven by the Nishi-Nagoya small modular reactors. This was a relatively new power plant that replaced the polluting coal and oil units that previously supplied the city and, due to their inherent operational flexibility, particularly suitable for support of a slowly recovering power distribution network.

The university itself was also recovering rapidly, with a focus on assuring local accommodation for both staff and students in order to reduce transportation requirements. As far as I was concerned, this move back to an older style of education where teachers and students mixed more intensively could only be a good thing. Even better, the focus was very much on technical subjects; predominantly engineering, but with an effort to expand physical, chemical and biological sciences. While I have the greatest respect for practical trades – without which we could not survive – their artificial incorporation into universities was a triumph of political correctness over common sense. Now the old apprenticeship system was re-established on a massive scale, with the pensioners who possessed critical late 20th / early 21st century skills drafted in to work with young recruits. *Learning by doing it – that's the way forward and the only way to capture the tacit knowledge that we so dearly need.*

Although my original contract as a visiting professor had long expired, this was never mentioned and, as soon as a first staff list for the University was produced, I was rather gobsmacked to find myself listed as an Emeritus Professor. I could have pointed out the mistake, but it seemed of little importance in the greater scheme of things.

Probably the development that really shook me was when Shoko moved out to take over a central role in international liaison, based in Tokyo. After only 2 weeks she was engaged, in eight weeks married and almost instantly thereafter pregnant to her new boss. *Even now I can't decide if that represented the biggest mistake or the luckiest escape of my life! I'm probably thinking about Shoko because I need to prepare a top-level presentation to JANA, covering an overview of the present situation and perspectives for the future. She'd have helped a lot – not least due to her irrepressible enthusiasm and confidence in my abilities and would be delighted by the good news*

301

of our influence already extending throughout Oceania and, gradually, South America.

Our relationship with the US was still strained, to say the least, after we identified one further CIA attempt to compromise our internet. Under intensive international scrutiny, extreme punitive actions were implemented, leading to death penalty for the entire top three CIA management layers, plus a number of prominent supporting politicians. As there has been absolutely nothing since, this seems to be no longer a threat – from the USA or any of the other former *powers*. Within the US, the situation was bad, but not as bad as I had expected it to be. Vast areas had been abandoned and were so highly polluted as to be unliveable for generations, but agreements forged with Canada and Mexico indicated that lessons had been learned from our successes in the East and cooperation was now increasingly more valued than ranking on the international political arm-wrestling podium.

The EU as an organisation was a shambles, but Europe was recovering reasonably well at a local level, especially after the larger cities had been abandoned. The resulting mosaic of small nations and independent regions functioned with only very loose control or coordination from outside. Despite being in a kind of political Limbo, the EU and NATO military networks continued to function and almost seemed to have developed an existence of their own – effectively as a regional communication and policing service-provider, but with negligible external defence role.

Although details were less clear, a similar situation seemed to have evolved in Russia and the CIS: recovering slowly, but with national and regional autonomy increasingly evident. The military role was still strong, but more focused internally than in any time in the past. Our subtle meta-analysis of developments suggested very strongly that the Russian security services had also developed a plan to attack Japanese infrastructure, but this had been quashed from above shortly after our face-off with the USA. I was unsure if this was fear of a similar action against Russia or simply passive backing of any country taking on their number-one opponent. In any case, since then Russia has been a vocal supporter of JANA and its plans.

Otherwise, the rest of the world seems to have gone to hell. China is still an enigma, ignoring all efforts to establish communication, but satellite imaging suggests that it has completely imploded and is now a tapestry of feuding regions without any form of central control. The military seem to have some residual communication infrastructure, but its role in the regional conflicts is unclear.

The Middle East, Africa and the Indian sub-continent are charnel houses, due primarily to their inability to provide food and water to their huge urban populations. Then followed the inevitable conflicts – including widespread use of chemical and biological weapons – and finally resultant plague, drought and famine. Current best guesses are that deaths exceed two billion so far, with no sign that the death toll is close to peaking.

There are, of course, local exceptions where impacts have been much less. For example, low tech green and survivalist communities scattered around the globe. Israel's resilience stood out from its Arab neighbours, with strengthened links to NATO and rapidly recovering infrastructure. It was, however, a nation under siege from all sides – suffering a series of attacks from Islamic radicals after the Incident, as if the Jews were somehow to blame for it. With typical ruthlessness, the Israelis cleared a 50 kilometre buffer zone around the entire country, using tailored bioweapons to render it uninhabitable. Whether due to this or the fact that the countries supporting terrorists were falling apart, the number of attacks decreased considerably thereafter.

Indeed, international terrorism had largely disappeared, indicating that much of this had been an artefact of the obscene inequalities of the pre-Incident world and deliberate exploitation of the weak-minded by a few leaders who had most to gain from the resultant destabilisation. Both of these drivers were now gone, in particular due to the disappearance of financial wealth. The Princes of Saudi Arabia and the United Arab Emirates, who had used their vast riches to support extremism worldwide, were instantaneously bankrupt and it did not take long before their hordes of serfs realised that their power had vanished and they were as vulnerable as other mortals. Despite the gaudy fortresses that they lived in, without money to pay guards it was soon recognised that they were vulnerable and, within a month, they had vanished as a caste – those not brutally murdered hiding within the hoi poloi.

My main recommendation will be clear: continuation of our polity of triage with no effort spent on any countries who could get by on their own or those that are beyond help. From a Japanese perspective, this means national recovery coupled to supporting developing of a synergistic network established under JANA leadership.

The tricky bit – where I would have liked feedback from someone like Shoko – is presenting a longer-term perspective, as we now have the luxury of planning for more than the very immediate future. I would not be able to present it in this way, but there is a definite silver lining to an event that rapidly reduced the human population. Anthropogenic climate change will certainly continue to cause massive regional – if not global – environmental degradation regardless of any political or engineering counter-measures attempted and, by this time last year, very few had gotten beyond the discussion phase.

This was a classic tragedy of the commons – at an individual level releasing carbon dioxide to the atmosphere was associated with immediate, clear benefits, so why forego these to avoid vague threats to the world as a whole sometime in the future. Even when the climate change chickens were coming in to roost, in the form of heat waves, droughts, more frequent and stronger storms, both powerful vested interests in the fossil fuel industry and mindless politicians – Merkel, Trump, Putin and their successors – worked to block any scientifically-based response to the problem.

It was clear to me that now there was a chance to get things on track towards gradual recovery. Despite the effective collapse of industry and the more polluting modes of transport, the last year had not significantly reduced greenhouse gas output due to the huge impact of the fires resulting from the Incident. Even when releases decrease in coming years, as they inevitably will, the inertia of the climate-controlling factors will cause warming to continue for decades to come. This will certainly give problems, but we might just have a chance of getting through them as long as we do not allow greenhouse gas emissions to return to problematic levels. There are two ways to do this and I really believed we had to aim for both in parallel: let population stabilise at a sensible level to allow sustainable use of resources, which would probably be about 2-3 billion maximum, and replace all use of fossil fuels to the extent possible. *The former is a topic that's so sensitive that it can't yet be openly discussed, so I need to focus on the latter.*

The tricky bit is to change a mind-set: we initially had to use all options available when we lost 21st century power, but now need to fight against a return to widespread use of oil, gas and, especially, coal. *The Australians are, as expected, pushing coal exports strongly – but that's a dangerous step in the wrong direction. All efforts have to be focused on any form of power that doesn't generate greenhouse gasses. In Japan we're lucky due to the existing facilities that can be brought online relatively rapidly, mainly hydro and inherently-safe nuclear. We can complement this with some geothermal and tidal or wave power, but it'll take time to recover the technology needed for photovoltaics.*

This is where I was caught in a dichotomy. I wanted my modelling toolkit to be accepted for objective assessment of different recovery strategies, but I also wanted to bias its output so that things were steered in the direction that I felt they had to go. After a month of wrestling with my conscience, I finally contacted Yoshi, who was more than happy to incorporate a dispersed Trojan into our database updates that would allow me to implement this bias as and when I wanted. Because this involved databases that were internal to the toolkit, he assured me that there was little risk of them being spotted by the cyber-war teams who now carefully reviewed our updates to avoid a repeat of our action against the US.

Apart from Yoshi, nobody else knew about this and even he could reasonably claim that he had no real understanding of the functionality of my routine – so the entire weight of any punishment would fall on my shoulders should this trick ever be discovered. I had made many enemies over the last year, so was sure that this would be branded as treason and there was a definite risk that it could be punished as such. Nevertheless, it was something that I had to do.

Although the impact was subtle, I had no doubts about the consequences of exaggeration of the benefits of alternatives to fossil fuels in terms of denying low tech energy sources to the more disadvantaged regions and the resulting suffering and death caused by this. At a global level this would contribute to my other goal of reducing population numbers, but I could not pretend that I was merely an observer here: I was actively encouraging a strategy that could be seen as genocide on a massive scale.

"Alea jacta est!" I muttered to myself as I added the initiation sequence to my monthly database update. I felt as if a weight had been lifted from my shoulders by this decision and I could view it as a fait accompli, a fixed boundary condition for our actions in the coming decades. I could now forget about the rest of the world and focus on helping accelerate the progress of recovery in Japan and its JANA partners.

***

Despite Shoko's absence, Akiko was still a regular visitor and, to celebrate this anniversary, I had invited her to dinner at my flat. Although I could no longer build up stocks of booze by raiding the refectory, local production of beer and sake had been re-established and I still had a few exotic wines stored away for special occasions like this one. The meal itself was rather pedestrian, featuring grilled fish on a bed of garlic rice, but we had Champagne as an Aperitif and a nice Burgundy to complement a New Zealand cheese that I had recently received as a gift from Shoko, who was still coordinating Japan's expanding trading Armada.

During the meal, naturally enough, our conversation had focused on the events of the last year and our hopes for the future. By the time we reached coffee, this was a form of verbal foreplay.

"Yes, despite the limitations of living in a basement, our time in the centre certainly had its highpoints," I grinned as I noticed that Akiko's usual schoolgirl outfit did not hide her prominent erect nipples.

"You're certainly thinking about that medical room and the antics we got up to on that gyno-chair thing. What was your favourite?" She turned towards me and, almost as if it was an accident, her short skirt rode up to flash a glimpse of her white knickers.

"Well, it's very difficult to choose between the many times when you and Shoko blew my mind..." I could feel my physical reaction to the memories, "...but that time with Yoshi was particularly kinky. What about you? What was your highlight?"

The little Japanese woman frowned as she carefully considered my question. "I guess our first time, which seems so long ago. Shoko was exactly how I expected her to be, but you were so naïve, innocent somehow."

I laughed aloud. "After six decades and two marriages, I would never have been expected to be described as innocent!"

"But you were: prim and shy and unexperienced." She smiled in a dreamy manner. "It was quite erotic, actually, especially as we were then able to make you less prudish."

"I'm not sure prudish is the correct term. I was more shell-shocked by the cornucopia of sexual deviation I was presented with, especially from young Shoko."

"In this day and age, that's prudish," she insisted. "Anyway, we now have to make do with a normal bed and just whatever toys I may happen to have in my handbag," she grinned salaciously and opened her legs to show that her little panties were already damp.

"That would work for me," I stood and helped her to her feet.

I then hesitated and received a quizzical stare. "What's up, don't you want to?" she asked.

I stood mute for a further moment, then I finally got it out. "Akiko, I really like you and would like to spend more time with you: not just occasional sex, doing other things."

"So you don't want more regular sex?" Her teasing grin reminded me immediately of Shoko.

"Well, certainly, to the extent that my old bod can handle it, but would you like... Would you consider moving in with me?"

She looked around the flat. "Well it's certainly nicer than the rabbit hutch that I'm assigned to at present, so I'll certainly think about it. But you know that this won't work if you think that we'll end up with an old-fashioned one-to-one relationship. Much though I like you – maybe love you – that's not for me."

"I realise that, but I think that's certainly something that I can handle. You can scratch your sexual itches any way you want – with or without me as a participant."

"Mmm, more is usually merrier, so all we need to do is widen your horizons a bit. Let's give it a try and see if it'll work out for a longer term."

"Perfect! Let's just get you out of your wet underwear and see what your bag of mysteries has for me."

While we slowly undressed each other, she pulled my head down and whispered into my ear. "I have just the thing to test your resolve. I know a couple of gay guys on campus who are into experimenting with couples. Should I invite them around next time?"

Fuck, walked right into this one! Anyway, in for a penny...

"Sure, love, anything you want, I'll give it a go. But why not invite pregnant Shoko also?" I couldn't help adding sarcastically.

"Actually, that's not a bad idea, Mike, I think she'll be in Nagoya next week."

I crushed the naked nypho to my chest, so that she couldn't see me rolling my eyes. *Me and my bloody big mouth. Although, then again...*

PA+1 Year, Cupecoy, Sint Maarten

I awoke to the glare of watery sunlight pouring through the open door to the balcony outside my bedroom. I looked at the empty space beside me and sighed. It was now three months since Lynn moved out – and in with Commander Konig of all people. I still saw her regularly, but it seemed that her hetero phase had been an experiment that did not work long-term and she was now much happier. My eyes were drawn to the polished wooden wheel mounted on the wall. I could just make out the gothic script: *Sapphic Dream*. It was all that had been recovered of the yacht and a reminder of the close friends I had found and lost over the year.

Despite the fact that it was still spring, we had just been hit by a small hurricane. Due to both improved early warning and more robust infrastructure, the impact had been minor: some local flooding and a few damaged roofs, but no catastrophic destruction or, so far, any deaths reported. I considered it a useful test of our natural hazard defence system before the main hurricane season and was feeling quite pleased with my contributions to it. Nevertheless, we were still only hovering on the edge of self-sufficiency as an island, but the situation looked better when seen in the light of the Lesser Antilles trading network. This was our inter-island partnership which was actually more important in terms of mutual aid in case of emergencies than trading under normal circumstances, especially as our trading products were generally similar.

The key to developing further was clearly establishing a wider link to one of the bigger players – with the obvious options being the US / N America bloc, due to proximity; the EU and NATO due to old colonial links; or JANA due to its apparent pre-eminence in post-Incident recovery. My personal preference was certainly JANA.

"Fuck!" While I had been daydreaming, I had forgotten that I had a top-level meeting this morning – with JANA, no less. Their delegation had arrived in Phillipsburg by submarine the previous evening and feted to the extent possible by the great and the good of the Lesser Antilles. Today a range of meeting would run in parallel, but I was supposed to be chairing the one on natural hazard resilience. "Fuck!"

I grabbed my automatic Rolex from the bedside – a present that I was sure Cecelia had liberated from one of the top-end jewellers pillaged after the incident – and was relieved to see that is was still only just after eight, so I had plenty of time to get myself sorted out and then cycle over to the meeting, organised in what had been one of the luxury hotels in Simpson Bay.

I set water to boil on the gas ring that Lynn had salvaged from a wrecked yacht and automatically checked the cylinder – *still about half full, so plenty of time before I need to scrounge up a replacement.* A quick pop to the *cludgy*, the basic outhouse constructed by my next-door neighbours, Steve and Alan – the precious gay sailors that I remembered

313

the girls being so scathing about. This was neatly built at the side of our beach – still known as the Loo – and provided a much more civilised way of utilising the sea for sewage disposal. Toilet paper was long gone, but a wet cloth acted as a sufficiently good alternative. The toilet was damaged regularly by hurricanes, but was easily repaired and a much preferable option to the buckets and pits used by those without access to a convenient beach.

Instant coffee was also something of the past, but there were plenty of sources of beans in the Caribbean, so all I required was my hand-turned grinder – again salvaged from a sunken ship – and my little cafetière could produce a perfectly acceptable brew. The caffeine buzz from the thick, black coffee immediately made the world seem like a better place. As I breakfasted on a couple of bananas, I thought of how, at least, my diet had improved post-Incident, with much more fruit and fish and almost no meat, sugar or dairy products. Also, despite my desk job, I was strict in keeping up my training routine, being well aware of how precarious our recovery was and how easily I could end up needing my fighting skills yet again.

I dressed up for my meeting, at least to the extent that this was possible: my best shorts, leather sandals and a somewhat worn but clean white linen shirt. I pedalled slowly to the hotel, a recently built – and even more recently abandoned – Hyatt. The accommodation blocks had been wrecked by our first post-Incident hurricane, but a low annex containing a ballroom and a number of meeting rooms was almost intact. Its particular advantages included large windows but also shading by surrounding trees, so that rooms were bright but did not get too hot during the day. It was also very close to the coastguard and police headquarters.

Despite taking it easy, I was still rather sweaty when I arrived at the empty meeting room, twenty minutes early. I had stripped off my shirt and was in the process of wiping myself down with a small towel that I kept with me for this purpose when I was shocked by the sound of a loud wolf-whistle. I spun to see a tall brunette standing in the doorway, smiling as she unabashedly inspected my naked torso. Given her neat grey trouser-suit, white blouse and shiny black shoes, I realised that she must be one of the JANA delegates and could feel myself blush, although it was probably hidden by my tan.

"Oops, sorry about that, I'll have my shirt back on in a tick," I gushed.

"Don't rush on my behalf," she responded in perfect English, although with a definite accent which did not seem traceable to the native Spanish that I expected of the delegation. "I suppose that you're one of the Antilles guys."

"Yes, I'm the Saint Martin host for this do," I struggled to button up my shirt, feeling distinctly under-dressed for the occasion. "I'm afraid I was here on holiday at the time of the Incident, so I don't have any business clothes to hand."

"I'm sorry for being so formal, probably more casual would have been better for this meeting. Anyway, my name is Anna-Maria, from Argentina." She extended her hand as she walked towards me.

315

I wiped my hands on the towel before we shook, feeling even more of a dork. "I'm Chris, originally based in Bermuda but now representing the Lesser Antilles for coordination of natural hazard defence and recovery."

"Pleased to meet you, Chris. I must say you seem in very good shape for a paper-pushing coordinator."

She smiled but I seemed to detect a lascivious glint in her eyes. *Now was that real, or just wishful thinking on my part?* "Well, I kind of fell into this position, rather than being properly qualified for it," I responded, "I was actually a cop in a previous incarnation."

"Mmm, I could believe that. Anyway, from what I can see Saint Martin seems to have weathered the last storm well, so you must be doing a good job."

I felt a wave of pride from this complement, which seemed to compensate a little for my scruffy appearance. "Yes, I'm certainly very relieved that we got off so easily there. Anyway, I should note that, from our side, we should have been joined by a couple of other island representatives but, due to the hurricane, they've had to call off. As you can imagine, the natural hazard guys are busiest at times like this. In any case, I am authorised to represent all of the islands in our trading group."

"Yes, well, that's understandable enough. It looks like the meeting is down to the two of us then, as this is predominantly a trade mission and I'm the only recovery specialist – with only a limited background in hazard assessment."

"Fine, but in that case, I don't suppose we need this meeting room," I waved at the table set with ten chairs, "or do you think we'll need the blackboard? I have all my stuff on bits of paper."

"I'm sure we won't need the blackboard," she gave me an enigmatic smile that suddenly reminded me of Cecilia, "and I guess I won't need this jacket."

I struggled to hide a gasp as her slim frame was revealed, contrasting with extremely large breasts. *Unless that's a miracle of brassiere engineering, she must truly be a sight to behold on a topless beach!*

Anna Maria smiled as if reading my thoughts: probably not a difficult challenge under the circumstances and one she must be well used to. "Anyway, let's have the coffee," she continued, "and I've got a nice surprise for you that might be received better if you're sitting down."

Given the surprise that I've just had, this has got to be a beauty! I led the well-endowed Argentinean to the tables set out under a sprawling chestnut tree while I frantically tried to guess what this surprise could be.

***

I was sure that it was to tease me, but Anna Maria insisted that we exchanged a bit more background before we went further with her cryptic promise. I went first and skipped over my re-insurance background before quickly covering my experiences after the Incident, leading up to my job as catastrophe manager. She sipped her coffee and listened without interruption, although nodding sadly when I mentioned losing two very close friends during our first hurricane. As soon as I started describing my approach to classifying threats and assessing options to reduce impact from them, however, she repeatedly asked questions aimed at both technical clarification and understanding my rationale for choosing particular options.

"So, as you can see, I've been just muddling along on the basis of common sense, using re-insurance tools that I've bastardised to fit this particular application."

"You shouldn't play this down. You've actually done a very nice job here, certainly in all the areas that I'm competent to assess." Anna Maria then went on to give her own background as a Professor of Risk Management in the Engineering Department of the huge University of Buenos Aires. I gasped when she mentioned, almost casually, that her husband, a pilot, had been in the air at the time of the incident. Although she herself had been at conference in Salta and had been little affected by the immediate impacts, her son had been staying with her parents in a suburb of BA that had been gutted by fire after a nearby oil terminal exploded. Her only sister had been on honeymoon in Europe. All were assumed to have perished, but there was no hard evidence in any case, which made things a lot worse. Despite putting on a brave face, from a tremor in her voice, I was sure that she was suffering still. *And to think I was feeling hard done to this morning, I haven't suffered a fraction of what this poor woman has experienced.*

In what I was sure would have been an epic story in itself, she simply stated that it took her more than a month to work her way back home and, once there, was immediately drafted into a military unit coordinating recovery actions. Because of her particularly good English and some basic Japanese, she was appointed to the international liaison team. I had previously heard a bizarre rumour about a Japanese professor shitting all over the president of the USA, but was amazed not only to hear the entire story, but that this was first-hand, as Anna had been one of the JANA observers following the action.

Since then, she had spent 3 months in New Zealand, organising knowledge exchange on rebuilding critical infrastructure and assessing evolving trade possibilities.

Ah, that's where the touch of an accent comes from – clear as soon as you know what to look for.

Now she was a member of the team planning long-term expansion of the JANA network. Although the primary focus for Argentina was on the other major countries of South America, these had generally been hit hard by the incident and would require a considerable time before they would be able to function as nations. This was a contrast to the Caribbean, and especially the Lesser Antilles, which had been hit less and recovered faster than other parts of Central America.

"In fact," she concluded, "your establishment of a trading network mirrors what we have done with JANA…"

"…although on a much smaller scale," I pointed out.

"Yes, but, as you explained, you did the critical planning using large sheets of paper. You didn't have anything like this…" At this point she withdrew a book-like object from her handbag with a theatrical flourish.

I stared at the object in disbelief. "That looks like a truly ancient ipad. I've only seen pictures of them. So, this is what you used to form JANA?" I couldn't keep sarcasm from my tone.

"Not the ipad, silly," her playful slap was accompanied by a joyous laugh, "it's what's on it. It's the recovery toolkit."

"The one developed by the Nagoya prof you mentioned?"

"The very one. We normally run it on much more powerful machines but, with all the other crap aps stripped out, this little toy can manage everything that you're likely to need it for." She leaned forward to place it into my hands, no doubt noting how they were shaking.

"What, you're just giving it to me? This must be worth a fortune!"

"Not really, Prof Mitchell distributes the tool for free and we've found quite a number of saveable machines like this to run cut-down versions of it. Older computers were actually less vulnerable to the EMP and, especially if unplugged, switched off and stored in a deep cellar, have survived quite well. A bigger problem was finding usable batteries and translation of relevant bits of our toolkit to fit the different operating systems. There are a couple of spare rechargeable batteries and the cables needed here," she passed over a small bag. "All you need is an occasional source of power and, ideally, a chance to link to a hardnet for monthly database updates."

"Well, the coastguard has power and access to the hardnet, so I can certainly organise something. Actually, my next-door neighbours are in the process of trying to build a wind-powered generator so, if that works, it would be another option." I grinned as this thought came to mind, deciding not to add that its main aim was to allow them to watch a cache of potentially undamaged video porn that they had managed to find somewhere.

We sat in silence for a moment, but a feeling of unease was slowly building up in me. "Anna Maria, this is very generous and I don't want to be looking a gift horse in the mouth, but what's in it for you: for Argentina or JANA? Even if you had dozens of these things, they're incredibly valuable at the present moment."

"Yes, of course, no such thing as a free lunch, is there? The official line is that it is a symbol of good faith and, if it helps your region recover faster, that can only be good for us and the rest of the world. There is, however, a bit of a particular vested interest in giving it to you."

I waited for a moment, but she seemed to expect me to see where this was going. "You said that you were more of an expert in catastrophe recovery and that seems to be what Argentina, New Zealand and Japan seem to be doing well. Here in the Caribbean, we'll tailor the tool to put much more weighting on natural hazard assessment and defence – so I guess this could be of use to you. You have seen how our recovery was set back by a hurricane and, with global warming, such hazards are going to become more likely in all regions. Could this be it?"

"Nail hit right on the head!" she laughed again. "The database updates are always two-way, so your experience will contribute to the knowledge that we'll need to assure that we're not caught out in the future."

"You know, the more I think about it, it's a clever investment on your side – just like the re-insurance I used to develop. The probability may not be high but the consequences are huge so, if you're rebuilding infrastructure anyway, why not make it robust?"

"Are you really as isolated as you claim to be?" Anna Maria looked at me now a bit suspiciously. "That's exactly what Professor Mitchell has been pushing."

"We're certainly so isolated that I hadn't even heard this prof's name until you mentioned it. But it's just common sense, really. Who could argue against it?"

"You'd be surprised," she muttered under her breath, indicating that the common front presented by JANA could be a bit more complex than it seemed.

"Actually, I wouldn't be in the slightest." Anna jumped, obviously surprised that her sotto voce comment had been heard. "If there's one thing that the insurance business tells you, it's that the general public – and even many organisations that should know much better – have a very poor grasp of natural hazards and how to manage them. Just

322

before the incident there was widespread outrage when we dramatically increased cost of insurance against flooding in many regions and, often, refused to provide insurance at any price. We knew about global warming, but they also knew about global warming and ignored all pleas to do something about it. The little chickens come home to roost and, somehow, they think it's our problem!"

"Oops, sorry, I got a bit carried away there," I apologised when I recognised that I had gone on another of my rants.

"Not at all – the more you talk, the more I can see why you've done so well here and am sure that our gift will pay dividends for us. I was actually intending to leave tomorrow, when we planned to push on further into the Caribbean and maybe also Bermuda and some of the other Atlantic islands. I don't think that there's anything for me there that's better than what you have already, so do you think you'd mind if I teamed up with you for a month or so. The sub can pick me up on the way back – if required."

If required? This is beginning to sound like the start of something good. "Of course, working together would be a win-win situation as you can get me up to speed on the toolkit faster and, in return, will be able to optimise my input to the database so that it fits your needs best."

"Well, I think that this has been one of the most productive meetings I've ever had – even if held in a coffee shop."

"It's actually a restaurant, so we could slowly slip on into lunch if you like," I suggested.

After a moment's hesitation, she smiled. "Why not – and maybe I can treat you?"

"That would be nice, but how are you thinking about paying?" I grinned at her look of annoyance.

"Shit! Keep on forgetting about that. How do you pay anyway?"

"Cash," my grin widened as I pulled some rather decrepit bills from my pocket.

"What on earth?" She grabbed a note from my hand. "Netherlands Antillean guilder," she read. "Where the hell did you get these from? You can't possibly have printed them!"

"We found boxes full of them in the basement of a bank – crated up for incineration when we formally adopted e-currency for all transactions, but apparently forgotten about. Not even in a vault, as they were worthless – but just the dab to replace all the scribbled bits of paper we were using as credit slips. Only useful on the island, of course, but we are already discussing an option for extension to all the Lesser Antilles."

"Mmm, it seems like I may indeed be here more than a month – so may need to find some long-terms digs."

"I think I might just have what you need," I smiled and waved at the waitress, hoping that they'd have some form of alcohol available to seal this deal. *Suddenly, out of the blue, the world looks like a very much better place!*

PA+1 year, Smokey Mountains, Tennessee

Joe "Hoss" Dean was in a bad way. When he looked back, the Incident had been the highlight of his life; the absolute proof that he and his compatriots were right and all the conventional assholes who called them insane, retarded or part of some kind of cult were burning in their riot-torn cities, starving in their towns or being preyed-upon by looting hordes in their farms. His survivalist camp had been set up with such an apocalypse in mind – intended to protect him and his family from anything from nuclear war to zombie plagues. This started with a remote location, accessible only by a single, easily-defended road. The stockade kept any wild animals from the fields therein, but would also defend against attack by any human who ever got that far. Despite being self-sufficient from farm land and animals and possessing a deep well, huge quantities of canned and otherwise preserved food was stored in underground bunkers along with an arsenal of weapons and munitions.

Joe was at the compound at the time of the Incident, along with his pregnant wife, son and daughter, taking their turn at maintaining the farm. The camp had been set up with an EMP as a precursor to a nuclear attack in mind, so the family moved into the bomb shelter and battened down the hatches as soon as its effects were evident. After a week with no sign of fallout and an eerie silence on the airwaves, they cautiously emerged and started preparations for the arrival of the other nine families – brothers, sisters, cousins and in-laws who shared the facility with them. Three weeks later, with still no signs of their arrival despite the heavy-duty, off-road vehicles they all possessed, Joe decided that the situation must be worse than anticipated and activated the access road defence system. This would not preclude use by those in the know, who would be able to find the hand-cranked walkie-talkie that could be used to allow safe passage, but anyone else would be confronted by the inbuilt booby-traps that protected the compound.

The protection provided by isolation worked for a further month, but it was inevitable that those who lived in the region knew of the survivalist camp's existence and, when things got critical due to lack of food and drinking water normally pumped from a distant reservoir, a first group set out to make contact and beg for help. The three women were blasted to bits by the claymore mines set only one hundred metres after the warning signs stating that this was *private property* and *intruders will be shot!*

That worked pretty well – and even better when I had the idea of mounting the bigger bits of the bodies as scarecrows, to keep the likes away.

It did indeed work for a while – the story spread, but what Joe had not reckoned on was the fact of the defence system acting as evidence that valuable resources were being protected.

The stupid fuckers then tried to get along the road at night, as if darkness makes any difference

326

when you hit a trip-wire linked up to mines. Of course, a couple of trails bypassing the road came next, as we expected, so they just hit the claymores we had planted there. Our thinking was spot on, we had it properly covered, although we probably could have done with a few more mines.

While external defences were still holding up, the claustrophobic situation in the stockade was beginning to have its impacts. Joe's wife, Elsie, successfully delivered her second daughter within the little clinic that had been planned with such requirements in mind. Unfortunately, the stress of isolation had led Elsie towards increasing use of anti-depressants and painkillers, which were beginning to degrade her hand-eye coordination and sense of balance. She tripped while nursing the baby, which was severely concussed by the fall. Despite all they could do, it died two days later.

Elsie went into free-fall rapidly thereafter, refusing to eat and living on a horrendous mixture of pharmaceuticals. She cut her wrists in the bath to end it all before the drugs did it for her.

Without their mother, the children became increasingly discontented, constantly complaining about lack of company and boredom within the confines of the camp. Joe tried his best to keep them busy, taking them with him on regular hunting trips and showing them how to rig traps on some of the less likely trespassing routes, including a couple of cliffs that would be climbable for someone with sufficient skill.

It was during one of these trips that they came on a scouting party, a young man and an older

327

woman who was noticeably pregnant. Both carried what looked like shotguns slung from their shoulders. From Joe's lookout on the ridge, he could watch the trespassers work their way along the thorn bushes intended to guide intruders onto the trails that had been booby-trapped. Unfortunately, a fallen tree now provided a route through this barrier and the pair had started to climb onto it.

"This is why we need to patrol regularly, even the best defences will degrade with time and we have to keep them maintained," he whispered. "OK, junior, you take out the boy and Lizzy can pop the women."

His children were expert shots and Joe was appalled to see bullets zipping around both targets without a single hit. "Shit, what're you kids doing, they're going to get away."

"It's just a boy, can't be much older than me," Joe junior protested.

"And the woman's pregnant, I can't murder her," his sister added.

Joe adjusted the telescopic sight on his own rifle and saw how, in their rush to escape the hail of bullets, the woman had fallen from the tree trunk into the thorns and the boy was struggling to extricate her. With unconscious cruelty, the sniper waited until the woman had been pulled free before he fired and the young man's head exploded. The woman fell to her knees to cradle the lifeless body and he lined up his shot. "Probably her son," he muttered, "so I'm just putting her out of her misery."

328

Just before he fired, Lizzy jostled his elbow, causing his bullet to go wide and hit a tree inches from the woman's shoulder. This seemed to bring her to her senses and she threw herself into cover of thicker vegetation and vanished from sight.

Feeling his face redden with rage, he spun to face his kids, who were standing together with matching looks of defiance. "What the shit is up with you two? That woman will now go back to her gang and tell them about this way into our home."

"So what? She'll also tell them that it's guarded. And she was pregnant."

Joe glared at his daughter, using all his willpower to restrain from slapping the annoying pout from her face. "We're fighting for our lives here," he roared, "can't you get that into your thick teenage skull? The woman's pregnant, she has a baby and that just means one more person up against us. And her son – only a boy," he tried to mimic his son's nasal tone. "That was a boy with a gun. Makes no difference how old the person pulling the trigger is, the bullet'll kill you just as dead."

"But you could just scare them off, you don't need to murder them," his daughter was not backing off.

"Christ on a bike!" Joe cursed, rolling his eyes to heaven to emphasise that he could not believe the stupidity of what he was hearing. "We're not going around killing people, we're only lawfully defending ourselves from armed trespassers. If they stay away from us, we'll let them alone. They're the ones provoking the trouble."

"If we just shared some of our stuff, then we wouldn't need to keep killing people," Lizzy persisted.

"And there would be more people, we wouldn't be alone all the time," her sibling added.

"Say we let a couple of people in, what will happen? There'll just be more and more until we're completely swamped. We did all the work to set up this place while slobs like those trying to take it from us sat on their complacent asses and laughed at us, calling us a nut-cult. But they'll all be happy to take a share now and, next thing you know, they'll be telling us what to do and deciding how we use our own stuff."

He was clearly having no success in getting his message over, so changed tack. "Remember how we got together to plan this place. It was all family that we knew and trusted. We loved each other, so didn't need to worry about crime or conflict. We never had any disagreements about how to proceed and so we'd welcome any of them if they ever make it here. But how can we expect this from a bunch of strangers?"

"Yes, but nobody else showed up. We're all alone," young Joe whined.

"They've not shown up yet, but we can keep hoping and make sure that there's a place for them if they eventually make it."

"After a year," his son muttered under his breath.

Joe decided to ignore this provocation, with the hope that, somehow or other, they'd eventually work this rebellion out of their systems and see it his way. *After all, it really is a no brainer, even without considering the burden that starved and probably disease-ridden outsiders would represent.* "Okay, gather up any bullet casings and you can reload them when we get back home."

"Why?" Lizzy asked belligerently. "We've got tons of ammunition."

"You can't possible have too many bullets," he answered with an air of finality and bent to pick up the casings from the couple of rounds he had fired.

***

For a few days it seemed that the situation had improved, no moaning from the children or attempted incursions from a small group who had set up camp just outside of the border of his land. He checked them daily, without the kids, his high-powered binoculars confirming that the pregnant woman was one of the party, along with four other women and about a dozen kids, ranging from babies to late teens, but no sign of any men. For a time, he actually considered offering the group shelter, but then realised that this could well be a trap. If there were some men who were keeping well hidden, such a sign of weakness could be exactly what they were planning on.

Following this decision, he decided to cut his normal scouting trip short, returning over an hour early to a strangely deserted camp. Immediately suspicious, he crept to the main housing block and glanced in, noting that the door to the section usually used by his younger sister was ajar. He flicked the safety off his rifle and slid silently into the building, hearing muffled sounds from the master bedroom. As he neared his goal, the sounds became clearer and a cold shiver ran up his spine. With shaking hands, he flicked the safety back on, laid down the rifle and peeped into the room.

He groaned when his worst suspicions were confirmed: his naked daughter with eyes closed and a look of ecstasy on her face, was writhing wildly while impaled on what could only be her brother.

"Fuck! Fucking Christ!" he screamed, grabbing Lizzie and throwing her to a corner of the room while he glared down at his son, who was scrabbling to cover himself with a sheet. "I cannot believe this, what the fuck're you doing."

"What do you think we're doing? We're fucking; have you forgotten how it goes?"

He was at her side in two strides and slapped her face hard. "You fucking little slut! You're only fifteen and that's your younger brother! Your brother, don't you get it? Never heard of incest and what happens as a result of it?"

"Fuck incest," she screamed back at him. "What else are we supposed to do, there's nobody else in this fucking jail. And I know what happens when you shag your kin, so young Joe was only getting rear entry. Of course, he could have had the whole shebang if, amongst your tons of supplies, you had thought to include some contraceptives, you redneck asshole!"

Rocked back on his heels by the virulence of her counter-attack, he raised his hand to slap her again and was momentarily surprised when it was grabbed from behind. "You just leave her be, you motherfucker! It's all your fault, you total bastard."

Joe backhanded his son and sent him crashing against the wall, blood spurting from his broken nose. "You, sir, get to your bedroom and, on the way, look out my black leather belt. I'll deal with you after I sort out this little tramp."

For a moment it looked like Joe junior was going to attack his father but, clearly, the difference between a rather slight, thirteen-year-old boy and a heavily build man convinced him that discretion was the better part of valour and he slunk off, slamming the door of this accommodation section behind him.

Lizzy was now on her feet, glaring at him and making no attempt to cover her nudity. He couldn't help noting her small but very well-formed breasts and thin bush of pubic hair that emphasised rather than shielded her labia. "So, what can you do now?" she challenged him. "I fuck my baby brother and I'll continue to do it until there's some other option for us in this hellhole."

In a rage he grabbed her wrists and fell backwards onto the bed, bringing her wrists together and pulling her face-down over his knee as he sat up. His free had now landed on her buttocks with a loud crack. Despite a scream of pain, or maybe of rage, she immediately stopped wriggling to free herself.

"So, this is what it's all about," she taunted him. "A bit of hanky-spanky to get you turned on, is that what you need? You're just like an ape that needs a red bottom to get you in the mood!"

Several slaps later her bottom was indeed red, but it seemed to have no effect at all; apart from grunts following each impact, she continued to bait him. "Incest is also father and daughter, you bastard! Don't you think I can feel your erection? Will you worry about the consequences and stick it only into my butt? I guess that was inevitable anyway, with an extended family group and not even a single condom. As long as we were in this fucking stockade it'd be parents fucking their kids, brothers and sisters. The remotest you'd get would be an aunt, uncle or first cousin. We'd all be playing banjos. You live in a world of the comics of your youth – I'm supposed to be trained up as Hit Girl while you're Big Daddy. I guess you expect little Mindy to have a bit of anal with her pop before she goes on patrol – is that what this's about?"

Joe was stunned into immobility. In all the discussions about setting up the survival camp and the catastrophes it would have to defend against, it was assumed that all couples would stay together and have lots of kids to grow the community, but the sexual needs of the kids themselves had never come up. Thinking about it, the loss of a wife or husband had not been considered either. *If I'd lost Elsie in a bigger group, would I share my brothers' wives? It'd make genetic sense, but I honestly can't imagine that working. Would I marry one of their daughters, a niece? Can't see that going down well either.*

He had tuned his daughter's ranting out while he thought her accusations through, but suddenly realised what she was shouting. "Lost you hard-on now, have you? The spanking wasn't enough?

334

Sticking your finger up my asshole – do you think that'll do the trick?"

With horror Joe realised that he had stopped paddling the well-tanned buttocks and his hand had started caressing them, with indeed a finger sliding slowly into a slippery rosebud anus. *She was well prepared in advance for her buggering.* His distracted thought came an instant before he threw the girl to the floor and put his head in his hands, feeling gutted by shame.

Lizzy ran from the room and he started to sob, painfully aware that all the plans that he had been so proud of had been ripped to shreds by a teenage girl. He went over all the discussions that accompanied the stepwise implementation of the camp and everything that had happened since things went tits-up, but could not see where mistakes were made, where anything could have been done differently. Even worse, he could see no possible way out of his predicament. Could he really accept his son and daughter living as man and wife? Even worse, could he ensure that the reactions that he felt when manhandling his daughter's naked body would never happen again, especially as she developed more towards womanhood.

Joe lost all track of time, but it was maybe an hour before he wearily made his way towards his own living quarters, still without a clue about how he was going to deal with his children. As it transpired, he did not have to worry about that. Lizzy was waiting for him when he entered his living room and shot him in the gut with a large calibre revolver.

Joe regained consciousness in a pool of blood, but a little probing indicated that the wound was not as bad as it could have been. Whether by luck or due to pity for him, the bullet had not actually penetrated his stomach but had passed through belly fat, leaving a big hole but not hitting any organs. He managed to crawl to the first aid kit that was located in every room and bound a compression bandage around his waist to stop the bleeding. He felt weak from blood loss but, after a few pain-killers and a couple of rehydrating drinks, was able to struggle to his feet and stagger to the workshop. One glance was enough to confirm his guess, the control panel that armed the mines and other traps on the routes to the camp had been wrecked.

The kids were gone. They could have simply disarmed the defences, but probably realised that he was not dead and worried about him re-arming them before they were clear. In any case, there was an open route for any attackers and, if his children were seen leaving, this would be fairly obvious. His pistol was also gone, along with the key for the massive steel door to the armoury. He was stunned for a while, before he remembered the rifle he had put down when encountering the shocking bedroom scene. Picking up a couple of reloaded magazines from the workbench, he slowly made his way to recover the gun. He was very careful to avoid looking at the crumpled bed, but the smell of sex still hung in the air.

***

Joe filled a backpack with bottled water and high energy rations and took up position in a lookout tower that guarded the entrance to the stockade. All was quiet until just before sunset, when a first shadowy figure emerged from a side path. He held his fire until he could make out that it was a man who was cautiously approaching, then let off the head shot. Joe gasped: he had missed. *Must be in much worse shape than I thought.* He switched to automatic and sprayed his victim as he attempted to runback to cover. It seemed certain that the man had been hit this time, but he couldn't be sure as he had to duck to avoid covering fire coming from at least two positions at the edge of the forest.

This is getting tricky, if I had another couple of shooters to take them out, I could draw fire to identify where these guys are hiding. As it is, they can move about freely while I can't risk leaving this outlook. With a sigh, he peeped out of cover and let off some shots into the exposed body, which was still showing signs of life. Before he ducked back into cover, he noted the positions firing on him. *They hadn't moved at all, the idiots.* Joe quickly changed magazines and then jumped up to spray one of these locations, rewarded by a scream of pain before he had to drop down again. He hadn't actually felt anything, but the warm flow of blood informed him he had been hit.

A chunk out of my ear, but adrenalin's a good thing under these circumstances. Even seems to be steadying my aim a bit. Joe repeated his pop-up, aiming a dozen rounds towards the second shooter location, but this time the return fire came from

337

twenty feet to the left. Another new magazine and he sprayed a further ten feet from the last location, eliciting another scream of pain. His momentary flush of success slowed him down sufficiently that a shot from a completely different location caught him in the shoulder, throwing him back into cover.

Now things are really dire. I can certainly fire one-handed on a range, but can't duck and weave as needed here to hold back these guys. Not only that, I've got only one magazine left. So basically, I've got nothing to lose.

Following this morbid thought, he raised himself up and started shooting in the general direction of the last shots and ignoring returning fire that was now coming from two locations. Just before he was hit again, once more on his injured shoulder, he noticed that his rifle did not seem to be handling properly, but he immediately discounted this as an artefact of his wounds.

Dropping back again, he checked the magazine and saw that he had only one bullet left. *Well, that means at least I go out quickly.* Without hesitation, he pointed the barrel into his open mouth and pulled the trigger.

***

The dull click was a lot more shocking than a bang would have been. *Not that I'd have heard the bang, my brain would have been gone before the sound reached my ears. So why am I not dead?*

As Joe slumped back in confusion, he was hit by a wave of excruciating pain. *I guess adrenalin and pain-killers can only do so much. I should have put a first aid kit in the rucksack, but I wasn't thinking straight then.*

He peered blearily at the last ejected shell casing in confusion. *I got this magazine from the bench, so it must have been recently reloaded.* "Those fucking kids," he groaned aloud, realising that this must have been part of their rebellion against his domination, reloading the bullets with negligible charge. *Well, they really got their revenge, although they'll never know it.*

Joe could now hear shouts as his attackers approached, but was far beyond caring. *I just hope it's going to be quick,* but deep down he knew it wasn't going to be.

PA+2 years, Costa Smeralda, Sardinia

At the time of the Incident, it was still off-season in Sardinia and the venerable Hotel Romazzino had not yet opened for business and was, like most of the surrounding luxury villas of the Costa Smeralda, lying empty. Of course, unopened and empty referred only to the mega-rich who made this their playground during the summer: numerous gardeners, groundsmen, cleaners and other tradesmen continued to work to maintain the properties and repair the wear and tear of a stormy winter. Dorothea, usually called Doro, was lockdown manager at the hotel and, during this time, lived in a staff flat in the hotel annex, so that she could be on call in case of any problems in the rambling edifice.

Doro shared the flat with her best friend, Sue. They had now been together for over five years, but neither considered herself as a *partner*, they were just good pals. Although often suspected as such, neither was a lesbian, or at least not straight gay. They had a mixed group of friends, but generally socialised with a pack of local single girls.

Tonight, she had a special dinner planned for Sue but, as usual, she started her day with an early morning swim in Romazzino Bay. Despite the rather cool water temperature at this time of year, the sun was bright and she wore only a small bikini

340

bottom. Although not using a snorkel, she swam with a diving mask and large fins, with a knife and net bag on a belt in case she saw an octopus, not common in this area but a favourite of both women.

The muscles of her arms and legs warmed as she powered through the water, but her torso was cool and she could see that her nipples were dramatically erect. She was proud of her large, firm breasts and the hard nipples looked good on her evenly tanned skin. *Despite that, maybe a reef shirt would have been a good idea, it's definitely on the chilly side today.*

To take her mind of her discomfort, Doro thought again of the events over the last two years while she cruised over the steep rock walls and deep canyons of the coastline to the north of her bay. Loss of electricity, motor-transport and communication had been an annoyance, but had little immediate impact on life at the hotel. Doro found hand work for the couple of gardeners who turned up on bicycles during the first week but, as time passed and it became clear that e-money to pay wages had also disappeared, the lock-down crew was reduced to Doro alone. A trek around the neighbouring villas revealed that, apart from a few managers like herself with accommodation on site, these had also been deserted.

Sue worked as a chef and masseuse, on call to hotels, villas and yachts, so she had little work off-season in any case. In the absence of electricity, she focused on sorting out cooking facilities in the beachside restaurant, based on a wood-fired pizza oven and a charcoal grill, while Doro made an inventory of available food. The large refrigerators and freezers had been cleared out at the end of the season, but a larder contained huge quantities of canned food and preserves, while a basement store had pallets of small bottles of mineral water. There was also a huge wine cellar, large quantities of spirits and thousands of bottles and cans of beer and soft drinks.

At the end of the first month, the couple decided that they had to assume that the situation would last indefinitely. It was clear that many others had come to this conclusion and, despite their remote location, the surrounding villas were plundered one by one. Apart from occasional break-ins by individuals on bikes, organised liberation of anything of value from the villas was carried out by groups using small boats. Doro learned that some form of organisation had been established in nearby Porto Cervo, which had decided that all empty houses or boats were now considered abandoned and their contents authorised for salvage. As there was no shortage of rich pickings in the region, Doro was able to argue that her presence meant the hotel was still occupied and hence it was spared from such raids.

The women fished in the deep water below the rocks that bounded the bay in front of the hotel, collected shellfish at low tide and snorkelled for sea urchins and the occasional octopus or lobster. After the second month, they dug up part of the lawn and planted vegetables and herbs, mainly transplanting these from the gardens found in surrounding villas. Although it was somewhat lonely, they were aware that this situation must be very much better than elsewhere in Italy.

Once a week they cycled into the market in Porto Cervo to barter for fruit and dairy products; initially with loads of jams, canned food and exotic spirits but, as time wore on and the stocks removed from supermarkets became depleted, soap, shampoo and toilet paper.

In the town square there was a large notice board that provided an overview of the evolving situation in Sardinia, neighbouring Corsica and the Italian mainland – with occasional mention of other parts of the world. One of the huge floating gin palaces docked in the marina at the time of the Incident had belonged to a neurotic billionaire and, apart from a helicopter on a pad towards the stern, contained a fully nuclear-hard power and communication system. The com links were originally set up to the head office of his engineering empire, but these had been commandeered and were now were fully integrated into the international hard-net. The local navy and coastguard commanders shared this resource with a recovery team, staffed mainly by the Sardinian police, and had managed to resist all calls to move the boat to a more central location at a port in the Italian mainland.

Dora had heard that the yacht's owner had been living in his penthouse in central London at the time of the incident, which had also nuclear-hard comms and power. Unfortunately for him, the wide-bodied jet that landed on top of it hadn't. *Maybe it was only*

343

an urban legend, but it would be somehow fitting if true.

Within a year, the remnant staff in the surrounding villas had also left, moving either inland to farming villages or along the coast to the villages and towns now focused on fishing the coastal waters. Dora and Sue were now the only residents of the entire Romazzino peninsula. *This probably recreated the situation before the Agha Khan had dreamed up the idea of the Costa Smeralda tourist centre in the first place. But with no prospects of tourists returning – and even the idea of mega-rich vanishing as a concept – the tricky thing was deciding if it was worth staying on in such a grandiose hotel.*

***

Sue was unsure, but Dora was convinced that isolation was not a bad thing, especially as recovery of infrastructure would certainly take a long time and northern Sardinia would probably be at the bottom of the list for support. To make the case better, Dora proposed that they move out of the staff accommodation into one of the villas on the grounds, set up for the richest of their customers. Not only was it much better furnished, but they had the advantage of a better lit living room with a wall of glass facing south, a pool that still remained reasonably fresh due to regular rain, a terrace perfect for sunbathing and even closer proximity to the sea and the beach restaurant. They moved a massage table from the hotel spa to a corner of the huge living room, so that Sue could not only work on her friend, but also teach her some of the skills

344

of her trade. With many farmers, fishermen and tradesmen no longer able to benefit from powered equipment, the demand for someone to sort out aches, pains and pulled muscles was continually increasing – so the business had gone from exotic aromatic oil massage, pandering to the rich, to basic physiotherapy for the poor.

Isolation was the factor that allowed us to live well when, especially in the larger towns on the island, life got tougher as food stocks were depleted, order broke down and outbreaks of cholera and typhoid resulted from complete failure of the sewage and water-supply systems. When I first heard about this, I had expected that we would be flooded with refugees, but white-collar townsfolk had no idea about the countryside and few were interested in venturing far from the urban centres. Fundamentally, the Costa Smeralda was a concept based beautiful scenery and beaches – which were no longer valuable commodities. The island, with its relatively small population and little mechanised agriculture and fisheries, was fundamentally in good shape – but needed re-organisation to cope with the loss of tourism as its biggest industry.

***

Now on the two-year anniversary of the incident, Doro had promised to discuss their future again. A clear option would be to move to one of the small communities nearby – Cala di Volpe or Pevero – or even to the larger town of Porto Cevero which was developing as a centre for regional recovery. This would certainly allow more social contact and avoid the long cycle trips to provide

345

massage services or visit the market. This had to be balanced with living in the relative luxury provided by the hotel and the resources in its cellars. *Sue is definitely much more of a social animal than me and certainly favours Porto Cervo, but maybe I've got a couple of cards up my sleeve that'll make her change her mind.*

The evening was cool with a bank of clouds making the view onto the Isola Mortorio, Isola Soffi and the other smaller islands in the bay even more spectacular in the light of the setting sun. Sue had prepared a fish stew that was slowly cooking on a wood fire and a plate of cheese, olives and salami was sitting on the table to provide nibbles while they waited. This was the setting for Dora's first surprise for her friend.

"Close your eyes for a minute, love, I've got something special for you," she left the table and moved into the candle-lit kitchen.

"Let me guess, you've dug out another bottle of outrageous Champagne from the cellars," Sue responded.

"Of course I have – a Krug Clos du Mesnil, which you don't want to know what it would have cost in the old days. But that isn't the surprise…"

Sue had not closed her eyes, so they widened immediately when Dora returned with the two condensation-frosted flutes. "Christ, Dora, those look cold. But they can't be…"

"Well, just try it," she handed over a glass. "Salute!"

"Cin cin," Sue responded automatically, before they clinked glasses. "My God, it's freezing cold! I never thought I'd ever have something like this ever again."

"Well, I know that you always liked sparkly and that it's not great at room temperature, so I got this sorted out."

"But how? You can't possibly have fixed up a fridge – we've still got no power."

"I did a bit of trading with an engineer from the nuke yacht, you know the English guy David that we've both given massages to. Seems that he found a working solar-powered wine cooler in a shielded store-room and I managed to snaffle it."

"What, for a massage? A working cooler is more than worth its weight in gold. Actually, much more than that, as gold and diamonds are fairly worthless now. That must have involved a truly mega *happy ending*!"

"No, I'm afraid that my abilities in that area don't match yours," they smiled at each other, aware that, for a number of their customers, both male and female, the *sensual massage* option was very popular. "I found out that David was a keen hunter and I traded a couple of guns for the cooler."

"Guns – where on earth did you get those?"

"David had managed to get hold of an ancient rifle somehow, but told me that he was worried that it would explode in his face someday. I remembered visiting the Hancock villa, the one at the end of the headland, for a reception at the end of the season. Old man Hancock took a shine to me and showed me some of his prized possessions, which included a couple of guns. They were kept in a chest in his bedroom – maybe why he wanted to show me them

– but when I popped in to have a look last week they were still there, so I salvaged them. It seems that they're a pair of Purdey shotguns: no idea what they are – or were – worth, but they were in an exotic wooden case so probably very valuable. In addition, there were five boxes of shells. David was totally delighted, and he was the one that suggested the trade."

"You lucky devil! Anyway, this is certainly going to make for a wondrous dinner. Look, despite being chilled, the Champagne has evaporated already."

Dora rose to top up the glasses. "Yes, well that's one reason now for staying a bit linger in the hotel."

"Why is that? Surely the cooler must be easy to move if you managed to get it here."

"Yes, the cooler is easy to move, but the Champagne is a bit trickier."

"Well, we've scoffed a few bottles over the last year, even if drunk warm," Sue screwed up her face with the memory and then immediately took a sip of the deliciously cold wine.

"We've hardly made a dent in the exotic Champagnes – remember this was a top-end hotel and some of the clients drank that stuff like lemonade. There are dozens of cases left."

"Wow, I don't need to hold back then!" Sue took a further, larger sip."

"Yes, that's not even counting the prosecco and other similar wines."

"How much of that?"

"Well, Ferrari was the house fizz and I estimate we have in excess of two hundred cases."

"Two hundred! You've got to be joking!"

"Not at all – on the wine side we've got enough to keep us going for at least the next decade."

"My God, that's a very pleasing thought. This place would be perfect if we weren't just stuck here alone."

"I've been thinking about that too..." Dora smiled mischievously and waited while Sue tried to puzzle out what she could have been planning.

After five minutes, Sue gave up. "Okay, out with it! I haven't a clue what you're on about."

"Well, again, it was when I was talking to David..."

"Post-coital or, at least, post-happy-ending, I assume"

"Not in this case. It seems that David was more or less confined on board as he was essential to running the boat's services. He has now trained up a Sardinian team and sees the writing on the wall. He will soon have to give up his comfy billet and move ashore, into the real world. He doesn't fancy Porto Cervo, so..."

"He wants to move in with us! I can see pros and cons, but I'm not sure about setting up home with someone we hardly know."

"It isn't quite like that. He has a steady girlfriend, also crew, who is now pregnant. We could offer them the villa next door. He's both an engineer and a hunter, so would certainly have his uses. She's a sailor and could also extend our fishing a bit as several properties hereabouts have sailing dinghies."

"Also sailing would make market visits a lot easier than by bike – I totally hate that hill between us and Porto Cervo." Sue grinned and waved her now empty glass. "We could celebrate this with another drop of Champagne, especially as we've got buckets of the stuff."

"That's a relief, I'd mentioned the option to David and Fred, his partner, and they were keen. I did say, however, that you had to agree."

"Fred? Is he gay? I thought there was a girlfriend."

"Frederica, she is. Definitely a girl: not only gorgeous, but noticeably pregnant. Also, I think that if all works out well, we might be able to interest a few more of David's colleagues, so could have the basis of a little commune here."

Sue clinked glasses again after she had been topped up. "You know, things are actually looking promising. I can see a way to building towards the future, not just getting by day by day. And it'll be nice to have some kids about the place."

"Kids, so we can think about that now?" Dora raised her eyebrows and smiled.

"Well, not totally out of the question. Anyway, do you fancy a short pre-prandial massage before I get any more slotted?"

"Would that be one with a happy ending?"

"Is there any other kind?" The women threw their arms around each other, laughing in a way that had been missing for the last year.

PA+10 years, Nagoya, Japan

I smiled as Akiko laid out snacks for our guests, setting out the array of small dishes with a diverse range of Japanese and Western nibbles. As a special treat, we were sipping glasses of Pelorus, an excellent sparkling wine that was a present of the young New Zealand couple, Sue and Simon, who were taking a crash course in Agricultural Engineering at the university. Our other guest, Trevor, was a tall, black South African visiting professor, who taught Sustainable Electrical Engineering. Although now middle-aged, Trevor had played rugby at a top level and looked fit as a fiddle. *Actually, given that he was still built like a brick outhouse, fit as a double bass might be more appropriate.*

Trevor was telling us that his 6-month stay was almost up and that he was looking forward to returning home to his family, a six-co-op living on a ranch near the Koeberg power complex on the outskirts of Cape Town. Akiko and Sue wanted to know more about his two husbands and three wives and their decision to adopt three teenage orphans rather than have children of their own. We had previously spent a couple of nights with Sue and Simon, but this was our first evening with Trevor, although I had encountered him a couple of times in disaster management workshops. Akiko had, however, been assured by her many contacts in the swinger network that he was hung like a stallion.

351

Apparently a very well-endowed stallion, as Aki put it.

I still lived in my original apartment in the Noyori complex, for which the rent was waived on the basis of my Emeritus Professorship. Over time, Akiko had modified our large upstairs bedroom to fit her group-sex fantasies, contrasting dramatically with the rather staid décor of the living and dining areas downstairs.

Now 10 years since young Shoko opened my horizons and 9 since Aki took over the job of pushing things even further. Where does the time go? I was feeling my age increasingly as, despite the impressive recovery of infrastructure in Japan, geriatric medicine was still far down the priority list. My role in supporting responses during the first couple of critical years had been acknowledged by awards of honorary Japanese citizenship and the Order of the Rising Sun, but even this was not enough to get me the hip and knee operations that I needed.

When we adjourned upstairs, Akiko and Sue first undressed me. They then allowed me to undress them while the other men watched, standing with arms around each other and occasionally kissing, which emphasised their height difference – Trevor being more than a head taller than Simon. I then settled in a leather wing chair, while the women undressed Simon and then the three of them focused their attentions on Trevor. The process was drawn out to emphasise that he was clearly going to be the focus of the night. It was at least ten minutes before Simon finally lowered Trevor's boxer-shorts, drawing gasps from the two women before their mouths were otherwise occupied.

Trevor did indeed sport a heroic erection. I had never seen its like, outside of Shoko's porn videos. *Just a shame she's not here – she'd love this. After all the times that I told her that these images just weren't real – examples only of the skill of those who photoshopped them.*

Simon joined the women and the oral action became frenzied. This, if anything, caused the humungous member to grow even further. Sue climbed up Trevor's torso, supported by her husband as she gingerly lowered herself down, grunting inelegantly as the head of the huge penis entered her vagina. "Hell's bells, that's big! Really, really big! Oh, God, slowly! Very, very slowly!"

Over the next 5 minutes, Sue was lowered further and Trevor began to thrust into the impaled woman, her screams becoming louder as his dick penetrated deeper. Simon was holding her buttocks apart and Akiko was squirming beneath the trio, active with tongue and fingers in some way that I couldn't quite make out.

"Jeez, double vaginal's not on the cards here," Sue groaned while she squirmed in what I wasn't sure was agony or ecstasy. *Maybe a bit of both by the looks of it.*

This clearly meant something to the others as Akiko immediately took Simon's penis in her mouth and soaked it with her saliva, while her fingers entered her own vagina before being rubbed into Sue's anus. She then gently directed the anal penetration, while Sue's back arched and her mouth opened in a silent scream.

I probably looked brain-dead as I watched the two men synchronise their thrusts into the slim woman. I noticed that Akiko had crawled over to me only when she took my own erection into her mouth and started slow fellatio, ensuring that she also had a good view of the ménage à trois action. Sensing that I was close to orgasm, she clambered onto my lap with her back to me so that she could watch the floorshow. I slid easily into her well lubricated vagina, but she held still while I struggled to delay coming. She nuzzled my neck and then nipped my earlobe. "So, this is going to be your treat tonight – you're going to get a good buggering from Trevor. I think Sue and I will be sitting on your face – but we just can't figure out what to do with Simon. I don't suppose you want to try double-anal?" she giggled.

"Perish the bloody thought. That sodding battering ram would split me in two on its own. I really don't know how Sue does that."

She chuckled lasciviously. "I'll let you know. Trevor's going to do me next and I'm going to try anal. So I just need to get ready for that." She lifted herself up and let me enter a tighter orifice, which caused me to climax immediately.

As I shook with the force of the orgasm, I suddenly felt an excruciating pain in my chest, which vanished before I could call out.

Well, if I've got to go, can't think of a better way...

354

Professor Mike Mitchell died with an ecstatic smile on his face.

PA+10 Years, Cupecoy, Sint Maarten

I was playing with my daughter on the terrace of my flat, telling her a story that was supposed to fit in with eating breakfast. This focussed on her favourite toy, a soft green turtle, which she insisted on calling *Tortoise*. "Tortoise is hungry, so you should give him your banana," I said, moving the toy towards her.

"No, silly, tortoises don't eat bananas," Lisa frowned in my direction.

"But Tortoise loves bananas, especially the ones that you have."

"No, this is my banana," she bit the end of it to emphasise her point. "Tortoise can have yoghurt."

I was in the process of working out a story that would switch the dialogue into German, as I wanted to keep her bilingual to the extent possible – or actually trilingual, as her mother often chatted to her in Spanish. *The only problem with this is that Schildkröte is German for both turtle and tortoise and getting over the difference between a Landschildkröte and Wasserschildkröte is a bit much for a 4-year old.*

Suddenly Lisa lost all interest in her toy, dropped the banana on her plate and scurried to peer through the glass barrier at the end of the terrace overlooking the sea. Initially confused, I gradually became aware of a strange deep humming noise that seemed to be approaching from the right, along the coast.

Slowly the huge airship came into view, shaped more like a huge flying saucer than a classic Zeppelin. The upper surface of the gasbag was covered with solar panels and the gondola below sported two large outrigger pods, which I guessed enclosed the propulsion units.

Lisa was amazed. "What's that, Papa? It's so big – like a flying house."

"It's an airship, which is like a flying ship."

"A flying ship is an airplane," my daughter corrected me. "That's not an airplane because it's got no wings."

"Well this is a different kind of flying ship. I haven't seen one before," I confessed, "but that's what it is."

"If you haven't seen one, how do you know what it is?"

I smiled proudly. *Bright as a button, this one – questions everything that anyone tells her. Not unlike myself as a kid.* "I've heard about these things, so I'm sure that's what it is."

"So, how does it fly if it's got no wings?" she smiled as if she had caught me out. "Airplanes have wings and birds have wings. Even flying fish have wingy things."

"Ah, yes, well, it kind of floats – like a bubble. Remember you blew bubbles from soapy water and they floated away in the air."

"It doesn't look like a bubble. And the bubbles burst." She was clearly unconvinced by my explanation.

357

"Well, that's what it is. It's a kind of a bubble that doesn't burst – which is the big bit on top. Underneath is the bit where the people are."

"People, like real people?" she gave me a frown of disbelief, but then peered at the gondola which was now passing directly in front of our apartment, maybe 500 metres offshore at a height of around 50 metres above the waves. "There are, there are, they're waving!" The girl jumped up and down in excitement, waving both of her little hands.

I lifted my daughter and held her in the crook of one arm while waving with my other. *I don't know why, but the return of air travel with this wondrous machine seems to indicate that we've not only recovered from the worst of the Incident, but are actually moving forward in a positive, environmentally-friendly way. Maybe this is the silver lining of the awful cloud that we've been under for the last decade.*

PA+10 years, Bataan, Philippines

Mina Villar had been promoted to Chief Engineer of the entire Bataan nuclear power complex only weeks before the Incident and she remembered clearly the first chaotic days after the loss of all external power links and all communication with the exception of a single hardened link to the IAEA emergency coordination centre in Vienna. Despite its age, the refurbished PWR had scrammed without problems and the ten younger SMRs had simply tripped to a backup mode that generated only enough power to supply all needs of the site. Bataan had also benefited from its relatively remote location, being isolated from the chaos that reduced Manilla and many of the other bigger cities and towns to smoking ruins. After rioting died away over the following months, malaria, typhoid and cholera began to take an increasing toll on the survivors – adding further to the misery caused by the super-typhoons that regularly ripped through the country from early summer until mid-winter.

Over the next couple of years, the industrial basis of the reactor site was rebuilt and power was even restored to a micro-network covering some surrounding resort towns, which became centres for refugees escaping from bigger conurbations. Although conditions were still rather primitive in the region, the tropical climate and coastal location meant that fisheries and agriculture were able to recover quickly, avoiding the famines that hit most of the globe over this period.

This oasis of relative comfort was a marked contrast to the rest of country, which was integrated only by the power of the military after declaration of Martial Law. Nevertheless, after 10 years, first steps towards establishing a formal government were being made – with the new Executive, comprising three military commanders and two civilians, setting up base in Bataan. Despite its remote setting, this was a logical choice due to both its high-tech infrastructure and international communications. Negotiations were ongoing to establish a formal link to Japan – exchanging technical support for food.

Strange indeed, a location that's been characterised by decades of political opposition to nuclear power will now become the political centre of the Philippines and, potentially, some of the surrounding lands that lack the infrastructure that we have established here.

PA+25 years, Atlantis 2, Atlantic Abyssal Plain

On board the international research ship
Atlantis 2, few of the technical support crew were
old enough to remember the Incident, at least not in
detail. Indeed, there was nobody who had actually
been involved in the initial response, with the
exception of Professor Mackenzie, who was
responsible for the radio-isotope work, and Hideki
Nakamura, the ship's captain. Despite this, the
justification for the cruise was well understood by
everyone on board – testing a speculation discussed
in the classic Mitchell and Tanaka paper
overviewing the Incident and subsequent responses
to it.

The bottom line was that, regardless of
hundreds of man-years of analysis by experts in the
field, there was no consensus on the mechanism that
caused the unexpected change in behaviour of the
sun and hence no soundly-based estimates of likely
recurrence times. Mitchell had always insisted that
the estimates by different solar physicists for a
Black Swan were guesses at best and had associated
uncertainties of many orders of magnitude – and
hence were fundamentally useless to serve as a
basis for guiding long-term planning or building of
critical infrastructure. The paper had suggested that
evidence could be gained from detailed examination
of records of environmental changes as preserved in

sediment or ice cores: the tricky bit was that the nature of the signal for a pre-industrial world would not be very obvious – as decades of pre-incident studies of the impacts of solar variability had yielded nothing suspicious. The best chance to be able to detect anomalous signals would be a continuous record of the environment extending tens or hundreds of millions of years – and hence this mission to what was expected to be one of the oldest and most stable portions of the Abyssal Plain – one of the least explored parts of the earth, despite covering about 50% of its surface.

Professor Mackenzie, generally known to his colleagues as Mac, was well aware of how tricky this would be. *A needle in a haystack would be trivial by comparison – burn the haystack and use a magnet to find the needle: piece of piss! I've got to find the unknown impact of a possible short duration solar event that might have occurred millions of years ago in sediments lying under 3 to 6 km of water in the middle of the ocean. If it wasn't so important, I'd just have said that it wasn't doable and walked away. But I was brow-beaten into giving it a go – and this with the kit that I've been able to salvage or rebuild post-Incident. It would have been touch and go with the analytical tools that allowed us to measure chemistry, stable- and radio-isotopes on nanometre-scale laser ablated material, but now we'll need kilograms of sediment for a wet-chemistry work up before we get stuck in with basic mass-spectrometry and radioanalysis. Even if there is a signal there, what's the chance of us seeing it?*

The vessel at his command was a refurbished drilling ship seized from a now-defunct oil exploration company. The rig had been modified to obtain much larger diameter cores from much deeper waters than originally considered, but this had been less challenging than stripping out and replacing all key electronic control and power systems – in particular those allowing the ship to maintain position in deep water.

Although the analytical hardware to hand was basic, to say the least, Mac had to admit that it was compensated to some extent by the software tools at his disposal. In particular, all data accumulated on a core – physical, chemical, mineralogical, biological and isotopic – was integrated in a central database and depth profiles subject to sophisticated pattern recognition tools. These tools were, in fact, closely related to some of those incorporated in Mitchell's original recovery toolkit. *A smart cookie that guy – if you suspect there is a signal, but you don't know what it actually is, this is the way to go. A bit more like cryptography than normal scientific approaches – but really seems to work.*

Mac forced himself to get back to the job on hand. They were now on site and the first core material would arrive soon, complemented by surface sediments that were vulnerable to disturbance by drilling and had to be obtained by their submersible. *Over forty years old and recovered from the basement of a museum. There's not any way they'd get me down in that bloody thing.* Dangerous as hell, he recognised, but the thin layer of sediment accumulated over the last 25 years

363

is the only material that we know contains a record of the Incident. *If, of course, there is any record that we're capable of detecting.*

***

The ship was already setting up for the second drilling site when the first database assessment became available. The entire scientific crew, along with the captain of the ship and a few of his senior officers, crammed into the small meeting room. Mac had only had a few hours to assess the preliminary results prior to this presentation, but he felt that he had to get this first feedback from his team before he posted his interpretation on the project website. Despite a couple of decades of lecturing and presenting to major conferences, he felt nervous. *I'm an academic, I don't do this political stuff.*

Bollocks, got to remember "ladies and gentlemen" is no longer PC, not inclusive enough. "Friends and colleagues," he started, hesitantly, "you all know what we're looking for – a core profile that gives us an interrupted record long enough to pick up the traces of past Incidents. It's probably serendipity, but our first site gave us a core that covers just over twenty million years, based on paleomagnetic dating. We've thrown every possible analytical technique at it, as all the guys and gals... all the folk," he corrected quickly, "who have been doing the heavy lifting know very well." There was some applause accompanied by backslapping and high-fives between the research team members. "And it looks like it has all paid off." The room was immediately silent.

"Ninety-nine percent of the massive database that we've created is focused on filtering out all the noise: the many signals in our record due to volcanoes, large meteorite impacts, climate change and stuff like that. I don't pretend to understand how the pattern recognition toolkit works but, based on changes we've seen in recent sediments, it can extricate similar signals in the past even if we have no technical understanding of what caused them." Mac hesitated, wondering if he was hedging his bets too much, but his audience seemed spell-bound, hanging on his every word.

"Anyway, it looks like we've got three good candidates – we can't be sure at present, but we'll sample at least a half dozen other locations and should be more confident after that. So, despite the huge investment of precious resources put into this project, it looks likely that we're going to come up with the goods." At that point, a collage of the synthesised data was projected onto the wall behind him and he was almost bowled over by those fighting to get a better look. *No point in even trying to go further at present, nobody'd hear me above this hubbub.*

It was almost a half hour before he could gradually coax the audience back into their seats and start the discussion session. After a dozen very technical observations, the key question came, to Mac's surprise, from the normally reticent Captain Nakamura. "Mackenzie-sensei, does this mean that you know when the next incident will occur?"

Immediately, you could have heard a pin drop. *It seems like everyone's literally holding their*

365

breath! How the hell do I answer this? "That is, of course, the key question, Captain. I'm a scientist, so inherently not good at giving straight answers," there were a few laughs at this, "but I'll take out all the arm waving and caveats and try to answer you honestly. But, do you want the good or bad news first?"

Captain Nakamura seemed bemused by this response. "Well, after everything that I've experienced over the last twenty-five years, good news would be a welcome change."

"Good news, okay, we have three signals over a period of twenty million years and the last one was three million years ago. So, without ifs, buts and maybes, I think there's little chance of another of these within the next few million years." The sigh of relief from the entire audience indicated that this reassurance is what everyone was looking for.

The captain was grinning widely. "Thank you, sensei, this is what I and my crew wanted to know." Now there was widespread applause and a lot of whistling and stamping of feet.

Bollocks! I didn't do that very well. "But, but, but…" he shouted until things quietened a little, "…there is also some potentially bad news." Silence again descended on the room. "We're no longer dealing with black swans, but are looking at events that we don't understand. If our tools analyse the raw data without any preconceptions, the signals actually look like double peaks in each case, a smaller peak followed by a bigger one very shortly afterwards – on this resolution a few hundred to a thousand years or so."

The looks of relief vanished and Mac was faced by a barrage of questions. He stood silently until the captain blew a whistle that finally restored some order. "Yes, that's bad news, but I had to answer the captain's question honestly. The technical guys... and gals of course... know that uncertainties are large at this stage so this could well be a statistical fluke. We have no technical reason to expect that an event as large as our recent Incident could be a precursor to something even bigger. Anyway, it's not a concern for anyone in this room, even if this double peak is real, we can be reasonably sure that nothing will happen for centuries."

Mac felt somehow remote from the discussion around him, almost sure that, no matter what the other cores revealed, the interpretation will be good or bad news depending on the viewpoint of the recipient. This brought to mind a conclusion from Mitchell's paper: *Interpretation of the historical record in order to determine future probabilities of rare events is fraught with difficulty, especially if the mechanistic basis of the processes influencing them are uncertain.*

PA+1328 years, Luleå, Sweden

The signs had been ambiguous for a decade: the next Incident was coming soon but, despite a millennium of study, the team had been guessing about the exact date until a week ago. Now the solar sonic tomography profile was clear – the reaction front had formed and was now progressing through the arenosphere, building power as the internal autocatalytic amplification occurred.

The defences were in place but, of course, they had never been tested in real life. Additionally, our actual recorded history of such events had a sample of one – all others were indirect based on interpretation of geochemical signatures. Our best understanding is that the 21st century Incident was at the upper end of the range and that impacts couldn't be greater than a factor of two or so larger. Then again, theories based on such a limited sample set have to be suspect. What if it was a magnitude greater, or two, or more? Then we're all dead, that's clear. Earth will be sterilised as far as man is concerned, although the deep biosphere won't be troubled in the slightest.

As an extremophile geomicrobiologist, Bror Jensson was aware that the microbial communities in both deep terrestrial and marine systems had survived much worse in the billions of years since life first emerged on Earth. *Even for mankind, this isn't an existential threat as we now have colonies both in the outer parts of the solar system beyond any worst-case impacts and also the first-*

generation ships heading for the nearest stars with
suitable planets.

Bror looked around at the scatter of islands, remembering that there had been a city here at the time of the last Incident – destroyed not by the loss of all power, but by the subsequent runaway global warming which had hit a tipping point before the sun had run wild. *There had certainly been a return to fossil fuels after the Incident, but this was more than compensated by the decreased population and the lower power requirements of the survivors.*

This really is a case of putting my money where my mouth is. As a member of the team working on global defence plans, I could've chosen to be somewhere safer – but I want to be where the fireworks are. North of Sweden in winter: our predictions are for amazing auroral displays. We did, however, also have a radiation monitoring network and a bunker that we could escape to if doses got too high. *Too high here was a factor of up to ten or twenty above expectations, more than that and we're screwed in a big way.*

I was aware of holding my breath as the seconds counted down. At zero it seemed to be an anti-climax, a first trace of veils of blue and green light, then the heavens exploded. ...

As I stared in awe, I couldn't help wondering if the original Incident had not actually been a blessing in disguise. *We're still suffering from the impacts of anthropogenic climate imbalance, but how much worse might it have been? Elimination of mega-powers gave us a return to small nation states, who grouped together to provide a basis for mutual survival. The Sword of Damocles over our heads forced nations to work together in a way that politicians would never have manged otherwise, especially without boundaries between the mega-rich and desperately poor being removed by the mutual need to survive.*

As Nietzsche put it – that which doesn't kill you makes you stronger! So, let's see what it's going to be…

THE END